THREE DEUCES DOWN

THREE DEUCES DOWN

A Donald Youngblood Mystery

KEITH DONNELLY

COURT STREET PRESS
Montgomery | Louisville

Court Street Press
P.O. Box 1588
Montgomery, AL 36102

Library of Congress Cataloging-in-Publication Data

Donnelly, Keith.
Three deuces down : a Donald Youngblood mystery / Keith Donnelly.
p. cm.
ISBN-13: 978-1-58838-227-6
ISBN-10: 1-58838-227-3
1. Private investigators--Tennessee--Fiction. 2. Male friendship--Fiction. 3. Cherokee Indians--
Fiction. 4. Missing persons--Fiction. 5. Rich people--Fiction. I. Title.

PS3604.O56325T48 2008
813'.6--dc22

2007039139

Design by Randall Williams
Printed in the United States of America
by the Maple-Vail Book Manufacturing Group

To Michele, Alex, Leigh Ann and Ryan
You certainly made life interesting

And to Tessa, my best destiny
To share is to live

Prologue

The summer of my high school senior year, a long hot summer in east Tennessee. Most of the graduates knew that one phase of their life was over. The unspoken truth in the air was that most of us would scatter to colleges around the country and make new friends, find new sweethearts. Most of our high school friendships and romances would fade. Only a few would survive and those would be the ones who stayed behind.

That night we had double-dated. Mike Brown and Marlene Long, Kitty Carr and me. We were all eighteen. Mike was in trouble with his parents and had lost his driving privileges. Marlene asked if she and Mike could double with us. I had immediately said yes because Marlene and I were great friends and because secretly I was in love with her even though in all the time we had known each other we had never dated. Mike and I were not friends but we knew each other and I thought he was an okay guy even though he was a brain. He had been voted most likely to succeed and was going to Duke on scholarships. He hadn't been dating Marlene very long and I could never picture them as a couple. Mike had to be home early as part of his punishment and so I dropped him first since he lived on the south side of town. Then I took Kitty home. She lived on the east side. Marlene lived near me on the lake north of Mountain Center.

We were alone in the car heading toward the lake when Marlene scooted over next to me and said, "I don't feel very much like going home right now, okay?"

I nearly ran off the road. "Sure!" I said.

She inched closer. My heart started pounding. *What the hell was going on?* I drove to a deserted lot very close to my house and backed the car into a shelter of trees so that we could not be seen. Marlene had not said another word. When I shut off the engine and turned toward her to ask what was going on she kissed me before I could say anything. It was a deep passionate kiss, the very best kiss of my life. I was having a hard time getting enough oxygen. We were kissing, slowly and passionately, locked in a slow sexual waltz, one I had never danced. I would have given everything to stop time and live forever inside that car with Marlene Long in my arms.

The car windows were down and I could feel the breeze flow through the car. Outside the cicada and cricket serenade faded from my awareness as life morphed into slow motion. Buttons were unbuttoned, zippers unzipped, clothes discarded, and my virginity was lost inside a 1975 Chevy on a magical summer night that would haunt me for years.

I LAID AWAKE that night replaying every move of my encounter with Marlene Long. When sleep finally came, it came deep and long and I slept until noon. On waking I thought at first that Saturday night had been a dream, but as I sat up on the edge of my bed I knew it had been real.

I got up and fixed a cup of coffee. I had been drinking coffee since I was six years old and because I started at such an early age I took cream and sugar. When I felt I was back in the land of the living, I picked up the phone and called Marlene. Thank God she answered.

"Hi," I said.

"Hi," she replied.

"Can I come up?" I asked.

"Sure," she said. She sounded normal. I was hoping that she didn't feel like she had made a major mistake.

"See you in a few minutes," I said. "I'm walking."

Marlene's house was about a half-mile walk. I took it slow. I needed time to think about last night and try to make some sense of it. When I arrived Marlene was waiting for me at the edge of her driveway. She came to me and kissed me as if to say last night was for real.

She smiled. "How are ya?"

"Confused," I said.

"Don't be," she said. "This has been coming for a long time. I had a sense of how you felt about me but I was never sure."

"It should have been pretty obvious," I smiled. Then the bomb dropped.

"Let's get married," Marlene proposed. She just blurted it out. "Let's just run away and do it. It will be great. We can attend the same college, live in a married dorm, study together, and everything."

She was babbling and my head was spinning. Even at eighteen I was a pretty good detective and I sensed that something was not right. I thought that I did love her, but I wasn't sure about her.

"I'll marry you only if you are really in love with me." I said.

She stared at me and did not reply. Tears started to form in her eyes and my world started breaking apart. Then it hit me. "You're pregnant," I whispered.

If a look could have killed, I would have died right where I stood. We stared at each other for what seemed like eternity. Then finally Marlene spoke in mean guttural sounds. "I never want to see you again," she hissed. "And don't ever call!" With that she turned and ran back to her house, leaving me standing at the edge of her driveway with a dumb-struck look on my face and a knot in my stomach.

THE NEXT DAY I called anyway. Marlene's mother answered.

"Hi, Mrs. Long. It's Don Youngblood. May I speak to Marlene, please?"

"Oh, hi, Don," Mrs. Long said pleasantly. "How are you?"

"I'm fine, Mrs. Long. Is Marlene around?"

"I'm sorry, Don, Marlene left for California early this morning to spend some time with my sister."

"When do you expect her back?" I asked.

"I really don't know, Don. She was talking about staying out there and going to college. If I hear from her, I'll tell her you called. I have to go now, Don, I think someone is at the front door." She hung up before I could say good-bye.

It was definitely a kiss-off. *If I hear from her* . . . So Marlene had been banished to California.

I spent the rest of the day trying to decide what to do and feeling sorry for myself. I had managed to have the best and the worst days of my life back-to-back. No easy task. Still, I wanted to figure this out. If Marlene was pregnant, who was the father? I doubted it was Mike Brown, but nothing would surprise me now. My best guess would have been Mark Lewis, who Marlene had dated a long time, but they had broken up months ago and she wasn't *that* pregnant.

I wandered around in a trance the rest of the day. When I went to bed that night I wasn't any closer to a conclusion than when the day had started. Little did I know it would be years before I discovered the truth, but I knew one thing for sure—Marlene Long was gone.

THREE DEUCES DOWN

1

I was in the inner office late one fall afternoon. Billy, my best friend and partner, was in the outer office working on his latest painting. The sign on our outer door read,

CHEROKEE INVESTIGATIONS
DONALD YOUNGBLOOD AND BILL T. FEATHERS
PRIVATE INVESTIGATORS

Billy and I didn't start out as licensed private investigators. We were basically just hanging out. The whole thing started as a joke. Then we got our licenses and in the years that followed a lot of people began to take us seriously. I didn't need the money but I did want to help people and bring some excitement into my dreary life. Becoming a private investigator seemed the perfect occupation to do just that. Besides, you can put anything you want to on an office door.

Billy, on the other hand, did need the money. His only other source of income was from his photography, painting, and drawing, where his reputation had far outdistanced his income. He had a small gallery where he sold underpriced original framed photos and his art. He also acted as a forensic photographer for a number of the smaller local police and sheriff's departments in the east Tennessee area. He lived frugally and he invested well. I know because I handled his investments.

I was playing solitaire on my desktop computer when the door opened to the outer office and I heard voices. One voice was Billy's. The other voice I did not recognize.

"Blood, you busy? Someone here to see you," Billy's voice rumbled back into my office. Billy did not have to talk loud to be heard. Billy had called me "Blood" since we became best friends in college. He says it is a spiritual thing. A few of my close friends have called me Blood since junior high school, but I didn't tell Billy. Best for him to think that it was his idea.

What Billy brings to our partnership is a deep understanding of the human condition and an air of danger. Billy is a big person. He seems to be in touch with life on a different plane than I am. It gives us a nice balance and a strong and unique friendship. Billy Two-Feathers is a full-blooded Cherokee Indian. I call him "Chief." I started that in college as a joke. It was not very original, but it stuck as sort of an inside joke. Billy finds the nickname rather amusing and teases me that it is racist, but I suspect he likes the bond that it creates between us. Only one other person calls Billy "Chief," though others have tried.

"Send them in," I answered as I shut down solitaire.

A tall, lean man entered my inner sanctum. I would guess six-foot-two. He had salt and pepper hair and steel gray eyes. Ruggedly handsome, a woman would say. He was dressed in an expensive suit and was maybe ten years older than me, but in really good shape.

"Mr. Joseph Fleet requests your presence as soon as possible at his residence," the man said in a monotone. He wore a deadly serious expression. He stood waiting for a response from me as I stared at him. He seemed in no hurry.

"I'm supposed to bring you now," he added, matter of factly.

I didn't know Joseph Fleet but I certainly knew of him. If he wasn't the richest man in Mountain Center he was at least in the top five.

"You have a name?" I asked the messenger.

"Roy Husky," he said. Upon closer inspection Roy did not exactly look like a typical employee. More like a bodyguard. He was polished and spoke with some education but I guessed that underneath it all he was basically a thug.

"So, Roy, it's take me or die trying?"

"Something like that," he said, with a tight grin.

"Think you could?" I smiled.

Roy looked over his shoulder toward Billy in the outer office. "Probably not," he said with a little larger smile. At least he was honest.

"You're in luck. I'm not busy. Let's go."

I FOLLOWED ROY out to a black limousine. He opened the back door and I got in. Once we were moving he lowered the privacy partition.

"You Fleet's chauffeur?" I asked.

"Among other things," he answered in a flat tone.

I didn't want to know what the other things were and so I kept my mouth shut.

After a few minutes Roy broke the silence. "The other man at your office, American Indian?" he asked.

"Yes."

"What tribe?"

"Cherokee."

"Been inside?" asked Roy. He wanted to know if Billy had been in prison. Billy had. I guessed that Roy already knew the answer. He was just looking for confirmation.

"For him to say," I answered, and paused. "You?"

"Yep," he nodded, and the conversation was over.

The drive took a while. The Fleet Addition was an exclusive neighborhood on the extreme north side of town. The rumor was that when Joseph Fleet developed the subdivision and built his mansion there he pulled some political strings and had the Addition annexed so that his children could go to city schools. Fleet was supposedly a devout family man. Actually, he had only one child, a daughter, Sarah Ann. She was a few years behind me in high school and I had not really known her and had not seen her in years. Fleet's wife died a few years back and he had not remarried, at least that I had heard.

As we drove I thought about Roy's interest in Billy. I suspected that Roy recognized and respected power and danger when he saw it. Billy was an imposing figure. At six-foot-six he didn't look so tall at first glance because his body was so perfectly proportioned. He did look immense.

Billy and I had met during our first basketball practice at the University of Connecticut. Billy was there on a basketball scholarship and trying desperately to get an education. I was there on an academic scholarship and trying desperately to forget about Marlene Long who had seemingly disappeared off the face of the earth. Since I was a pretty good high school player, I had decided to take my just over six-foot frame and walk on to the UConn basketball team. I hoped to win a guard position, but two weeks later I was told my services were no longer needed.

Billy and I sat next to each other in a freshman Geography class. Billy was very quiet. I think he was afraid of saying something stupid, so he said nothing. I rarely got more than a one-word response to anything I said to him. But I hung in there with him and one day after class he asked if I wanted to go someplace and get something to eat. I said yes and that was our start.

Billy gradually opened up. In fact, sometimes I could not shut him up. I don't think he had anyone else to talk to. We became the dynamic duo, the basketball star and the playboy scholar. For countless hours I helped him study. He was brighter than he gave himself credit for, but he was deliberate and he was afraid of books. It took him a while to get things, but when he finally understood he didn't forget. We both graduated in the spring of 1980, Billy with a degree in Art and I with degrees in Finance and Economics. We went our separate ways vowing to stay in touch.

I ended up on Wall Street. Billy made some bad decisions, kept some bad company, and ended up in prison. I visited Billy on a regular basis while he was in Danbury prison for the entire five years I worked in New York City. It took years for Billy to tell me what he was in for and up until that time I never asked or tried to find out. When he got out, I quit the rat race and we headed south. I was amazed that Roy had spotted Billy as an ex-con. *It takes one to know one* ran through my mind.

At the driveway to the Fleet mansion, the big iron gate magically opened. The drive was long and gently winding between well-placed trees that hid the big house from the road. It was early October and the leaves were beginning to change color. When the leaves were gone I suspected the house might be seen from the road. The house was splendid in a facsimile of the old Southern tradition. Four giant white columns framed the double-door front of a three-story center section flanked by two-story side sections. I looked for a Marriott sign but didn't see any.

Roy turned back toward me and said, "Stay in the car. I'll let you out."

I'm not too fond of taking orders of any kind, but I let it pass and waited until Roy opened the door. After all, opening doors was part of a chauffeur's job. He led me up the steps and into a large tiled oval foyer. To the right were double doors that were shut. Just to the left of those doors was a circular staircase to the second floor. To my immediate left was another set of double doors, also closed.

"Wait here," Roy said as he walked down a wide hall in front of me and just to the left.

More orders. I obeyed. Roy's job description was becoming increasingly clear. Part chauffeur, part butler, and part bodyguard. I wondered if he cooked.

Roy returned.

"Mr. Fleet will be with you in a moment. You can wait in the study. Come," he said as he turned and walked back down the hall.

I followed.

Roy nodded toward a doorway to the right and waited until I was inside the study and then shut the door behind me. I smiled to myself and wondered if he locked it to be sure I stayed put.

The room was a typical rich man's study. Bookshelves were everywhere and full of books. Leather-bound classics, books on politics, novels, and reference books. Facing away from a picture window obscured by sheers was a large leather-topped desk with a big overstuffed black leather chair behind it. The chair was showing some wear. Evidently Joseph Fleet spent a good deal of time at his desk. A computer desk was on the right within swivel distance of the main desk. Fleet had basically the same setup as I did: monitor, hard drive, modem, CD player, and printer. A fax machine and answering machine were within reach on a small table to the left. There was a large leather couch, a large coffee table, two leather chairs, two end tables with matching lamps, and a floor lamp that serviced both chairs, all set strategically around an ample fireplace. In one corner was the obligatory freestanding globe. I gave it a spin. It seemed to be current.

"I cannot resist doing that from time to time myself," said a large man entering the room.

Caught in the act.

"Joseph Fleet," he smiled, extending his hand. It was a solid, firm handshake. "Thanks for coming. I hope Roy wasn't too enthusiastic with his invitation."

"Nice to meet you, Mr. Fleet," I said. "If I hadn't wanted to come, I wouldn't be here. What can I do for you?"

"I heard you were to the point. Would you like a drink?"

I looked at my watch to see it was a little past five o'clock. It's a personal discipline never to drink before five.

"A beer would be fine," I replied.

Fleet pressed an intercom at his desk and ordered two beers. He turned back to me and leveled an impressive stare. "I need to find somebody. Or rather two somebodies," he said.

He paused as if wondering exactly how to proceed.

"Anything you say to me is confidential," I said. "And I only share confidentialities with my staff on a need-to-know basis."

Fleet looked forlorn. "My daughter Sarah Ann and my son-in-law are missing. And a lot of money."

I noticed he didn't refer to his son-in-law by name or as Sarah Ann's husband.

"How much money?"

"Nearly three million dollars." He sat down on the couch and took a deep breath.

"How could they get their hands on that much money?"

Fleet looked me right in the eye and began to lay it out.

"Sarah Ann met Ronnie on a cruise—Ronald Fitzgerald Fairchild, of Greenwich, Connecticut. I didn't like him when I heard the name, but she was in love and they had this whirlwind courtship and ran off and got married. I thought he was a fortune hunter so I had him checked out. Plenty of money in the family and he always seemed to have plenty of money, so I didn't think it was money he was after. Maybe he loved her, but they just didn't seem to fit as a couple. Ronnie is a real handsome devil, I have to admit, and glib. Could charm the spots off a leopard. Sarah Ann is attractive enough but not in his league in the looks department. There was just something about him I didn't trust, but after a year or so the marriage seemed to be working so I offered to bring him into the business and he accepted." Fleet was rambling a bit and I just let him ramble.

Roy arrived with two beers in large pilsner glasses and set them on the coffee table. Fleet nodded. Roy left without a word.

"They have been married almost five years and Ronnie has done a good job in the business. With his charm and looks, he is a natural-born salesman. I was beginning to think I was wrong about him."

"Did you ever meet his family?"

"No. Ronnie said they weren't speaking. According to him, he was the black sheep of the family. I didn't have much desire to meet some snobs from Greenwich, Connecticut, anyway."

I smiled inwardly. Fleet was good-ole-boy rich. A son of a bootlegger, he had gone to college, taken the family spoils, and built an empire. Fleet had polished his act, but the rough edges were still there. Hiring Roy Husky certainly fit. He would have little use for the Fairchilds of the world.

"Could anyone else have taken the money?" I asked.

"No way," Fleet said raising his voice slightly. "Only Sarah and myself had that kind of access."

"Not Ronnie?"

"No. Him I trusted only so far."

"When is the last time you saw them?"

"Thursday night. They were going to our condo in Destin, Florida, on Friday morning for a two-week vacation. They never showed up. I haven't heard anything. No call, nothing."

Today was Monday. "When did you discover the money missing?" I asked, though I already guessed it was today. That's why he was panicked.

"This morning. I noticed a large withdrawal from one of our business accounts. I started checking other accounts. Sarah Ann had secretly cashed in stocks and securities and made withdrawals early in the week. Then I got really concerned, so I made a few phone calls and came up with your name."

"Anything else missing? Items that you would not expect them to take on a vacation?"

"Maybe. It's hard to tell. I haven't had the chance to do an inventory."

"What were they driving?"

"A brand-new white Jeep Grand Cherokee Limited."

I sat and thought about what he had told me. Joseph Fleet watched and said nothing. He knew I was processing the information. If Ronnie and Sarah Ann had wanted to disappear with the money, what better day to leave than a Friday? The banks were closed for the weekend. By the time Fleet became suspicious, they had a two-day head start.

"If they planned this together—"

"They didn't," he cut me off. "I know my girl. Something is wrong and I want you to find her." His stare was chilling. I didn't necessarily agree, but I felt compelled to help him.

There was another long silence. All parents think they know their children. The fact is that some parents don't have a clue. Others know their kids as well as they can, but there are always those dark recesses that parents do not and should not know about. We sat staring in different directions and sipping our beers. I had the feeling this was not going to turn out well.

I didn't see any reason to stay longer. "I can't make any promises, but I'll see what I can do."

I got up and held out my hand. He rose and took it.

"Thanks," he said. He looked tired and troubled. "If you have any questions or need anything," he said, "call Roy."

Fleet reached into his inside coat pocket, took out an envelope and handed it to me.

Inside was a check for $10,000. "Too much," I said.

"Doesn't matter. Find her."

"I may want to talk to you again."

"Just call Roy. He'll set it up."

Roy appeared from nowhere and stood at the door waiting to escort me out. We walked back out to the car and Roy opened the right rear door for me again. In the car, Roy turned around and handed me his card: Roy Husky, Fleet Industries, Special Projects Coordinator. It meant bodyguard, strong arm, and a lot more. There were two handwritten numbers on the back, beeper and cell phone.

"How long have you been working for Fleet?" I asked.

"Long time. Since jail. He took me on when nobody else would. I saw an ad in the paper for a chauffeur. I was supposed to send a resumé. What a joke. I was young and full of the devil and had just got out of prison. So I sent a note saying I didn't have a resumé, but I could drive like hell. I couldn't believe it when he called me to come for an interview. He asked me if I had been in jail and I said yes. He asked if I was tough and I said tough enough. He asked if I could take orders and I asked him what the job paid. When he told me, I said I damn sure could take orders. He taught me how to act, how to dress, even how to eat. He made me go to night school and get an associate degree in business. Joseph Fleet changed my life. He's like the father I never had. I owe him." Roy's voice was intense, his eyes piercing. "Don't let him down."

He turned back to the windshield and put the car in gear and headed back toward Mountain Center.

I decided I would not want Roy Husky for an enemy. I knew when someone was telling me the truth and his loyalty to Fleet was genuine.

Joseph Fleet was harder to read. He had no reason to lie to me but I felt something was missing and I was sure sooner or later I would have to know what it was.

My mind wandered. I was a long way from Wall Street and there were times I missed the frantic pace of the city. The move from the University of Connecticut campus to Wall Street was a dream come true. I had always been interested in high finance and the way it worked. I graduated magna cum laude and set my sights on the Street. I knew it was a long shot. I made my resumé as provocative as possible, even including the imaginary fortune I made in an advanced finance class when they gave us an imaginary $10,000 to play the market with. According to my interviewers it was the single most impressive thing on my resumé. So much for grades! I received four offers, took the best one, and my career began. I played with my money and everyone else's. I had considerable funds. During my junior year in college my parents were killed in a commercial airline accident in South America. Dad was on business with IBM and had decided to take Mom along. I was devastated. We were a very close family. I had no siblings. In one tragic moment I became a very rich orphan. Between their personal assets, the IBM insurance, and the airline settlement I was financially set. Seven figures rich. I had total disdain for the money and so I gambled it boldly in the market on things that I thought made sense.

Timing is everything and mine was perfect. I worked long hours and had almost no social life. In truth I was still in mourning and work was my therapy. On the Street, I could do no wrong. I made a name for myself along with a lot of connections. In five years I amassed a fortune for many, including myself, and called it quits. I was burned out, rich, alone and except for Billy, I had no nearby friends. I needed to be around friends and people I knew and so I took Billy and went back to the only place that felt safe and familiar—home. Looking out the Fleet limo window on a beautiful fall day, it seemed like a lifetime ago. Actually it was only ten years.

"You getting out or do I have to throw you out?" Roy asked. He was standing outside the car with my door open. Thank God he was smiling.

"Sorry. Lost in thought."

Roy got back behind the wheel and the driver's side window went down.

"I'll need pictures," I said. "Lots of them and as soon as possible."

Roy nodded without question. I think he understood what I was looking for. I sensed a lot of intelligence behind those steel gray eyes.

"I'll call," he said.

Billy was still in the office.

"Hey, Chief. Gym time," I said.

Today was a gym day and I needed to work out and think about the case I had just received and didn't really want. So what did I expect? I couldn't be an investigator if I didn't want to investigate!

MR. MOTO'S FITNESS SOLUTIONS was an expanding and well-equipped fitness center in the heart of Mountain Center. Every time I went in it seemed Moto had added something new. Billy and I had worked out at least three times a week for years and it showed. I was slightly over six feet one inches tall, one hundred ninety-five pounds and in excellent shape if I do say so myself, except in comparison to Billy, who was a solid rock. I wasn't sure what Billy weighed because he would never get on any scale. I, on the other hand, was obsessed with weighing every day. Billy found that amusing. In fact, Billy found a lot of things I did amusing. *Blood, you are strange,* he always said.

"Donnie!" Moto semi-shouted as I walked through the door, always the same greeting. He half-smiled at Billy and nodded and Billy grunted back. They never exchanged pleasantries. Billy and Moto carried on a fake feud that each found amusing and each perpetuated. Occasionally they argued for the sport of it. All the regulars in the gym understood what was going on between them and added fuel to the fake fire whenever possible. Truth be known, they liked each other a lot as evidenced a few years back when Billy came to Moto's aid on Spring Street. Moto was being hassled by a group of bikers, maybe four or five. Billy happened on the scene and before Moto could protest, Billy had put two of them on the ground. Moto is a black belt and really didn't need any help. Billy knew this but the scene made him angry. It was definitely motivated by racism and Billy had been there before. He couldn't help but get involved. *Mind your own business*, Moto had said. *I can handle this.*

Then handle it, Billy had replied and left the scene, but not before the bikers had gone.

Moto told the story to me later that week out of earshot of Billy. He would not admit it but he was really very proud and very moved by Billy's intervention. "Dumb Indian!" he said at the time. That was his pet name for Billy and always brought a smile to Billy's face. Billy in return called Moto a "dumb Chinaman," which infuriated Moto, which amused Billy. Moto, as Billy well knew, was Japanese.

There were days I had to drag myself into the gym, but Billy never complained about going in. Once I started my routine, I was fine and glad to be there.

"What did Joseph Fleet want with you, Blood?"

"To find his daughter," I panted from the exercise bike beside Billy. I told Billy what I knew.

"What can I do?" he asked.

"Check the obvious—planes, trains, buses, rental cars. Cover all the smaller airports within a hundred-mile radius for planes, commercial and private. Also check Roanoke, Nashville, and Atlanta. I'm almost positive they drove out of here to a major airport but you might as well cover everything. We are being well-paid."

"How much?"

"Twenty thousand," I lied. Billy whistled. I always lied about how much we were being paid. Cherokee Investigations was the major source of income for Billy and I certainly didn't need the money. Billy loved our business. It made him feel important and gave him a sense of purpose. As the pedals turned, I could see Billy was already thinking about the case.

"If it was me, I'd drive to Atlanta and fly out," Billy said.

"Good place to start," I agreed.

We worked out hard for an hour and a half, each in our own way. We started on the exercise bikes for about twenty minutes to get a sweat going and then worked on abs. From there I went to chest and arms, then to back and shoulders, and finished with legs. Sometimes I went back to the bike for about ten minutes at maximum effort or into the side room to work on the speed bag or heavy bag with Billy. I always finished rubbery-legged and feeling justified that despite some of the unhealthy food I continued to eat, I was taking care of my body.

That day we went to the side room to finish our workout. I worked on the speed bag and Billy thumped the heavy bag. Dust flew every time he made contact. After ten minutes on the speed bag and sweating heavily, I took a break. Billy finished his heavy bag workout and reached into his gym bag and took out three knives. They were all large type hunting knives with different blades and handle designs. Billy walked back to the far wall and turned and threw the first knife into a life-sized wooden cutout of a man that was attached to the opposite wall. Billy had made the target himself and Moto, with feigned reluctance, had let Billy mount it in the side room. The knife lodged into the target in the approximate area of the heart. The second knife zipped through the air seconds later and thudded in beside the first. The third knife followed with similar results. Billy repeated this practice in silence while I watched. Sometimes he aimed at an arm or a leg, but mostly the heart. About once a month he had to replace the wood in the chest area. I guess that is why he originally made the target in three pieces, although I never asked.

Billy ended every workout with knife-throwing.

BILLY AND I LEFT the gym at 7 PM and parted company. I drove back to my condo at the Mountain View condo complex. I walked up two flights of stairs to unit 5300, a penthouse corner unit on the top floor. The five was for building five. The three was for the third floor. The double zero meant corner unit, left side of building. Upon entering I was mauled by Jake, my big black standard poodle, who couldn't contain himself to a proper greeting. He had to jump, spin, nuzzle, and perform an assortment of other acrobatic wonders. Did he really like me that much or did he have to pee? I never felt like putting Jake to the test, so I grabbed the leash and we went for a walk. I ignored the beeping answering machine. I knew it didn't have to pee.

Jake and I stayed in town during the week and at the lake house on most weekends. Occasionally we had company of the opposite sex, mostly my company. The lake house is a good hour's drive and belonged to my parents before they were killed. The house and property was and still is immaculate and sprawls over ten acres, a lot of it lakefront on Indian Lake. The lake house is my favorite place in the world but too far for a daily commute, and so I bought the luxury condo at Mountain View in the woods on the outskirts of town.

Every night Jake and I spend a half an hour together outside, weather permitting. Our routine begins with a walk while Jake takes care of business, and ends with a game of soccer-basketball on the tennis court that has a basketball goal.

Standard poodles need daily exercise and quality time with their masters. Fifteen minutes of our game leaves Jake winded and ready for a nap. It doesn't tire me out at all. Jake does all the work. It proceeds like this. I dribble the ball behind the three-point line and try to shoot. Jake tries to steal the ball and occasionally does. When I try to shoot Jake defends. It is not easy trying to score from three-point range with a standard poodle in your face. Especially one that appears to have pogo sticks for legs. I shoot and occasionally score. Jake tracks down the ball and maneuvers it around the court with his nose until he has finally rolled it back to me and the process starts over. We went through our routine and when I thought Jake was sufficiently winded we went back inside.

The answering machine was still beeping. I punched the button and was greeted by a familiar sexy voice. "Hey, Donnie, what's happening? Call me when you and Jake are finished horsing around."

Cassandra Alexandria Smith, a.k.a. Sandy, was my current love interest although the "L" word had never been used and wasn't likely to be. I teased her about her name suggesting that her parents must have been looking for something complicated to go with Smith. An exercise they chose not to go through again. Sandy was an only child. She stood about five foot four inches tall with a very muscular, athletic and well-proportioned body. In a word, Sandy was built. She worked out three times a week. We liked each other a lot, enjoyed spending time together, had great sex, and for the most part led separate lives. Sandy was an investment broker. We met on the telephone when she tried to sell me on her services. I was intrigued by her voice and therefore granted an appointment hoping the rest of the package looked as good as the voice sounded. It did. She was single and "taking a sabbatical from men." I asked her out anyway. She said yes. That was a year ago.

We never demanded each other's time. If getting together wasn't convenient for both parties, neither got offended. "Not tonight" was okay. We rarely planned far ahead. I liked her a lot but I wasn't in love. I was still carrying a twenty-year-old torch that seemed to burn brighter as time passed, no doubt fueled by adolescent hormones left unsatiated. I think something in Sandy's past haunted her also, but so far it had been left undiscussed.

I called her back. "Do you need to be investigated?"

She laughed, "Absolutely!" Sandy had a great laugh.

"Tonight?"

"No, not tonight." she said. "I'm beat. I couldn't give you my best tonight and I have an early appointment tomorrow."

"No problem," I replied, although I did feel a pang of disappointment in my lower extremities. I asked about her day and she told me in a language of fine detail that only Wall Street junkies would have understood. She had had a good day, a very good and stressful day that had left her limp. A day I understood very well. Once upon a time I had been on that roller coaster. I listened intently and interjected at the right moments. She had to tell it to someone who understood. She had to share the excitement, get it all out, unwind.

Finally, Sandy ran out of steam. "God, I'm talking a lot tonight," she said.

"It's okay. You had a big day. Besides, we private investigators need to hone our listening skills."

She laughed again. "Tell me about your day."

I told her and she was fascinated. "What are you going to do? How do you start?"

"Ma'am," I mimicked in my best Bogie, "I haven't a clue."

2

Early the next morning I was in the office playing PC solitaire and pondering a plan of attack. I always played solitaire when I wanted to think something out, usually something like a big stock purchase. I had done some police work for "Big Bob" Wilson, my high school buddy who now happened to be the chief of police, and some investigative work for a few lawyers in town and for an insurance company on an insurance scam. None of it would have taxed anyone with half a brain. I had never tried to find a missing person, so the solitaire had its work to do.

Meanwhile, I had a ten thousand dollar check that I wouldn't cash until the job was done, and a half-finished second cup of coffee was cooling on my right-hand mouse pad—I had long ago trained myself to use the mouse with either hand, so I had mouse pads on both sides of my keyboard. I was playing solitaire using Vegas rules, one look at the card. Use it or lose it. I had four aces up early, caught a few breaks, and ran the deck for the entire $208. I was up $174 when I paged Roy Husky. He called minutes later.

"Cherokee Investigations," I answered most officially.

"I have a Cherokee I need investigated," came the reply. I didn't know Roy had a sense of humor. I might like this guy.

"Jeep or person?" I replied.

"Funny!" he deadpanned

"You too."

"You paged me," Roy said.

"Pictures?" I questioned.

"On my way with them now," came the reply.

"Cell phone?"

"Yeah."

"I'm in the office," I said.

"Ten minutes," Roy said and hung up.

I went back to solitaire and promptly ran the table and won another $208. Back-to-back wins are not uncommon even though winning once sometimes takes twenty or thirty hands. I was up $382 when Roy walked in.

"Where's security?" Roy cracked.

"He's over there in the corner asleep," I said pointing at Jake, but I knew Roy was asking about Billy. "What have you got?"

"Nice dog. Take a look at these," Roy said, handing me a stack of photos.

What Roy had was a lot of pictures of Sarah Ann Fairchild and not that many of Ronnie. Sarah Ann obviously liked the camera and Ronnie did not. The best pictures of Ronnie were the wedding pictures, but even in those he was not looking into the camera. There were only a few good candid shots of Ronnie, when he wasn't aware of the photographer.

"Ronnie disliked cameras," I commented.

"Evidently."

"Thanks, I'll get these back to you later."

Roy nodded and left, a man of few words.

I studied the pictures and thought. If I were Joseph Fleet and had a daughter who was heir to his fortune, I would want to know everything I could about the man she was marrying. I pulled out Roy's card and dialed his cell phone number.

"Yes sir," Roy answered.

Either Roy had developed tremendous respect for me in a very short time or he assumed Joseph Fleet was calling. I assumed the latter.

"Relax. It's your friendly gumshoe. Did Fleet have his son-in-law checked out when he started dating Sarah Ann?"

"Of course."

"By who?"

"I think you mean by whom," he said. "Some guy in Knoxville."

"That helps a lot," I bantered. "Find out."

"I thought you were the private investigator."

"Yeah, right," I replied in my most sarcastic voice and hung up.

I went back to my game of solitaire and almost got shut out on the next deal, losing $47. By the time the phone rang again I was down to $208.

"Thomas Slack Investigations, on Gay Street in Knoxville."

"Gay Street?"

"Knew you would like it," Roy chuckled.

"Thanks," I said. "And don't let him know I'm coming. And I'll call you if I need more smart remarks." I hung up before he could retaliate.

3

The next morning, after an early workout at Moto's, I worked my new Pathfinder LE over to I-81 and south to I-40 West and on into Knoxville. I knew the area well from having attended so many University of Tennessee football and basketball games when I was younger. I had not called ahead. If Slack had a file on Ronnie Fairchild I wanted it intact. I had no reason to believe it wouldn't be, but why take chances?

The day was cool and overcast with battleship gray clouds that threatened rain. I was dressed to the nines in a blue pinstripe suit, white shirt, and a red-striped power tie. My trench coat lay over the passenger seat and my briefcase with laptop securely inside lay in the passenger-side floorboard. A suitcase packed for two days nestled behind the driver's seat—I didn't plan on spending the night but it paid to be prepared. With my radar detector on, I made Gay Street in an hour and fifteen minutes.

Thomas Slack Investigations was on the second floor of an older but well-kept office building. Why did private investigators always have offices on the second floor, I wondered—life imitating art? I opened the door and encountered a very pretty young blond receptionist. Cherokee Investigations could use one of those, I thought.

The phone rang. "Tom Slack Investigations," said a pleasant voice. A pause and then, "I'm sorry, he's on another line. Can I take a message? Uh-huh, uh-huh, right, okay."

She smiled at me and started to say something and the phone rang again and the scenario repeated itself. Before she could hang up it rang again and she put the call through to someone. Then it was quiet.

"Sorry, can I help you?" she asked.

"Busy day, Emily?" I asked. I guessed her name not because I am such a crack investigator but because the nameplate on her desk read Emily Wright.

"Not really," she replied.

I was witnessing a thriving investigations business for the first time. Can't say that I liked it. I handed her my card and requested, "Tom Slack, please."

"Is he expecting you?"

"No. As a professional courtesy I thought he might work me in," I continued. It was meant as a joke. She didn't laugh.

"One moment, please." She walked down the hall and around the corner—not an unpleasant sight. She returned quickly.

"Mr. Slack is with a client. He said to wait and he will see you."

I hung up my trench coat and waited. Then I waited some more. I am not good at waiting. Fidgeting in someone's waiting room is almost as bad as sitting in traffic. I am notorious for walking out on appointments that make me wait and for exploring secondary roads when traffic is backed up. My doctor gives me his first morning appointment for my annual physical since a few years ago I walked out of his office after having waited an hour. He actually called to apologize. My doctor does not want to make me angry. As a personal favor, I handle his investments. His investments are doing quite well.

But I was going to wait for Tom Slack for as long as it took. I may be impatient, but I am not stupid. I had driven a considerable distance to see Slack and I had come unannounced for a reason. So I waited.

It wasn't long before a fortyish-looking man with close-cropped blond hair came walking purposefully down the hall. He wore a slight smile. He stopped and considered me. "Mister Youngblood?"

I stood and shook the extended hand. "Don will do just fine," I answered.

"Tom Slack. Call me Tom. Come on back."

I grabbed my briefcase and followed him down the hall and around the corner and down that hall to the end where we entered his office. It was, of course, a corner office and as far from the reception area as he could get and still be in the building. His office was about twenty feet square and immaculate. It was tastefully decorated in a male persona and everything was in its place. Slack had rugged good looks on a frame that appeared to be in very good shape and stood about five feet ten inches tall. His eyes were ice blue, bright and intent. A picture on the wall explained it all. Tom Slack was an ex-marine colonel.

"I didn't know Mountain Center had a private investigation firm," he said.

"We don't really," I replied. "I just kind of dabble. Small stuff."

"Well what brings you to Knoxville?"

"I need to ask about someone your firm investigated a while back. A Ronald Fairchild. You were hired by Joseph Fleet or more probably by Roy Husky."

"I really cannot comment on any case unless the client gives permission," Slack said. "You should know that."

"No problem," I said as I took my cell phone from my coat pocket, "What is your direct number?" He gave it to me.

I dialed Roy's beeper. We sat and stared at each other as we waited. It wasn't long before Slack's phone rang. "Put it on speaker, please," I said. He did.

"Tom Slack," he answered.

"This is Roy Husky," came the voice through the speaker.

Before Slack could reply I interjected, "Roy, Youngblood here. I need Fleet's permission to see the file we discussed."

"Permission granted," came the reply with a tint of humor. I could picture Roy smiling.

"How do I know this is Roy Husky?" Slack asked.

"Remember the bar we met at, Mr. Slack? Remember the girl . . ."

"Okay, okay," Slack said hurriedly. He picked up the phone. "I'll be sure he gets everything we have." He listened for a moment, smiled, said "Okay" and then hung up and pressed the intercom button. "Emily, get me the file on Ronald Fairchild. It's five or six years old."

We waited.

"How long you been a P.I.?" he asked.

"A few years," I smiled. "Although there is still some doubt that I really am one."

"I might need your help in your area sometime," Slack said. I couldn't tell if he was serious or just making idle conversation while we waited on the file.

"Anytime," I said.

The door opened and Emily came in with a file. Slack briefly looked at it and then passed it to me as his phone rang. He answered and got absorbed in the conversation, as I got absorbed in the file. There wasn't a lot there. By the time Slack was finished with his telephone call, I was finished with my first pass through the file. Slack's investigator on the case had been an ex-cop, Ed Sanders, who had spent two days in Connecticut a few weeks before Ronnie and Sarah Ann were married. According to the file, Ronnie Fairchild was who he said he was and from a rich and prominent Greenwich, Connecticut, family. Trent Fairchild III, Ronnie's father, headed a very successful investment firm. Ronnie had one older brother, Trent IV. Obviously, Joseph Fleet had been pleased with the report. "Any chance of talking to Ed Sanders?" I asked.

"Not unless you believe in seances," Slack cracked.

"Dead?"

Slack nodded.

"When?"

"A few days after he came back from Connecticut after working this case."

"How?"

"Car wreck. Drunk."

"Anything suspicious about the accident?"

"You think it's connected to this case?" He looked skeptical.

"I don't know," I said. "I'm just asking questions."

"Well, forget it. Ed Sanders was an alcoholic. It was the reason he had to leave the Knoxville police force. He did good work and promised me he would never drink on the job and as far as I know he didn't. Sometimes when he wasn't working a case he would go on a bender. Then I'd call and tell him to sober up, that I had a job for him. The next day he would show up sober and ready to work. That's pretty much the way it went the entire three years he worked for me. I was sorry when I heard the news, but not surprised. If he hadn't been an ex-cop he would probably have had a dozen DUI's.

"Do you know any of the details?" I asked.

"Single-car accident late at night. No witnesses."

"Can I have a copy of this file?"

"No need for a copy, take the file. Send it back when you're through with it."

I thanked Slack for his time. We shook hands and I left his office. The reception area was empty as I gathered my trench coat from the coat rack.

"In town long?" Emily queried with a smile beyond friendliness.

I smiled back. "It does look like I might have to stay at least one night."

She handed me a card. "Call me if you're free, and I'll buy you a drink."

I pocketed the card. "I'll do that," I said and left.

The times, as Dylan said, *they are a changin'.*

NOT LONG AFTER LEAVING Tom Slack Investigations, I was in a downtown coffee shop doing major damage to a loaded cheeseburger and a large order of fries. I had commandeered a booth in the back and was deeply engrossed in my food, a *USA Today,* and a *Knoxville News Sentinel.* My beloved Tennessee Vols were entrenched in the top ten after wins over UCLA, Arkansas, the hated Florida Gators, and LSU. Visions of another national championship danced in my head. Georgia was next. Then my cheeseburger almost did an about-face as I read that our star running back was out for the season. My visions of a national championship vanished.

I had not lied to the lovely Emily when I said I might be spending the night. I disliked coincidences, even when they made sense. Ed Sanders could have died after working on any case, but he died after working on the case I was now investigating and my naturally suspicious nature was working overtime. I used my cell phone to call Big Bob Wilson.

Big Bob was my best high school friend and we had stayed in touch after graduation. His nickname was bestowed by teammates after the local paper repeatedly reported that "Big Bob Wilson" had done this or that when referring to a win by our high school basketball team. Big Bob went on to UT on a basketball scholarship. In his senior year, he made All-SEC and Tennessee went to the NCAA tournament, an occurrence that came around about as often as Halley's Comet. The Vols made it to the sweet sixteen.

Big Bob graduated with a degree in criminal science but he still let his very close friends call him Big Bob even though he was now Chief of Police in Mountain City. Big Bob's father was also one of the five richest men in town and many thought this was why Big Bob was police chief at such a young age. I didn't think Big Bob was all that young. We were both pushing forty.

"Mountain Center Police Headquarters," announced a female voice on the other end of the line.

"Hi, Susie," I said. "Let me speak to the Big Bob."

"Hey Donnie. How you doin'?"

Susie was Big Bob's sister. After small talk, she got him on the line.

"Hey Blood! What's going on?" Big Bob's voice matched his nickname. He was a serious man with a subtle sense of humor. He had become more serious after being appointed Chief. Crime and all that went with it had had its effects on the big man. Big Bob had ulcers.

"Investigating," I replied. "Remember, I'm a private investigator."

"Like shit you are," he teased. "Investor gator is more like it."

"I'm on a serious case and surrounded by comedians," I said. "Listen, Big Bob, I need a favor. Do you know the Knoxville Chief of Police?"

"Of course. What do you need?"

"I need to talk to the officer who investigated a traffic accident about five years ago if he is still with the force. If not, then I need to know where he is. I need to know something today if possible. Call me on the cell phone."

"Will do. By the way, we're expecting you for dinner Friday night." Before I could accept or decline, Big Bob hung up. I took out my day planner and wrote *Dinner@Wilsons* under Friday. Big Bob had spoken.

I HAD FINISHED with *USA Today* and was well into my second cup of coffee when my cell phone rang.

"Ask for Captain Liam McSwain," Big Bob commanded.

"An Irish cop. How quaint."

Big Bob ignored the humor. "He'll see you as soon as you get there."

"Thanks," I said. "He must owe you a favor."

"Everybody owes me a favor," he said and hung up.

I opened the Fairchild file and re-read it. Then I looked at the late Ed Sanders's expense account. His written report about the trip said he had spent two days in Connecticut but there was a receipt for only one night at a Holiday Inn in Darien. Other than that one discrepancy, I found no other information that I had not found the first time I looked at the file. I tucked the file in my briefcase and left a tip and the newspapers behind as I paid the check at the front register. The police department was in a municipal building near the Tennessee River, not far from the University of Tennessee campus. I decided to walk. I needed to walk and think. It took fifteen minutes.

I RODE THE elevator to the fifth floor where the lobby directory informed me I might find the Chief. I introduced myself to the receptionist, handed her my card and told her that I was expected. I was shortly sitting in front of the Knoxville Chief of Police.

"So how is Big Bob?" Liam McSwain asked with a heavy brogue.

"Big," I said. I resisted the temptation of asking the Irishman how he had ended up in Knoxville, Tennessee, as the Chief of Police.

"He certainly is that," McSwain said. "What can I do for you?"

McSwain was no lightweight himself. He was about six foot two and probably weighed two-fifty but did not look fat. He had a ruddy complexion and premature gray hair with eyebrows to match. His hands were large and meaty and a barrel chest tapered to relatively slender hips. I imagined him to be one of those graceful big men whose agileness and coordination belied his size. Even at his age—mid-fifties, I guessed—he was not a guy I would want to mess with. I also guessed that when he gave orders they were followed. I told him what I needed.

"Sanders, you say," McSwain said as he turned sideways to his computer. I could listen to this guy talk all day, I thought. "About five years ago?"

I nodded.

The big hands moved deftly over the keyboard. He brought up the accident report. Seconds later his printer whirred into action and spit out a page. McSwain glanced at it and handed it to me.

"Looks routine," he said.

I scanned it. Two AM, single-car accident, dead drunk, etc. Ed Sanders was just another statistic. The investigating officer was Hoffman.

"Where can I find this Officer Hoffman?" I asked.

He turned back to his computer and opened another file.

"Left the force last year," McSwain said.

"Know where he went?"

"Doesn't say," he replied, glancing at the screen with a sigh that said my time was up.

"Any chance you can find out for me?"

He gave me a quick annoyed look that let me know I was pushing it, but then he smiled and said, "Sure, where can I reach you?"

"I'll be moving around a lot in the next few days," I said. "But I'll be at Big Bob's on Friday for dinner."

"Fine. I'll let Big Bob know and he can pass it along Friday night." He wrote Hoffman with a question mark on a note pad on his desk. Under that he wrote, **Call Big Bob**.

I could have given him my cell phone number, but only a few people knew it and I wanted to keep it that way. I didn't think the information was so important it couldn't wait until Friday night. I hoped Hoffman wasn't dead. Then I really would be paranoid.

I stood and extended my hand. "I appreciate your time and your help. If you get up my way, we'll grab Big Bob and I'll treat for dinner."

He shook my hand and replied, "It's a date."

I RETRIEVED THE Pathfinder and headed for the Residence Inn on Kingston Pike. I wanted to do some more poking around and I had a few ideas. I felt like a barnyard rooster scratching and pecking, scratching and pecking, hoping to turn up something worth finding. By the time I got inside my penthouse suite, it was 5:05. I quickly changed into my running gear and headed back to campus. Ten minutes later I was doing laps on Tom Black track. Running helps me think and thinking helps me forget that running is really work. An hour later I was back in my suite with a beer, a box of white cheddar Cheez-Its and my laptop, checking out the stock market. It had been a very flat day on the Street.

I called Sandy and talked to her machine. "Staying over," I said. "Probably back tomorrow night. Want to get laid?" My rule was to leave as few words as possible on any machine. I also left my telephone and room number. Then I made one more phone call and headed to the shower.

THE REGAS IS one of Knoxville's oldest and best-known restaurants. I valet parked the Pathfinder and double-checked my attire in the entrance hall mirror. Black turtleneck, gray herringbone sport coat with a touch of beige, and tan slacks accessorized by a black belt, black socks, and black shoes. I was trying to be modest but I liked what I saw. Private investigators, after all, do need confidence.

There was a half-hour wait for dinner. I put my name in for two and went to the bar. I ordered a Rolling Rock and had no sooner taken that first cold delicious swallow than I felt a hand on my shoulder. I turned and was almost nose-to-nose with a very pretty, blond haired, blue-eyed face.

"Hi," I said. "First round is on you. What will you have?"

"Rolling Rock looks good," Emily replied.

Emily was gorgeous in a black leather jacket, white turtleneck, tight jeans, and high heels. If I had been a wolf I would have howled. Instead I smiled and took another swallow of Rolling Rock. We finished our first round exchanging small talk and as promised Emily bought the first round. She had just paid for the drinks when my name was called for dinner.

"You hungry?" I asked. "Dinner is on me."

"Sure," she smiled.

I left the bartender a five and we followed our waiter to our table. We took our time accessing the menu. Finally, Emily looked up. "Too many choices," she said. "What are you having?"

"Salmon."

"Sounds good to me."

When the waiter returned, I ordered two salmon entrees and two small Caesar salads. I looked at Emily as I ordered the salads and a slight nod of her head told me I had made the right choice.

We engaged in more small talk. I mostly listened as Emily told me her life story. Occasionally I asked a question to keep her going. I wanted her talking freely. We ordered another round of drinks. The Caesars came and went. Delicious. The salmon arrived.

"How long have you been with Tom Slack?"

"Eight years," Emily answered. "I was attending UT and getting bored. I answered an ad in the paper for a part-time file clerk-typist. I worked about twenty hours a week and continued school. Mr. Slack liked my work and kept offering me more hours. The more hours I worked, the fewer classes I took. After two years I was working full-time and going to night school. I finally graduated two years ago with a degree in business. My official title now is office manager. I run the office, do payroll, manage the secretaries and sometimes play receptionist."

"Which I am glad you were doing today," I smiled.

"Me, too," Emily smiled back. "The salmon is delicious."

"Indeed it is. Do you remember Ed Sanders?"

"Ed? Sure. Nice guy, but he drank too much. It was a real shock when he was killed. Mr. Slack was very upset."

"Was Sanders married?"

"Divorced, I think. I saw his wife at the funeral so I know he was married, but I believe I heard they were divorced."

"Any children?"

"One at least. Ed had a son he was very proud of. The kid was a real jock for Knox Central, football and basketball. Ed talked about him all the time. If he had other children, he never mentioned them. Why all the interest?"

Something tugged at my memory as I tried to make a connection but then it was gone. "A case Ed investigated is tied to a case I am working now," I answered. "It's probably nothing. I'm just tracking down leads. Do you know the wife's name or where she lives?"

Emily arched an eyebrow and gave me a wicked smile. "I get it. I'm being pumped for information. A little beer, a good meal, and the lady will tell you anything, right?"

I was beginning to like this woman.

I laughed. "You did give me your phone number."

"Touché," Emily said. "And I'm glad you called. Call me at the office tomorrow and I'll pull Ed's personnel file and see if I can help."

"Deal. How about dessert or coffee?"

OUTSIDE IN THE cool autumn evening I turned to Emily and asked, "Did you valet park your car?"

She smiled and said, "I took a taxi."

I gave my parking receipt to the valet and within minutes I was downtown on Cumberland Avenue and out Kingston Pike obediently following the directions Emily had given me. Eventually I took a right into an elaborate condo complex.

"Building G, to the left past the tennis courts," Emily instructed. "There," she pointed. "Any place in front of that building."

I parked. I got out and went around the back of the Pathfinder to open the passenger side door, but Emily was already out and searching for her keys.

"One flight up," she said as she led the way.

We stopped in front of 2G as Emily unlocked two locks and opened the door. I stood in the threshold.

"Coming in?" she asked with an inviting smile.

"Better not this time."

"Guess I'll have to settle for a good-night kiss," she said as she slid against me.

It was more of a statement of fact than a question and we were kissing before I knew what happened. It was not that unpleasant. I could feel her breasts against my chest and her hips pressing against mine. Her mouth was relaxed and inviting. I let go of her reluctantly.

"I'll call you tomorrow, if that's OK."

"Sure," she smiled.

"Good-night," I said.

I left as casually as I could, thinking that I probably should have stayed and wondering why I didn't. I hadn't slept with anyone but Sandy Smith in more than a year. Sandy and I have an unspoken understanding to be mutually exclusive. Since it remains unspoken, I'm not quite sure, but that's the way I was playing it. One woman at a time is enough. Why make life more complicated than it already is?

4

My favorite time of day is early morning after a good night's sleep. I was up at six and in the lounge of the Residence Inn getting that first cup of elixir and devouring the sports pages. Tennessee was a six-point underdog against Georgia. The game was in Athens. Both teams were ranked in the top ten and Georgia considered it their biggest game in years. Big Bob and I were going to the game and I felt nervous already.

I went back to my room, hooked up my laptop and went online to check the market. I went through my various portfolios surveying the winners and losers. My luck—intuition, gift, or whatever it was—was holding. I made one purchase and one sell, checked all my e-mail and logged off. It seemed as if I had been online maybe a half hour. Actually it was two. I shaved, showered and dressed in a fresh shirt and different tie and checked the time. It was after nine.

I called the lovely Emily. "Tom Slack Investigations," she said answering the phone in a very businesslike voice. Not the voice she had used on me the night before.

"Good morning," I said, curious to see if she recognized my voice. I have been told I have a rather distinctive voice. I would guess it is because of my southern upbringing and my northern schooling and the fact that I worked hard to lose some of the drawl that caused me to be unmercifully teased in my freshman year at UConn.

"Hi, Don," she answered. "Is this a personal call or business?"

"Both," I answered truthfully. The market had taught me always to keep my options open.

"I have something for you."

"Shoot."

"Ed's ex-wife is Mary Sanders. They divorced six months before Ed was killed. She lives in the Green Tree Apartments off Sutherland Avenue. Telephone 476-6484. Two kids, both in college at Wake Forest."

"Hold it," I said. "Is one of the kids named Jimmy?"

"Yes. How did you know?"

"He's an All-ACC quarterback. Might make All-America this year."

"The only football I follow is UT," Emily said, scoring points with me. "Anyway, the other kid is Susan. She's a couple of years younger than Jimmy. Plays basketball. Anything else you need?"

I had a bunch of smart remarks for that question, but I decided to play it straight. "Did Mary Sanders know that Ed was working for Tom Slack?" I asked.

"Yes, she knew."

"Would she remember you?"

"Maybe."

"Ask Tom if you can call her and arrange an interview for me. Tell her that I'm a private investigator working on an old case that Ed might have worked on and that I would like to ask her some questions. Be as vague as you can."

I WAS BEGINNING to understand the art of investigation. Ask a question and get an answer that leads to two more questions. Follow a lead down a single path and the path invariably forks. This case was getting too geometric. The questions and leads were piling up and I could see at least two opposite directions to take. A lot of the leads would probably prove to be a waste of time. So be it. I still didn't like the coincidence that Ed Sanders died so soon after investigating Ronnie Fairchild. I figured I had at least another week of work before I exhausted all my leads. I also figured that, unless they found me, I was not going to find Ronnie and Sarah Ann Fleet Fairchild. People who work hard at not being found are very hard to find, and the Fairchilds had nearly three million reasons not to be found. My philosophic daydream ended when the phone rang.

"Youngblood."

"Mary Sanders has agreed to see you. She will meet you in the lounge of the Residence Inn at one-thirty," Emily said.

"Thanks, you've been a big help."

"When are you leaving?"

"Right after I talk to Mary Sanders."

"When are you coming back?"

I didn't know how to answer that one. I had a strong urge to see Emily again but I had an unspoken commitment in Mountain Center. I gave Emily the best answer I could.

"I don't know, but I hope I see you again sometime," I said.

"Call me if you need anything, Don," Emily purred.

AT ONE-THIRTY I was in a corner of the Residence Inn lounge that I had staked out fifteen minutes earlier. Mary Sanders had not yet made an appearance. The Pathfinder was in the parking lot, packed for the drive back to Mountain Center. The vision of Emily Wright was shoved into a back corner of my mind and I was ready to go home and ravage the lovely Sandy Smith. As I was about to pursue this carnal fantasy, I was interrupted by reality.

A tall, attractive blond woman walked into the lobby and paused at the registration desk looking around. Mary Sanders. She was not at all what I expected. She turned, spotted me and approached with an air of confidence and purpose. She was in the uniform of her profession and her nameplate confirmed who she was. Mary Sanders was a cop.

"Officer," I stood and nodded offering her a chair and handing her my card.

"Mary," she smiled.

"Don," I countered.

She looked much younger than I had expected. With a son who had to be near twenty-two, Mary was probably no younger than forty but I would have guessed thirty to thirty-five. She was close to six feet tall and even the uniform could not hide all of her very attractive assets.

She had clear blue eyes that stared straight into mine. This was not a lady to be messed with.

"Thank you for taking the time to see me."

"I was curious," she countered. "What are you working on?"

I told her about the disappearance of Ronnie and Sarah Ann Fairchild and about the fact that her ex-husband had checked out Ronnie Fairchild's background a few days before he died.

"You think there is a connection between Ed's death and this case?"

The question surprised me. "You don't think Ed's death was an accident?"

"Never have, never will," she said shaking her head. "Ed was an alcoholic, but he would never drive drunk. He would take a cab, call me, call a friend but never drink and drive. I knew him almost all my life and I am sure of it."

Her stare was intense. Her sincerity was compelling. It didn't jive with what Tom Slack had said, but maybe he was just guessing.

"So, who do you think killed him?"

"I don't know. Ed and I had not lived together for two years before the divorce. He drank a lot and might have been into some things he shouldn't have been into. Drugs maybe." She paused as if trying to decide whether to tell me more. "I've never told anyone this, and if you repeat it I'll deny it, but I have this feeling I can trust you." Mary moved closer and lowered her voice although there was no one else in sight. "A few days before he was killed, Ed mailed me a package with a note saying it was some money for the kids to help with college. The note said to put it in a safe place and that there probably would be more money later. There wasn't."

"How much money?"

"Ten thousand dollars," Mary said slowly. "No way he comes up with that kind of money unless he is into something wrong."

"Did you ask him about it?"

"Never had the chance."

The look on Mary's face was a blend of sadness and anger. I let her words hang for a moment and then asked, "What did you do with the money?"

"I was going to give it back, but before I could Ed was killed. I didn't know what to do with it so I bought each of the kids a five thousand dollar CD and put them in my safety deposit box. They are still there."

"You did the right thing," I assured her. "Were you at the scene of the accident?"

"No. The so-called accident happened around 3 AM. I had gotten off work at midnight. I came straight home and went to bed. I found out the next day."

"Did you see the scene later?"

"Yes," she answered. "I couldn't help myself. The more I thought about it the more I did not think it was an accident. The kids were really upset and Ed didn't have any family other than us so I had to make all the arrangements. By the time I visited the scene it was cleaned up, but it was the perfect place to stage an accident if someone was trying to make it look that way. All the components were there—a fairly long curve, late at night, drunk driver with a history of alcohol, steep embankment, no guardrail. Car goes straight when road curves. Car leaves road, rolls over five or six times, gets torn all to pieces and explodes."

Mary's monotone described the scene as if she had been over it many times in her head. She rattled off the details with the blank stare of someone who was not in the present. Mary paused and the stare continued. I reached out and put my hand on her shoulder and brought her back to the here and now.

"Sorry," she said.

"It's OK. Were they able to get a blood alcohol level from the body?"

"Yes. Ed was thrown from the car, official cause of death, broken neck. His blood alcohol level was point one five. I screamed for an autopsy and got it. The ME said he thinks Ed was alive when the car left the road but he could not be sure. Nothing he found was inconsistent with the wreck."

"He could have been unconscious," I observed.

"Without a doubt," Mary said.

"Did you try to check out his whereabouts before the accident?"

"Yes. Once I got things settled down with the kids. I never told the kids that I didn't think Ed's death was an accident. It would have killed Jimmy. He took it the hardest. Jimmy and his dad were pals. It hurt him so bad he quit the basketball team in mid-season and he was all-city as a freshman. Then he refused to go out for football. Said he would always be looking for his dad in the stands. It took him a while to accept Ed's death and when he did he went back to sports. Susan and Ed weren't getting along very well at the time of Ed's death. Ed wasn't treating me very well and Susan disliked him for it. She felt guilty that she never resolved the conflict. Anyway, I'm rambling," she said with a little embarrassed smile. "I loved Ed once and he was the father of my children. If anyone took his life, I want to find out who and why.

"A few days after the funeral I asked Bud Hoffman to check out his local hangouts to see if he had been at one of them the night of his death. Bud was the first on the scene of Ed's accident and I know him casually. Anyway, no luck—dead-ends everywhere. In fact, he could not find a single person, other than Tom Slack, who had seen Ed alive since he returned from that Connecticut trip."

My ears perked up. "How did you know Ed went to Connecticut?"

"He told Jimmy. Jimmy was all excited. Ed told him he was going into New York City while he was there and would get Jimmy a Yankees baseball cap. I found the cap in Ed's apartment when I went through his things."

I was running out of questions but I was enjoying talking to Mary Sanders. "I was told Bud Hoffman left the Knoxville police force last year. Do you know where he went?"

"New Orleans. Bud was from Louisiana and always wanted to be a part of the New Orleans PD."

In my mind, I went over everything Mary had told me. Our eyes met in a contemplative stare. Two very different, yet very attractive, women in two days, I needed to get out more often, I thought.

Mary smiled. "Want another case?"

"No, thanks," I smiled back. "The one I've got is tough enough, but if I find out anything else about Ed's death, I'll let you know."

She took out a card and wrote her home number and beeper number on the back, then handed it to me. "If I can ever be of help or if you find out anything, give me a call," Mary said as we stood up.

"I'll do it. It was nice meeting you, Mary. Thanks for your time and your honesty."

She looked directly at me with those piercing blue eyes. "I hope I see you again sometime."

Before I could think of a reply, Mary Sanders turned and was gone. I watched her disappear out the front door. Now I had two reasons for wanting to come back to Knoxville. I've really got to get out of this town, I thought.

I WAS ROARING up I-81 with an urgent need for close female contact in the person of one Sandy Smith. I reached for my cell and speed dialed her work number. "Cassandra Smith," she answered.

"You might want to record this. It's going to be an obscene phone call."

"Great, those are the best kind."

"Please tell me that we are on for tonight."

"You too, huh? Damn right we are. Better be well rested."

I slowed to seventy-five miles an hour and put the Pathfinder on cruise. "No problem," I said. "But cut the sexy talk before I run off the road."

She laughed. "I can't talk now, lover. Got to run. See you around seven?"

"Count on it," I said and hung up. The drive home had just become a whole lot more enjoyable. I never did believe the old saying that *anticipation is ninety per cent of satisfaction*, but it sure has its place.

I OBSERVED DAYLIGHT making its slow retreat behind the Great Smoky Mountains as I knocked on Sandy's condo door. She lived in the same complex that I did except at the other end in building one. It was a very long walk that Jake and I both needed. The nights were getting progressively cooler and the mountain air was fragrant with autumn smells, my favorite time of the year. Sandy opened the door and I forgot all about weather and seasons. She was wearing sandals, jeans, a T-shirt, and a big smile. A faint hint of nipples from her ample breasts accented her T-shirt suggesting she was not wearing a bra. Her black curly hair glistened in the fading sunlight that peeked over my shoulder and her turquoise-blue eyes sparkled. I resisted the urge to grab her then and there and instead kissed her lightly on the mouth. At that moment Jake, who had waited patiently behind me, bounded in.

"Jakie!" Sandy squealed. She immediately knelt and began to give Jake a good rub around his neck and ears.

"Boy, I see who ranks around here," I teased.

"You'll get yours later big guy," Sandy grinned.

"My ears rubbed?"

"Yes, and more. Now get in the kitchen and fix that famous Caesar salad. I'm starved."

Jake went immediately to the living area and lay down in front of the fireplace even though there was no fire. It was his favorite spot in Sandy's condo. I went obediently to the kitchen and began preparing Caesar salad. Sandy began working on fettuccini with a light Alfredo sauce and garlic bread. A bottle of Kendall Jackson Chardonnay was on the kitchen island, opened and breathing. Sandy poured two glasses. I usually drank beer but I could not pass up a bottle of "KJ" as she called it. I sipped the wine and began to create.

Youngblood's recipe for terrific Caesar salad goes something like this: Start with the best head of romaine lettuce you can find and tear off the bottom, thereby separating the leaves. Wash in ice-cold water and pat dry with paper towel. Tear the leaves into eatable size portions while scrutinizing for any flaws in the lettuce. Be liberal in what you throw away. Split the stalk where it is too large. Place the lettuce in a jumbo salad bowl and add an appropriate amount of Cardini's original Caesar salad dressing. Yes, I know I should make my dressing from scratch using an egg and anchovies, but what do you expect from a bachelor? Toss the lettuce until the leaves are lightly coated. Using a brick of Parmesan cheese, grate an appropriate amount over the lettuce. Add homemade croutons (which I made earlier). Be sure and crush some of the croutons so that you have some nice size crumbs spread throughout the salad. This will enhance the flavor. Toss until all ingredients are well mixed, then eat your heart out.

WE WERE IN bed and it was well past midnight. Dinner had been a rousing success. After dinner had been even better. When we had finished the last of the wine I kissed her. Seconds later Sandy and I were hurriedly undressing each other on the way to Sandy's king-size bed. We had urgent, physical sex followed by a less aggressive period of very tender sensual lovemaking. After a rest and a long conversation about stocks and my case, we made love again. Sandy lay asleep in my arms and I was on the twilight of sleep trying to figure out my next move on the Fleet case. The last thing I remember was thinking that maybe I should find Bud Hoffman.

5

I woke to an empty bed and the smell of fresh coffee. The hum of the air conditioning beckoned me to roll over and drift off again. I reluctantly ignored it. Sandy was showered and dressed when I stumbled into the kitchen wearing only the white robe I kept at her place for when I stayed over.

"Good morning," she said cheerfully.

I waved weakly. I prefer total silence between getting up and having my first cup of coffee and a shower, after which I feel human enough to speak. I took a mug of coffee offered to me by a smiling Sandy, added cream and sugar, and headed for the bathroom. Although amused, Sandy understood me well enough to accept my morning ritual. She would wait patiently while the hot water, soap, shampoo, shaving cream, razor, and toothbrush performed their magic and I reappeared a new and more responsive man. Fifteen minutes later I was sitting at the kitchen bar having a second cup of coffee and eating a whole-wheat English muffin.

"Has Jake been out?" I asked.

"Of course. We had a very nice walk."

At the sound of his name, Jake the dog came over for a morning rub. When he had lost my attention, he went to Sandy for more pampering. When Sandy dismissed him, he went back to his favorite spot and lay down.

"We have to talk," Sandy said seriously.

I stared. Not good, I thought.

"I'm moving," she said calmly.

I was stunned. "Where?"

"Atlanta."

"Why?" I asked, but being the great detective that I am, I was reasonably sure of her answer. Only one thing would draw Sandy away from Mountain Center.

"I have accepted a new offer of employment," she said quite pertly.

"Who with?"

"Wachovia."

"Damn," was all I could muster as a reply.

We kept silent as we finished our pseudo breakfast. Sandy had been in my life for a year and I very much liked our arrangement. I enjoyed all of her with no commitment. As the words *I'm moving* echoed through my brain, I slowly began to realize that maybe I cared for her more than I was willing to admit. I did not want her to go anywhere! I did not want another woman in my life. On the other hand, I did not want to hold back her career. She had obviously given this some thought and decided the move was right for her.

Or was she giving me an unspoken ultimatum? It was my experience that most women wanted commitment. Was I, a confirmed bachelor, capable of making a commitment? My head was spinning.

"Atlanta's not so far away," I said.

"No, it's not."

"How soon?"

"Two weeks."

Two weeks, I wanted to scream. Instead I said, "We could see each other a lot."

"Yes, we could."

"Jake would miss you," I added.

"And I would miss him," Sandy said with a slight smile. She was very mechanical and proper in her responses.

The next words out of my mouth were supposed to be *I'll miss you too*, but what came out was, "I have to get to the office."

"Me too," she said.

I clicked Jake's leash onto his collar, gave Sandy a light kiss and headed for the front door.

"I'll call you," I said as I closed the door behind me.

JAKE AND I went to the office. Over the last year I had taken Jake to the office on the average of twice a week. Lately, he seemed to be going every day. The building management had not bothered to restrict dogs in my lease since they undoubtably thought a dog in my office would not be an issue. So far no one on the second floor had complained. In fact the entire female population of the second floor always seemed to come by to pet Jake once the word was out that he was in.

I parked in my reserved parking spot in the back lot. As soon as I was out of the Pathfinder, Jake jumped out the driver's side and ran to the back door of the building and waited. He knew the routine. The Hamilton Building was a five-story stone office building built in the 1920s and recently restored to near its original look inside and out. I punched in the five-digit code that gave me access to the back staircase. Jake was at the top of the stairs in a flash. When I joined an impatient Jake at the second floor entrance, I punched in a four-digit code, which allowed us entry to the second floor. Lots of security—the first floor of the Hamilton building was the Mountain Center National Bank.

Jake's claws clicked on the marble floor as he cantered the length of the hall to our office. He did his hurry-up spin in front of the office door while he waited for me to get there and open up. Once inside, Jake ran around to inspect both offices and the bathroom to make sure he wasn't missing anything. He would have inspected the supply room but the door was shut.

When Jake was convinced all was as it should be, he went into my office to his favorite spot, circled three times and plopped down on his dog bed.

I went through my early morning office ritual. I turned on all the lights in the front office that were supposed to be on, omitting the glaring overheads. Then I made coffee. As the coffee brewed and the aroma filled the office, I turned on the lights in my office and all the computers and the printer that they shared. There were two desks in the larger outer office with computers and plenty of workspace. There also was a refrigerator, a microwave, a toaster oven, a fax machine, mostly empty filing cabinets, and two large tables for additional workspace should we ever need them. One desk was Billy's and one desk was for a yet-to-be-hired receptionist. Hiring a receptionist was not so much a question of money but a question of the moral principle of hiring someone knowing they would die of sheer boredom in a few weeks. I was not optimistic that we would ever have a receptionist but it's the thought that counts.

As I heard the coffee machine sputter to a stop, I grabbed my favorite cup off my desk and headed to the outer office, inspecting the cup along the way. There was a light brown film in the bottom. I momentarily debated going to the bathroom and washing it but the aroma of the fresh brewed coffee was too tempting. I blew hard into the cup to remove any dust that might have settled there during the few days I had been gone. Clean enough, I thought. I poured my coffee and headed back to my desk and began playing solitaire as I pondered Sandy's news. I was surprisingly depressed and was confused at my depression. Was I not Mister Love 'Em and Leave 'Em? Solitaire was not so kind today either. One ace up was all I could manage from the first game. The next game I managed to get all four aces and a deuce up, but there were three deuces down and that wrecked the hand. I gave up and logged on to AOL to check the market.

The bell had not sounded on today's action as yet and the market was down almost two hundred points from yesterday's opening. A few years ago this would have constituted a mini-crash. In today's market it was a common occurrence. I knew the market was heading for thirteen thousand and beyond. It was only a matter of time. Who knew where the ceiling was? Certainly, not I. I did know the waters of the Street were shark-infested and unless you were willing to watch your investments on a daily or even hourly basis, you best stick to good mutual funds and leave stocks to the players. To be a player you had to have good timing, good instinct, lots of money, and the nerves of a bank robber.

I looked at my portfolios and was pleased to see minimal losses compared to yesterday's downslide. Three of my stocks even gained. I navigated from finance to sports and checked the latest odds on Saturday's college football action. Tennessee was still a six-point underdog to the Georgia Bulldogs. Good, I thought, we play better as an underdog, having won twice in that role already this year. I looked at the baseball playoff lineup. The Reds weren't there and so I had only a passing interest. My mind was wandering as I surfed around aimlessly. I gave up and called Sandy.

"Cassandra Smith," she answered.

"Want to join me for dinner tonight at Big Bob's?"

"Sure. What time?"

"I'll pick you up at seven."

There was a pause. Dead air brought about by unfinished business.

"Can you take a few days off next week?" I asked.

"I think so. What do you have in mind?"

"I have to go to New Orleans. Want to join me in the French Quarter?"

"Sounds promising. Count me in," Sandy purred in her sexiest voice.

"Great. See you tonight."

"Tonight," she said and hung up.

The outer door to the office opened and Jake raised his head for a moment, then resumed his snooze. I knew it was Billy. Anyone else, other than Sandy, and Jake would have been on his feet in a defensive posture. Jake could not see the outer door and I was constantly amazed at how he could distinguish one person from another. Dog radar, I concluded.

Billy walked in and sat down.

"How was Knoxville?"

"Enlightening," I said. I proceeded to tell Billy everything I had learned from the trip.

"Sounds like Ed Sanders's death might not have been an accident," Billy said. "Too many coincidences."

"I agree."

"What's next for you—Hoffman?"

"Hoffman," I confirmed. "What did you learn?"

"Not much. Woman I know works for East Tennessee Travel. I bought her dinner Tuesday night and then we went back to her office and spent hours on her computer looking for possibilities that would match the Fairchilds flying out of any airport within a three hundred mile radius. Anything that fit we tracked down. Confirmed home addresses and made a few phone calls pretending to be customer service. Everything checked out. If they flew out then they probably flew separately, which would make sense because it would be almost impossible to track down that many possibilities. Wednesday I drove to Tri-City Airport and checked the parking lot for their white Jeep Cherokee. No luck. Then I followed my hunch and drove to Atlanta and checked all their parking lots for a white Jeep Cherokee Limited. I found ten, none with Tennessee tags. I'm convinced that they didn't fly anywhere."

"Maybe the Cherokee didn't have Tennessee tags."

"Figured you'd get around to that," Billy smiled. He reached into his hip pocket, pulled out his wallet and extracted a folded piece of paper.

"Tag numbers," he said, obviously pleased with himself.

"Smart," I said. Billy smiled.

I picked up the phone and paged Roy Husky. He called immediately.

"Speedy Gonzales, I assume," I said as I picked up the phone.

"You got anything better to do than try to be funny?" he snapped.

"Not really. I do have a question though. Were the tags on Ronnie's Jeep Tennessee tags?"

"Probably, but I'll check to make sure. And it was Sarah Ann's Jeep, not Ronnie's. Call you back," Roy said.

Billy went to get coffee and I followed to get a refill. He poured mine and then his and we both added sugar and half-and-half. I remembered the first time I saw Billy drink coffee. *Didn't know Indians drank coffee*, I had teased.

This Indian does was Billy's rumbling response.

The phone rang and I put it on speaker. I was sure it was Roy.

"Youngblood," I answered.

"Tennessee tags," Roy barked. "You guys getting anywhere?"

"Yes and no," I answered. "Drop by sometime and I'll fill you in. How is Fleet?"

"Keeping busy but the suspense is killing him. He still thinks Sarah is dead or he would have heard from her."

"What do you think?"

"I think maybe they took the money and skipped, but something doesn't feel right. I can't talk now. Just find her," he added and then he was gone.

"What now, Blood?" Billy asked.

"The Big Easy, Chief, the Big Easy."

6

Sandy and I were on a Monday afternoon flight to New Orleans, and she was asleep with a book in her lap, while I revisited Sunday's sports pages. We had spent much of the weekend together at the lake house. Dinner at Big Bob's Friday night had been a welcome relief from the emptiness I was feeling about Sandy's impending departure.

Sylvia, Big Bob's wife, had fixed a huge pot roast with new potatoes, carrots, and delicious brown gravy, baked apples, and homemade yeast rolls. Big Bob and I ate to the point of gluttony and then sat on the front porch with our feet up sipping after-dinner drinks and discussing the upcoming football game between Tennessee and Georgia that we were attending Saturday.

We drove down in Big Bob's marked Chief of Police car, which gained us access to parking next to the stadium—professional courtesy and all that. Big Bob knew a few Athens policemen and Georgia state troopers, which led to more introductions and a lot of good-natured kidding. All the Georgians were positive this was going to be their day. I was introduced as a detective on the Mountain Center force. PIs were not necessarily held in high esteem.

Our box seats were in the loge level of Sanford Stadium. The tickets had been sent to me by an Atlanta publisher whose IRA account I was still handling as a favor, and my reward was Tennessee-Georgia tickets every other year.

Big Bob and I were both nervous about Tennessee's chances but as game time grew near I was feeling an unexplainable sense of calm. Seconds before kickoff I turned to Big Bob and asked, "What do you think?"

"The Georgia fans are entirely too cocky," he said. "I think it filters down to the team. I believe we will kick butt."

"You may be right," I responded. Kick butt we did. Tennessee dominated from start to finish in a rout that could have been worse. Reading about it now as we winged to New Orleans was just as sweet as it had been on the ride home from the game with Big Bob.

I looked at Sandy and wondered what life was going to be like after she left for Atlanta. There was only one way I could keep her from leaving and I was not ready to make that commitment. *Absence makes the heart grow fonder* or *out of sight out of mind*? Very soon I was going to find out.

I RENTED A car at the airport and we drove into the city. I took the Poydras Street exit and cut over to the Residence Inn on St. Joseph in the warehouse district right next to the French Quarter. We unpacked and settled into our suite by opening a bottle of KJ and sharing it in our kitchen that overlooked the courtyard. When the wine was gone we checked out the four-poster bed.

Later Sandy and I had dinner at a corner table of Mike Anderson's Seafood Restaurant on Bourbon Street. We arrived late and the dinner crowd was thinning out, which let us dine in relative quiet. We talked about everything except her move, but the essence of it hung in the air creating a subtle tension that had not previously existed between us. Our parting was not going to be easy.

7

Bud Hoffman was about five feet ten inches tall with dark complexion and the serious look cops have to cultivate to be successful on the street, especially if your beat is Bourbon Street. He looked trim and fit and I would guess his age to be early forties. Perps would think twice before messing with Officer Hoffman.

We were having early morning lattes at a table in a back corner of Café Du Monde, the world-famous open-air coffee house beneath the Mississippi River levee on the edge of the French Quarter. We were deep in conversation about Tennessee football and last week's game. Having worked the Knoxville police force for nine years, Hoffman had become a fan even though he had grown up in Louisiana.

"So," he finally said. "You didn't come all this way to talk Tennessee football. What's on your mind?"

I slid my file and personal notes on the Ed Sanders accident across the table. While he read it, I quietly sipped my latte that was just beginning to cool enough to drink. When Hoffman finished he slid the file back and stared at me for a few seconds in silence.

"Mary Sanders ask you to look into this?"

I nodded. It was, at least, a partial truth.

"She never thought it was an accident," Bud said.

"What did you think?"

"Initially, there were some things that I thought didn't add up."

"For instance?"

He looked out toward the levee and let out a deep breath.

"I'm out on I-640 cruising toward Broadway early in the morning," he began. "I come around this long sweeping curve and I think I see a flash. Then I see car taillights about a half mile up ahead on the side of the road. I get a little closer and it looks like a fire, so I hit the lights. The car at the side of the road takes off. I get to the spot where the car was and I see another car engulfed in flames down over the embankment. At that point I have a decision to make."

"Chase the car or look for survivors."

"Exactly! So I decide the car that left probably just stopped to see what was going on and I spooked it when I hit the lights."

He was a lot more animated than when we first started talking.

"Didn't make much difference," I interrupted. "You would have still had to check out the accident."

"Exactly!" he said again with emphasis.

"So I go over the hill and look and see if I can find anyone and I find Ed Sanders who was apparently thrown from the car. I check for life signs. None. Looks like a broken neck. So I call it in and while I'm waiting I look for skid marks. None. So I figure he must have fallen asleep at the wheel and run off the road."

"Did you check the car for other passengers?"

"Tried to. The fire was hotter than hell and had already set the brush around it on fire, so I couldn't get that close. Wouldn't have made much difference. Nobody could have survived inside that inferno."

"What made you think it might not have been an accident?"

"No one particular thing," he said and paused. "Combination of things. No skid marks but upon examining the grass on the side of the road it appeared the car was going very slow. You follow?"

"Yeah. If the car had been going at least the speed limit it would have sailed some distance before touching ground," I answered.

"Exactly! And the fire was extremely hot and there was already a lot of burning around the car."

"Like it had help," I offered. "And it had only just started because you saw the flash."

"Exactly!" Bud said. He was in love with the word. I imagined he drove some people at the precinct crazy. Maybe it was why he was no longer in Knoxville. Still, he seemed to have a good grasp of what had transpired.

"And then I started thinking about the car pulling away and later Mary came to me convinced it was murder. I guess she told you her reasons?"

I nodded. He was winding down.

"So for Mary I did some checking and could find nothing to support murder. He certainly had been drinking. The history was there and everyone was convinced it was an accident. If it was murder it was well concealed and there were no leads."

He paused again. "But, it could have been an accident."

"Did the coroner's report confirm the broken neck?"

"Yes. And head injury consistent with being thrown from the car."

We sat in silence and drank our lattes and watched one very well built young lady pass by on the sidewalk not far from our table and smiled that knowing smile at each other that only men can share.

"Why did you leave Knoxville?" I asked.

"Change of scenery."

"Politics?"

He started to say "exactly" but caught himself.

"Politics," he nodded.

I RETURNED TO the Residence Inn to find Sandy hard at work trying to balance her checkbook. I had witnessed this scenario before. I knew enough to keep quiet so I tiptoed to the couch with the latest Spenser novel and sat down to read. I occasionally heard "shit" or "damn" and then I heard a rather loud scream.

I buried my head deeper in my book and tried to look inconspicuous. It didn't work. I felt Sandy sit down beside me. I looked up. She was wearing that expression I had seen before, a sweet, sexy, helpless look.

"I need help," she purred.

"No way."

"Please," she pleaded.

The "please" was dripping with female seductiveness. I was destined to cave in but I wanted to put up a good fight.

"How long has it been since you balanced that thing?"

"A couple of months," she said weakly.

"Couple of months!"

"Help me do this and there will be a reward for you after," she said, rubbing up against me. I had to bite my tongue to keep a straight face. She knew she had me.

With as much seriousness as I could muster I asked, "What reward?"

"Use your imagination," she whispered close to my ear.

"I have a very *active* imagination," I said.

"I know. So do I."

"Then let's take a look at this checkbook of yours."

8

We stayed in the Big Easy the entire week, finally leaving the following Sunday. Each day after Tuesday we decided to stay "one more day" until Sandy finally said she had to go home. I felt like we were on our honeymoon rather than what it was, a final fling. We made love twice a day in every conceivable way. We walked every block of the French Quarter and I felt like we stopped in every store. We spent hours at the flea market. I say *we* when I really mean Sandy. I was just tagging along enjoying watching her delighting in all the things to see, to touch, to decide upon. Every night we picked out a different, but equally famous, French Quarter restaurant and had exquisite meals. We talked about everything except the move and what was to become of us. Sunday came all too soon.

On the flight home, Sandy was staring out the window apparently lost in thought.

"Good time?" I asked. She turned toward me.

"A very good time," she smiled. It was a sad smile. "I love you, Don," she added and waited for a response. Caught off guard, I had none. I was totally unprepared. She smiled the sad smile and turned away looking out the window once again.

We landed at Tri-Cities Airport shortly after four o'clock. Since we had not planned on staying a week, we had packed for only a few days. Luckily for Sandy, when she packed for a few days she had enough for a week. I, on the other hand, had had to do some laundry at the hotel. I carried my bag off the plane and went to get the Pathfinder while Sandy went to baggage claim to claim the wheeled suitcase that I jokingly called the moving van. I picked her up at curbside and we rode in silence back to Mountain Center.

I parked in front of her building. We took the elevator to her third floor unit and I wheeled Sandy's suitcase to her front door while she searched for her keys. She opened the door, wheeled in the suitcase and stood in the doorway. She took a step forward and put her arms around me and buried her head in my chest. I held her for what seemed like an eternity. Finally she let go and stepped back.

"I had a great time," she said. "I'll talk to you before I leave." She turned and went inside and closed the door.

I STOOD THERE for a few moments and looked at her condo door with a sense of utter confusion. I turned reluctantly and went back to the Pathfinder and drove to my own parking space. I went inside and called Billy and told him I was back. In a few minutes he showed up with Jake, who did his welcome home dance for me.

"How was New Orleans?" Billy asked.

"Great!"

"Learn anything?"

"Hard to tell."

I filled him in on my conversation with Hoffman.

"So he's suspicious but he can't put his finger on anything," Billy said.

"That's about it, Chief. What have you been up to?"

"I checked all the limo services and private cars in the area to see if I could turn up a lead. Nothing."

"I had another idea on the plane back," I said. "Private charters or rentals. Check all the small airports. We might get lucky."

"No luck involved," Billy smiled. "Crack investigating."

"I've got to go to the gym," I said, heading to the bedroom to change. "I think I ate half of New Orleans. Want to join me?"

BILLY AND I were in Moto's for almost an hour before we uttered another word toward each other. We had finished with the weights and were in the side room with the speed bag and the heavy bag. Billy was holding the heavy bag for me and I was pounding away. I normally worked on the speed bag because the heavy bag hurt my wrists, but tonight I felt like hitting something substantial. I was working hard and the sweat was pouring. Anger and frustration were flowing through my punches. I had been at it for a while grunting and groaning but I couldn't stop. I had to let it all out.

"Something bothering you?" Billy asked.

"No," I said and kept swinging.

"Bullshit," said Billy.

After a few more minutes of all-out assault I stopped, mainly because my arms were about to fall off. Sweating profusely and breathing heavily, I grabbed my towel and my water bottle and sat down. Billy joined me. He was quiet and I knew he was waiting for me to say something. I told him Sandy was leaving. I told him how I felt or at least how I thought I felt. I told him I was very confused.

"What should I do, Chief?"

"Giving advice is bad medicine," he said, trying to be serious.

"Oh, cut the Indian crap," I snapped.

We sat there for some time toweling off and drinking water. No words were spoken. My breathing was returning to normal. Billy motioned to the heavy bag and I went and held it for him as he went through his routine. When he had finished we sat down again saying nothing and drank more water. Finally Billy broke the silence.

"I'm done," he said. He put his hand on my shoulder and added,

"You'll work it out, Blood. You always do."

He left me sitting there alone with my thoughts. I tried to let my mind go blank and almost succeeded until Marlene Long skipped through the back of it. From time to time thoughts of Marlene popped into my head at the most unlikely moments and for no explainable reason. I wondered if the spectre of Marlene Long was keeping me from saying to Sandy all the things that needed to be said. I hadn't seen Marlene since the summer of my senior year, but I could not purge that one magical moment from my memory. *Ecstasy's curse.* I pushed Marlene Long back into my subconscious and concluded that I couldn't spend the night at Moto's. I got up to leave. As I left the side room I glanced to the right and spotted Sandy at the far end of the gym hard at work on an exercise bike. She had her head down buried in a book. We were so much alike in so many ways, I thought. Feeling the same anger and frustration that I was feeling, she had come to the gym to deal with it the same way I had. She did not see me and I slipped quietly out to the front desk where Moto was ogling female body-beautifuls in the latest *Muscle* magazine. He looked up.

"Does she know I'm here?" I asked, tilting my head toward Sandy.

"Don't think so. I was in back office when she came in. Did not talk to her."

"Do not mention that I was here," I said slowly for emphasis.

Moto nodded grandly with a bow of his head. "Everything okay between you two?"

"No, it's not," I muttered as I walked out into the cool darkness.

9

The time had come to visit again with T. Elbert. My mentor, friend, and ex-TBI agent, T. Elbert Brown, was now confined to a wheelchair thanks to a drug dealer's bullet five years ago. T. Elbert lived in an old turn-of-the-century two-story on Olivia Drive. The house was immaculately kept inside and out.

A few years after I moved back to Mountain Center, I met T. Elbert at an accident scene Billy was photographing. It was soon after I had been granted a private investigator's license by the State of Tennessee. T. Elbert had been chasing a suspected drug dealer who had lost control of his car, hit a tree, and instantly ended his drug-dealing career. T. Elbert was searching the car for drugs and I was standing around waiting on Billy to finish photographing the scene. I asked if I could help and he said I could. He was dismantling the outside of the car so I went to work inside. I was about to cut into the driver's side seat when I got a faint whiff of coffee. Further sniffing led me to the passenger-side headrest.

"Think I got something," I said, removing the headrest.

I tossed it out of the car and T. Elbert cut it open. Coffee poured out and then a Ziploc bag of white powder. T. Elbert did the wet-finger test.

"Cocaine," he said. "Good find."

One backseat headrest was also loaded with coffee and cocaine. We continued to tear the car apart but found nothing else. By that time the scene was crawling with TBI agents. When we were finished he gave me his card and told me if I ever needed a favor to give him a call. I called him a couple of weeks later to run a license tag for me. Someone was parking illegally at the condo complex where I lived and the manager had asked me if I could find out who it was.

T. Elbert ran the plate and asked me out to lunch and that started our friendship. We talked sports, women, cops and robbers, and life in general. T. Elbert was my senior by fifteen years and had many stories to tell. He was a year from retirement when he caught the bullet.

In the early morning hours I always knew I could find T. Elbert on his front porch in his rocking chair. T. Elbert was about five feet eight inches tall with light brown hair flecked with gray. He was a slight man who always had a smile on his face and a twinkle in his eye. T. Elbert told his tales with great humor that always made me laugh and he delighted in telling them. He was a disarming man with great insight and I was certain those qualities had helped him be a very good agent for the Tennessee Bureau of Investigation.

I parked in front of his house and got out of the Pathfinder. T. Elbert gave me a small wave and a smile as I walked up his front steps with a bag from Dunkin' Donuts that contained large coffees and various weight gainers, a ritual I performed every Wednesday I was in town. If I were going to be out of town, I would send T. Elbert an e-mail. T. Elbert loved e-mail and he loved Dunkin' Donuts coffee as much as I did. He had few friends and no family and although he never said so, I do not think he had many visitors.

"What's happening, Donald?" T. Elbert asked.

He had always called me Donald. He had first read it from my business card and although I had told him a few times to call me Don he seemed to like the fact that he used my real birth name. *I'll call you what your parents named you*, he once said.

"Too much," I said.

"What are you working on?"

I told him about the Fairchild case from the time that Roy Husky walked into my office through the trip to New Orleans. He listened intently. When I was finished we drank coffee and ate our fill of various donuts, croissants, and muffins. I was in the other rocker enjoying the morning while T. Elbert was digesting not only the treats I had brought, but also what I had told him. I waited. I knew not to interrupt. Finally he broke the silence.

"You trust this Husky?"

"Not sure. But I think so."

"The money has to be somewhere."

"Yes, it does."

"Probably in the Cayman Islands."

"Probably."

"What are you going to do next?" he asked.

"Connecticut."

"Seems like the next logical step," T. Elbert said.

We were quiet again, rocking and drinking our coffee. At six AM the October morning was cool and windless and there was little noise other than the chirping of early rising birds and the muted creaks of our rocking chairs. Except for occasional car headlights in the predawn dimness we could have been the only two people on earth, friends sharing a special moment.

T. Elbert glanced over with a twinkle in his eye and asked, "How's your love life?"

He always asked me that and I always said it was none of his business. It was a big joke between us.

"Going down hill," I said.

"What?" He was startled.

I spilled my guts. I couldn't believe it. It was as if talking it out would somehow purge my anger and frustration. T. Elbert knew about Sandy and Sandy knew about T. Elbert, but they had never met. I gave him the complete history from the time I first talked to her on the telephone to my walking out of the gym last night. He listened as if I was discussing a murder case, occasionally nodding or smiling that he understood. He seemed completely enthralled and in no hurry for me to finish. T. Elbert, after all, had no place to go and I on the other hand was in no particular hurry to leave.

I finally finished my manic monologue and we sat again in the silence of the morning. The sun was making its usual slow appearance signaling that soon the noise of early morning traffic would infringe on our quiet time.

I waited for T. Elbert to say something but he just rocked and sipped the remainder of his early morning coffee.

"Any advice?"

"Nope."

I took another sip of coffee.

"Ever been married?" I asked.

"Nope."

He was, all of a sudden, a man of few words. I figured I must be close to something.

"Ever been close?"

"Once," he said.

He rocked. I waited.

"And?"

"And she thought I loved the job more than I loved her and she didn't want to be number two, so she walked."

Being the great detective that I am, I wanted to probe further but thought better of it and stood to leave.

"How are you doing, T. Elbert?" I asked seriously. "Really."

"I'm doing okay," he sighed. "I've got my books, my computer, my TV, my VCR, my portable phone, my cell phone, two wheelchairs and every once in a while I get laid." He grinned widely when he said the last part and I had no reason to disbelieve him.

I ended our visit the way I always did. "If you ever need anything or need me to take you anywhere, just holler."

"Hell, I can take myself. You know I can still drive the black beauty. Just keep me in the loop on this case you're working on. Sounds like you've finally got something you can sink your teeth into. Send me e-mails. I like e-mails."

"I'll do it," I said as I walked down the stairs and out the front walk.

T. Elbert waved and I tapped the horn as I drove away.

WHEN I WALKED into the office at seven-thirty, Billy was already there and the coffee was brewing. He was pouring the first cup as I walked in. He raised the pot in my direction and I shook my head. Billy never spoke when a gesture would suffice. I went into the office and turned on my computer and promptly got on AOL. I pulled up Orbitz from my favorite places and booked a flight to White Plains. I needed to get out of town.

Billy came in and sat down and waited until I logged off AOL. I didn't look at him for a few minutes as I was making a list of things to do before I left town. He sat quietly sipping coffee and waiting. He was the most methodical, patient person I had ever met. Billy was almost never in a hurry and when he was he could move like the wind. I looked up and made eye contact.

"I'll start checking the small airports today," he said.

"Good," I nodded. "I'm going to Connecticut in the morning. Will you look after Jake?"

"Of course," he rumbled.

I stared at him. I had nothing more to say and he sensed it.

Walking out of my office he said over his shoulder, "See you when you get back."

10

Small, newly remodeled, and conveniently located twenty-five miles north of Manhattan, White Plains Airport is a terrific alternative to JFK or LaGuardia if your final destination is Connecticut. I picked up my keys at the Hertz Gold desk and made an escape any bandit would have envied. Half an hour later I was resting comfortably in the Residence Inn on Barker Avenue in White Plains. It was five o'clock in the afternoon. My mission was to interview Trent Fairchild, Ronnie's father. The Ed Sanders file on Ronnie had given the telephone number.

"Fairchild residence," a voice on the other end of the line answered. With the trained instincts of a seasoned P.I., I guessed butler.

"Trent Fairchild, please," I said trying to resurrect my Connecticut accent from days gone by.

"Whom shall I say is calling sir?"

No doubt that it was a butler's voice.

"Donald Youngblood," I said. "Insurance investigator."

I expected more questions about the nature of my call, but instead I heard, "One moment please."

"This is Fairchild."

"Mr. Fairchild . . ."

"Yes, I know. Are you people finally going to get around to paying this claim?" he said rather testily.

I was caught off guard by this twist, but I took the opening.

"I certainly hope so, sir," I replied. "However, there are a few final questions I need to ask you about and a signature I need to complete my investigation. When would it be convenient to see you?"

I held my breath. Any one of a thousand questions from Fairchild and I was not going to get an interview.

"The sooner the better," he said. "How about nine o'clock tomorrow morning at my office?"

"That would be fine," I said and he gave me the address.

11

Trent Fairchild's office building was in downtown Greenwich near the Metro-North train station. The building was mostly glass and sparkled in the early morning sun of a crisp Connecticut day. I inhaled the cool air and promised myself this would be the year I resumed my college passion for skiing. And when I actually found a parking place on the street, I smiled to myself at my good fortune.

Fairchild, Addison & Clark, Investment Counselors, was on the ninth floor. A pretty brunette receptionist announced my arrival and showed me into Fairchild's office. The man behind the desk rose to greet me with a cordial if not warm smile and offered me a chair positioned in front of his desk. Surprised and confused, I sat down. I was obviously staring at Trent IV, not the father I had expected. I guessed this Trent was about my age. He was about six feet with prematurely gray hair and appeared trim and fit. He was well-groomed and well-dressed and I suspected women found him quite handsome.

He got right to the point: "What do you need to ask me about the accident?"

I was all of a sudden in deep water with no life preserver. I could try to bluff my way, but I sensed that Trent IV would smell a rat before I could find out what I wanted to know. So I did the only thing I could think of that might work—I handed him my private investigator's license and hoped to take advantage of his curiosity.

"I'm investigating your brother," I said, hoping they might not be on good terms.

"My brother's dead," he said angrily. "And you misrepresented yourself over the telephone. I think you better go."

He stood up. I stayed seated, trying to take in this latest piece of impossible information.

"Your brother is alive and until a few weeks ago was living in Tennessee," I said calmly.

"Impossible!"

"Why would you think he was dead?" I asked.

"I *know* he is dead," he said convincingly. "He died in a private plane crash with my mother and father a little over five years ago."

I felt as if I had been slapped. I was reeling from the realization that Trent Fairchild IV and I had a very unpleasant common bond, losing our parents in a plane crash. I took a deep breath and moved on. If he noticed it didn't show.

"Where was the crash?"

"In the Atlantic. They were on the way to Bermuda."

"Are you absolutely sure he was on the plane?"

"Positive. There was a lot of insurance money involved and there was a lengthy investigation. The final report concluded that all three were on the plane when it took off. The insurance company said we would have to wait seven years for the money since neither bodies nor wreckage was recovered. I didn't care about the money so I didn't push it. However, a few months ago some wreckage was recovered off the coast of Bermuda that was identified as pieces of our plane so I am now trying to get the claim settled. I assumed your call was about the claim."

"I'm sorry about that. But if you will bear with me, maybe we can make some sense out of all of this. What month did the crash occur?"

"March," he said.

I opened my case and handed Fairchild a newspaper article Billy had blown up, with a picture from a party celebrating the wedding of Ronnie and Sarah Ann Fairchild. The article was dated June the same year of the crash. Trent IV looked at it in disbelief and sat down. His brow wrinkled and his eyes narrowed. He read the article and studied the picture for a very long time. Then he looked up at me and frowned.

"It's not Ronnie," he said.

"You're sure?"

"Positive. This guy looks like Ronnie, but something is a little off, especially around the eyes. See for yourself."

He swiveled a framed picture on his desk so it faced me. I looked at the real Ronald Fairchild and then back to the enlargement. I studied them for a minute. He was right; the faces were close but they were not the same. I sat back and took a deep breath.

"Now, would you mind telling me what is going on?" he urged.

"It's a long story."

Fairchild touched his intercom and spoke, "Alice, get Andy to take my nine-thirty appointment and bring in some coffee and danish, please." Then, turning to me, "I'm all ears."

"Well," I started. "It appears someone is impersonating your brother. We don't know why, but I am going to find out."

I saw no reason not to level with Fairchild. Coffee and danish arrived and we moved to a small conference table as I recounted my investigation from the time Roy Husky walked into my office. I omitted some details but all in all I gave him a full account. He listened in amazement.

"Why would anyone want to impersonate Ronnie?"

"This guy wanted a new identity," I said. "I'm guessing he saw your brother's picture in the paper after the accident and thought he and your brother looked a lot alike. He probably did some research on your family, had some phony IDs made and then headed south with his new identity looking for a new life. He might have even had plastic surgery. He succeeded in making a new life for himself, but something went wrong and now he is either running again or he is dead. I have to find out which."

"Is there anything I can do to help?" he asked, as I was standing to leave.

"I'll let you know."

12

There was no way I was going to Greenwich without making a twenty-mile side trip to Wilton, Connecticut. I knew Wilton because Billy grew up there. He first took me home to meet his parents on a short break during our freshman year.

How or why an affluent, childless, white couple adopted a Cherokee child, I never figured out, but Billy was certainly the better for it. His parents were loving and caring and wore their wealth well. They took great pride in teaching Billy about his heritage and their home was filled with Cherokee artifacts and related books and art.

The last time I was in Wilton was two years ago for Billy's father's funeral. His mother had since moved to Florida. Those sober thoughts were weighing on me, but not enough to dampen my anticipation of Orem's Diner, the legendary breakfast institution that had served Wilton's locals roughly since the flood, to hear them tell it. Billy introduced me to Orem's. More meetings are held at Orem's than at the town hall, and though no one paid them much attention, it wasn't unusual to spot one of the celebrities who live in Wilton or the surrounding affluent towns which had become bedroom communities to Manhattan.

So you can imagine my disgruntlement when I pulled up to Orem's and found it closed with a map on the door to their new location. A local landmark just ups and moves? How ridiculous. But I drove down the street and found the new Orem's, a beautiful new fifties'-style diner bigger and better appointed than the original.

Soon I was sitting happily with a *USA Today* and a cup of coffee, waiting on a feta cheese omelet with home fries and rye toast. Heaven on a plate.

Thankfully, the food hadn't changed, and I wolfed it down. Then I sat back with my second cup of inimitable Orem's coffee and tried to piece my case together.

Pictures can be deceiving and Trent Fairchild IV had a lot to lose if Ronnie were alive, but I suspected he was right about the man in my picture not being his brother. If Sarah Ann's husband was not Ronnie Fairchild, then I had to find out who he was. I was sure his identity would lead me to the reason they disappeared. I wondered if Sarah Ann knew who her Ronnie really was. I would bet big money Ed Sanders knew, and that knowledge got him killed.

I pulled out my cell phone and dialed Roy Husky's beeper. He called back within two minutes.

"Thanks for the quick response," I said.

"No problem. You in Greenwich?"

"Not now."

"Learn anything?"

"Enough. I need you to get me something with Ronnie's fingerprints."

"What are you thinking?" Roy asked quietly.

"Our boy may not be who he says he is," I said.

There was silence on the other end. I started to wonder if we had been cut off when Roy finally spoke.

"Okay. I'll have to give it some thought. When I have something, where do you want it?"

"I need it tomorrow," I said and gave him the address of the Residence Inn.

"You going to tell me all of it?" Roy asked.

"Let me make sure of some things first," I said. "See you later."

I hung up. I needed to make one more phone call.

13

When I am 33,000 feet above the earth sealed inside Boeing's latest marvel and looking down at an apparent perfect miniature, I find it is easy to forget all the problems I left on the ground. When my life is entrusted to some unknown pilot and a machine I know little about, I can become very philosophical. I was flying to Baltimore to meet an old friend, and while doing so, trying to solve the meaning of life.

I had spent the rest of Wednesday changing my flight plans and tracking various stocks through the Internet on my laptop and trying not to think about Sandy Smith. A long run and a few beers had allowed me to drift easily into a dreamless sleep. Thursday I was up early performing my morning ritual and waiting for Roy's package.

When it finally arrived I found in it a coffee cup, a stapler, a staple remover, a calculator and some floppy disks Roy had obviously pilfered from Ronnie's office. There was also a note from Roy. *If you can't find some fingerprints on something in this box, you're fired.*

Which brings me to Scottie.

Scott Glass, a.k.a. Scottie, a.k.a. Professor, was an FBI agent working out of central headquarters in Quantico. I met Scott at UConn even before I met Billy. Scott was also on the basketball team. Except for his six-five height, Scott looked nothing like a basketball player. He had a geeky, lanky, awkward, studious look that belied the fact that he was one of the finest shooting guards ever to wear the UConn blue and white. Scott had dark curly hair and always wore glasses. He was quickly nicknamed "Professor." He smiled widely as he approached my table in the Marriott dining room. Scott was always grinning as if he knew something no one else did.

"Hey, Professor," I said as we shook hands warmly.

"How are you, Blood?"

"Fine," I said as we sat down. The waitress appeared and we ordered drinks.

"How is Billy? I haven't talked to him in a long time."

"Billy is doing very well," I said.

The drinks arrived. We exchanged small talk. We covered family, friends, love life, the stock market and sports as more drinks appeared and were consumed, then the salads, followed by the main course and finally coffee. Time never diminishes old friendships. Scott and I always picked up right where we left off.

"I have a feeling this is not entirely a social call," he finally said.

"I have a present for you," I said, handing him the box from Roy.

"You shouldn't have," he smirked.

"Don't touch," I added.

Scott cautiously looked inside and rummaged through the various items with a pen from his shirt pocket. "Explain, please."

"Fingerprints."

"Oh, come on, Don. You know I can't do that. That's against policy."

"Bullshit, Scott. You can do anything you want to do if you want to."

We both knew that he would help me but we had to engage in this mock argument as foreplay to his agreeing. Scott loved to argue and debate. He would never agree to anything without tearing it apart and looking at it from all angles.

"What's this about?" he frowned.

"Missing persons case," I said. "I want to find out if these fingerprints prove the guy wearing them to be who he says he is."

"I don't know, Don," he paused.

"Looked at your portfolio lately?" I teased.

"Oh, come on! That's bribery."

I smiled. "Well, have you?"

Scott was one of a select number of people for whom I still handled investments. His portfolio had grown well into the six figures since I talked him into letting me plan for his future.

He couldn't contain a laugh. "Yeah, I have. How in the hell can you be that good?"

"Ouiji board," I said.

He laughed again and looked at the box.

"OK," he acquiesced. "I'll run the prints and let you know what I find. Then you tell me the whole story. Agreed?"

"Agreed. How soon?"

"When is your flight out?"

"Tomorrow morning."

"Change it," he said. "I'll pick you up for dinner tomorrow night."

It was obvious that the Professor's curiosity had gotten the best of him.

14

I was sitting in the lobby of the Baltimore Marriott reading the sports pages and waiting for Scott to pick me up for dinner. Tennessee was a three-point favorite over undefeated Alabama for Saturday's game in Tuscaloosa. The Vols were also undefeated, highly ranked and the hard part of their schedule was almost over. I quickly suppressed a flicker of hope for a national championship, fearing that I would jinx our chances. A figure looming over me broke my concentration and I looked up into the face of a very serious Scott Glass.

"We have to talk," he said before I could utter a greeting. "In private."

"I have a suite on the top floor. And I have beer."

"My hero," Scott said. "Lead the way."

There was a lot of activity in the lobby and we were not alone on the elevator, so we kept silent. I noticed that Scott was carrying his briefcase. Inside the suite, Scott took off his jacket and tossed it and the briefcase on the couch. I poured two beers from the mini-bar into tall pilsner glasses and handed one to Scott as we sat down.

"So what the hell are you into?" Scott asked.

"I told you. Missing persons. What did you turn up?"

"The FBI is looking for this guy. His name is Joey Avanti. He was a New York wise guy who ran with Carlo Vincente. Avanti was busted on drug trafficking and agreed to testify against Vincente if we took him into the witness protection program. We had Avanti under protective custody when he disappeared from under our noses. We thought he was dead or had skipped the country. Now please tell me everything you know and don't leave anything out."

I told Scott everything. I filled in the parts I had omitted with Trent Fairchild and took Scott through my investigation step-by-step including Billy's work. I showed him my file on the case and Billy's blow-up of Ronnie's picture. When I was finished Scott smiled.

"What?" I asked.

"Not bad," he said. "I think you've turned into a real private eye."

"Well, I haven't found anybody yet."

"True, and I doubt that you will. Believe me, Avanti knows how to cover his tracks."

He opened his briefcase and took out a file and handed it to me. We sat silently, drinking beer and reading each others' files on Ronnie-Joe.

Joey Avanti was a very bad boy. He was suspected of a number of mob hits that were never proved. He was also a real ladies' man and had a history of abusing women. He was smart and well-educated, compliments of a father well-placed in the Vincente crime family. Joey had a reputation as a charming but violent man, who would kill if it suited his purpose.

We spread out the pictures of Ronnie Fairchild that Billy had enlarged and the photos of Joey Avanti from the FBI file on the coffee table. There was a definite resemblance but I would not have known it was the same guy. The nose was different, the lips fuller and there was something about the eyes.

I took a deep breath and put aside Scott's file. I got up and got two more bottles of Michelob Amber Bock.

"How much do you want this guy?" I asked.

"Not as much as we once did. Vincente has cleaned up his act. He is out of the drug and prostitute business. Mostly now into garbage, restaurants, restaurant supplies, and protection. We'd still go after him if we could get our hands on Avanti, but Vincente is not as high on our list of priorities as he once was."

"How did you nail Joey in the first place?"

"Joey was heavily into the drug business. We infiltrated his business

KEITH DONNELLY 85

and had enough to send him away for life. Vincente wanted out of the drug business and he and Joey were at odds about it. I don't think Joey would have agreed to testify against Vincente if not for the infighting. Maybe he had second thoughts and that's why he took off."

We drank our beers and I picked up Scott's file for one final look as Scott's cell phone rang. He took the call and walked into my bedroom.

"Ready for my deductions?" I asked as he returned a few minutes later.

"Okay, Sherlock, lay it out for me."

"This is what I think I know. The dates all fit. The FBI has Joey Avanti in protective custody and since the word is out, they probably think Joey is not likely to plan an escape. Joey is reading the paper one day and sees an article about Ronnie Fairchild who has disappeared in a plane crash. He notices that he and Ronnie look somewhat alike and a plan begins to take root. Since Ronnie is probably, but not officially, dead, this is the perfect opportunity to assume a new identity and skip out on the Feds, sort of a do-it-yourself witness protection program. He gives the FBI the slip, finds a plastic surgeon to do the minor face changes, gets some forged papers in the name of Ronald Fairchild and heads for parts unknown. Joey Avanti is now Ronnie Fairchild. Then the new Ronnie Fairchild meets Sarah Ann Fleet. The new Ronnie is charming and good-looking and she is attractive enough and rich. He sweeps her off her feet and they set the wedding date. Joseph Fleet is a little suspicious and so he has his future son-in-law checked out by Tom Slack Investigations. Ed Sanders finds out Ronnie Fairchild is not who he says he is and shakes Joey down. Ed promises a glowing report on Ronnie Fairchild in return for ten thousand dollars. Joey pays and waits for Joseph Fleet to get the bogus report from Tom Slack Investigations. Ronnie realizes it is too risky to let Ed Sanders live and so he kills him and by all appearances thinks he will live happily ever after. Then recently something happens. Probably Carlo Vincente finds out where Joey is. I don't know how, but he does. Maybe Carlo sends a hit man and Ronnie finds out. Maybe some old pal spots him and figures it out. I don't know what, but something made Ronnie run."

"Hold it," Scott interrupted. "How do you know Ronnie finds out someone is on to him?"

"The money. Ronnie decides he is going to have to run and to run he needs funds. Three million is an excellent stake."

"Not bad, Sherlock," Scott teased.

"Yeah, so far. But there are some things I don't know. Was there a hit man or did Ronnie decide it was time to move on for another reason? Did the hit man, if there was one, get the job done or did Ronnie give him the slip? And what happened to Sarah Ann?"

"Maybe he loves her and took her with him."

"Maybe. Either way this plays out does not look good for Sarah Ann."

"What if there was no hit man?" Scott asked. "What if Ronnie told Sarah Ann everything and they just took the money and disappeared?"

"That wouldn't make any sense. Why run if you are not being chased? Unless there is something Fleet is not telling me. He did say that only he and Sarah Ann had access to that kind of money. That tells me that Ronnie told Sarah Ann something to get her to steal that kind of cash from her father. Either that or Ronnie found a way to get at the cash."

I got up in silence, went to the bar and brought back two more beers and some peanuts. I poured the beer and we both sat for a few minutes with our own thoughts.

"There is a way to find out about the hit man, if there was one," I said.

"How?"

"Ask Carlo Vincente," I said.

"Oh, shit!" was Scott's reply.

15

W hat's up, Chief?"

"Hey, Blood. Where are you?"

"Baltimore airport, getting ready to board a flight for Tri-Cities. I'll call you when I am on the ground. Go ahead and take Jake over to the condo. You and I will have dinner somewhere and I'll fill you in."

"Be safe," Billy said. "I'll take Jake and wait to hear from you."

The plane was nearly empty, the service friendly and the flight uneventful. I retrieved the Pathfinder from the airport parking lot and began the thirty-minute trip of curvy two-lane highway to Mountain Center. I activated Bluetooth and speed-dialed Billy on my cell phone.

"Good trip, Blood?" Billy answered.

"Yeah, Chief, very interesting," I answered. "Meet me at The Brewery in about thirty minutes and I'll get you caught up."

The local micro-brewery had a few really good beers and excellent food. I ordered a pint of Black Bear ale and a bacon-cheeseburger with fries. Billy ordered salmon with rice and a bottle of spring water. We were tucked in a quiet corner booth far away from the bar. The drinks arrived and I took a long drink of the cold dark brew. I could feel the fatigue of the last few days envelop me like a heavy blanket as the ale worked its way into my system. In silence, Billy took a long pull on his water and waited. I knew he could sense my exhaustion and would let the tempo go at my pace. I took another drink.

"How are you, Chief?" I asked.

"Hungry," Billy said as if I had asked a stupid question.

"You are always hungry," I teased. "What have you been doing since I left?"

"Checking airports, photographing crime scenes and accidents, usual stuff," he said nonchalantly.

"Any luck on the airports?"

"No."

"Well, I have had some luck, maybe too much. We've stumbled into something far bigger than a simple missing-persons case."

I started my tale with my visit to Trent Fairchild. I teased Billy with my side trip to Orem's Diner. He feigned jealousy. The food arrived as I recounted my first meeting with Scott Glass.

"Scott says hello, by the way."

Billy nodded and began to attack the salmon. I took an ample bite of my burger and proceeded to my second meeting with Scottie. Every few sentences I would pause to take a bite and a quick drink. Billy listened in silence, his face serious as his food disappeared, clearly focused on my story. I finished my account, ate the last of my burger and washed it down with the last of my ale. Timing is all.

"So you're going to New York?" Billy asked with a frown.

"Looks like."

"I don't like it. It could be dangerous."

JAKE WAITED PATIENTLY in the master bedroom as I changed into an old white turtleneck with black sweats and beat-up Nikes. By the front door, I pulled on a gray fleece and retrieved the basketball from the floor of the front hall closet. Jake did a little playtime dance and off we went to the tennis courts. When Jake was sufficiently tired we took the long route back to 5300 which took us by Sandy's apartment. As we cut through a breezeway and emerged in the parking lot adjacent to Sandy's building, my heart sank. I stood face to grill with a moving van. The door to Sandy's third-floor penthouse apartment stood open. A man came out carrying a large brown corrugated carton and disappeared into the elevator. Seconds later he reappeared on the ground and disappeared into the trailer. I walked over to the back of the van and peered in. He was busy stacking the box against one wall of the trailer and tying down the entire load. I recognized a couch, then a chair and then the headboard to Sandy's bed.

"Excuse me," I said. "Is Miss Smith still around?"

He looked up a little startled. "Naw. She left 'bout an hour ago driving to Atlanta. You Don?"

"Yes."

He handed me an envelope.

"She said to give you this if you showed up. Said to tell you she was sorry she missed you but she had to get going before it got too late," he said with an accent that was hill country thick.

"What if I hadn't showed up?"

"I was supposed to drop it in your mail slot."

"Thanks."

"You the boyfriend?" he twanged.

"Sort of."

"Nice lady," he said. "I don't see why you'd let her run off to Atlanta."

It's none of your fucking business is what I wanted to say but didn't, I suppose because I tended to agree with his observation. And besides, I try not to use the "F" word.

"Thanks again," I said rather weakly and walked away with Jake leading before the mover could offer further comment.

Inside 5300 I opened Sandy's envelope. The note was short and bittersweet: "It was fun. I'll be in touch. Love, Sandy."

16

I was wide awake. Glowing red letters on my bedside alarm clock glared 3:15. Jake, on the other hand, was sound asleep. Unit 5300 could be stripped clean by a motorcycle gang in the middle of the night and Jake would sleep through it. Watchdog was not in his genetic makeup. Nothing short of a good shaking would awaken Jake, except thunder and lightning. Jake was afraid of thunderstorms.

I lay staring into the darkness with my mind racing around and around my current personal events. I replayed the Tennessee-Alabama game in my mind. Jake and I had watched it earlier that evening. Jake slept through most of it, a 20–7 Tennessee win. Jake was not a big football fan. I mentally made my best and worst guesses on a number of pending questions. Where was Ronnie Fairchild? Where was Sarah Ann? Where was Sandy Smith? For that matter, where in the hell was Marlene Long? Finally, what do I do next?

I had to admit I was feeling less cocky about going to New York and tracking down Carlo Vincente. I lay an hour trying to force sleep to return but sleep had long departed. I gave up and got up. A hot shower convinced my body, if not my mind, that it was later than it actually was, and so I got dressed and took myself and a rather uncooperative Jake to the office. I made coffee and turned on the computer to check e-mail, hoping that Sandy had left a clue as to her whereabouts. No such luck. I had a lot of garbage mail and one personal e-mail from T. Elbert:

> What the hell is going on? You promised me an update.
> T

I smiled; he was a man of few words. I sat back and enjoyed my coffee and wrote T. Elbert an involved e-mail updating him on the Fairchild case. Then I played solitaire for thirty minutes, couldn't win, gave up, and went out to breakfast leaving a sleeping Jake to guard the office.

The Mountain Center Diner was only two blocks from my office and I made the walk in minutes. I had my own table in the back and Doris Black, the owner, made sure that no one sat there until after I left or nine o'clock, whichever came first. I bought a copy of the Sunday *Knoxville News Sentinel* and sat down with another cup of coffee. Doris had always waited on me personally ever since I had given her a tip on America Online stock when it was still affordable. When I finally recommended selling it, the AOL stock was worth about twenty times what Doris had paid for it. Although she had never told me how much she had invested, I knew it was considerable. Soon after she sold, it took a tumble. From time to time I gave her tidbits and she always followed up with a purchase.

"Good morning Mr. Youngblood," she smiled. I had given up on trying to get her to call me Don. Doris considered me a celebrity because I had worked on Wall Street. That made no sense to me, but it did to Doris. I just enjoyed the status.

"Good morning, Doris. Feels like French toast and sausage patties today," I answered.

"You got it," she said as she scribbled on her pad. "Have you been watching that Aspect Development stock that you told me to purchase? It is going nuts."

"Now, Doris, I didn't tell you to buy it. I said it might be a good gamble."

"Yeah, yeah. I know, but anytime you say good gamble I run to my broker. He keeps asking me where I am getting my information and I keep saying that I guess I'm just lucky. Anyway, thanks a bunch. I'll get that breakfast."

Doris scurried off. She reminded me of Shirley Booth on the old *Hazel* TV show. Doris was in her mid-fifties, slightly overweight, and attractive in a matronly way. Her husband had died many years ago and she had two grown sons who had moved away and one more who was a senior in high school.

Doris was very proud of the fact that she had put the two oldest through college. The diner was her life and she loved seeing all her regulars. She had a great sense of humor and was always cheerful. God had smiled on the people who could call Doris a friend.

I dove into the *Sentinel* sports page and read all the articles, stats, and interviews about the big game. Tennessee had pulled away from a scrappy Alabama team in the final quarter and covered the spread. I checked out other college action and tried to determine where the Vols would be in the upcoming polls. Doris appeared with my breakfast.

"When do you think I should sell Aspect?" she whispered.

"When you have made so much on it that you are scared to death," I said as if I were talking in church. "Then sell half and I'll try to advise you on when to sell the rest."

"It's gettin' close," she chuckled and bustled away.

I was rearranging my breakfast and the paper when I caught sight of a front-page headline. "Wounded Officer's Condition Improving." I was about to put it aside when Mary Sanders's name caught my eye. I read from the beginning.

> The physical condition of wounded Knoxville police officer Mary Sanders has been upgraded from critical to serious. The officer, wounded in a shootout during an attempted bank robbery on Wednesday last, is expected to fully recover from two gunshot wounds. Two of the holdup gang were killed during the shootout, one by Sanders and another by Officer Arnold E. Wiggins. Their names have not been released. Wiggins, who was also wounded, died late Friday night. Services with full honors were held for Wiggins on Monday.
>
> Police are still searching for two suspects who managed to flee the scene of the shooting. While police search for the remaining suspects,

Sanders remains in a local area hospital under guard. All of the money taken from the bank was recovered at the scene.

I flashed back to the interview and the image of the very attractive Mary Sanders. I had liked her immediately and had intended to call her regarding the Bud Hoffman interview. Now she was in the hospital fighting for her life and I was feeling a little guilty that I hadn't called. I put the front page aside and returned to the sports page and my breakfast.

My quiet little table in the corner gave as much privacy as you could expect in a local diner, so I decided to make a phone call. I took out my cell phone and dialed Big Bob. The phone rang twice and Sylvia answered.

"Hey, Sylvie," I said.

"Hey, Donnie. How you doing?"

"Fine, Sylvie. I need to speak to the man."

"Hang on, Donnie. I'll get him."

I took another gulp of coffee. I could almost feel the caffeine surge through my body.

"Hey, Blood, what's going on?" came the rumble on the other end of the line.

"Did you read anything about the bank robbery shootout in Knoxville last week?" I asked.

"Sure, it was in all the papers and I even talked to McSwain. Some bad apples took part in that fiasco. Why do you ask?"

"I interviewed the female officer that was wounded in the shootout as part of my investigation of the Fairchild case. I liked her. I'd like to give her a call and see how she is doing, but it sounds like they have her under lock and key."

"Yeah, they do," Big Bob said. "She capped Larry Elroy during the shootout and they are certain that one of the two guys that got away is his older brother, Teddy Earl. Teddy Earl Elroy is one crazy mean son of a bitch, and they think he may take a run at Mary Sanders sooner or later. They want to find him before she is released from the hospital."

"Can you get me a number?"

"Probably. I'll leave you a message at your office if I can't track you down."

"Thanks, Big Bob. See you later."

WHEN I GOT back to the office the door was unlocked. As I opened it and went in, Jake greeted me with his usual nudge and ran back to my office as I followed. Roy Husky sat in the chair in front of my desk. He was drinking the last of my morning coffee and reading the newspaper. He looked up and smiled. *That Jake, one hell of a watch dog.*

"Hey, gumshoe," he deadpanned.

"You comfy?" I shot back.

"I'm fine."

"I thought I locked that door."

"Just showing off," he smiled. "I'm here for an update."

"Sorry," I said. "I don't work for you."

Roy did not reply. He simply took out his cell phone and quick dialed a number.

"Roy here. Would you give your private investigator permission to update me on the case? Yes, sir," Roy said and handed me the phone.

"Youngblood," I said.

"Don, please give Roy everything you've got on my daughter's disappearance at any time," he ordered. "OK?"

Fleet did not sound very happy and I could not figure out why he wouldn't want to hear it directly from me, but who am I to question a rich man whose missing daughter might be dead?

"Sure thing," I said, and the line went dead.

I handed the cell phone back to Roy.

"Curious," I said.

"Why he does not want to talk to you direct?"

I nodded.

"Mr. Fleet is having a hard time with this," Roy said. "He is very emotional. He won't even talk to me. I have to record everything and give him a tape. He considers tears and emotions a weakness, and he will not put them on display in front of me or anyone else."

I nodded. Roy took out a small tape recorder from his breast pocket and placed it on my desk. I stared at it as I collected my thoughts and then I punched the record button and went over everything I had found out. Roy sat in silence. When I had finished I punched the stop button.

"That's it," I said.

"Son of a bitch."

We sat in silence for a few minutes while Roy digested all the information. There was a hard and distant look on his face.

"You think Sarah Ann is dead?" he asked.

"She is either dead or she knows everything. I do not know which at this point. Maybe Joey changed. Maybe he really loved her and they ran off together. I just don't know."

"I think she is dead," Roy said softly.

There was sadness about him that I had not seen before and I was suddenly seized by a revelation. Could Roy Husky be in love with Sarah Ann? We sat in silence while I pondered that question and Roy stared at the floor, seemingly off in some distant place.

"What are you going to do next?" he finally asked.

"Go to New York."

"You're nuts. You are getting in way over your head if you start getting mixed up with the mob."

"Maybe," I smiled. "Maybe not."

Late in the day I went online to check e-mail, I had two. The first was from T. Elbert saying thanks for the update and let him know if he could help in any way with the investigation. The second was from Sandy. The subject of which was "Hello there!" I sat and stared at the computer screen trying to figure out what I really wanted. The committed part of me was desperate to hear from Sandy. The uncommitted part was telling me maybe it was time to move on. I double-clicked it open.

> Hi Don, Sorry I haven't been in touch sooner but I had to sort out my thoughts and of course I am going crazy trying to settle in. I am staying at the company apartment in Marietta until I find a place of my own. My stuff is in storage. I start my new job tomorrow. At this point you have to decide what you want. I know what I want and it is not a long distance relationship. Say the word and I'll be back tomorrow. You know what the word is don't you, Don. It's the "M" word, Don. It happens to the best of us. I'm not getting any younger and I love you very much but I cannot just be your "steady girlfriend." I need a future. I hope it's with you. Sandy

An ultimatum. I didn't do well with ultimatums. In a way it took the pressure off. I could decide about this later. Besides, I was slowly being consumed by the Fairchild case. With a combination of fear and excitement, I decided it was time to go to New York. I wrote T. Elbert another e-mail to let him know where I was going and what I was up to in case things didn't turn out the way I hoped. Then I called Scott Glass.

17

The next morning I got up in the wee hours and drove to Knoxville to catch an early flight to New York's LaGuardia Airport. By the time my cab dropped me at Marriott's Marquis Hotel at Time Square, it was almost lunch time. I checked in, then grabbed a quick bite to eat and spent the rest of the day walking the streets absorbing the energy, sights, and sounds of an old friend.

That evening in my room high above Broadway's street noise, I was scanning the room service menu and the in-room movie guide. Daylight departs early in the east as winter approaches. I looked down on the glittering lights of Broadway and watched the evening theater crowd jockey for position on the congested sidewalks. Showtime was approaching and I considered going to a play. Last-minute single seats in a good location are not that hard to find, but I decided I wasn't in a theater frame of mind. I located the TV remote and began flipping through the channels until I stumbled upon Monday night football. It was minutes before the start of the game. I ordered room service as the opening kickoff was in the air. My food arrived near the end of the first quarter. I went to bed at halftime.

TUESDAY MORNING I WAS under the big clock in the hotel atrium having my first cup of coffee and reading the late edition of the *New York Times*. It was a little past six and few people were stirring. I put down the paper and pondered how a missing-persons case in east Tennessee had led me back to New York and trying to contact a mob boss. I had a few leads on how to find Carlo Vincente from a reluctant Scott Glass. I had to promise Scott that I would share anything I learned from talking to Vincente if I found him and survived the interview. The smart thing to do would be to catch the first flight back South and forget the whole thing but I knew I wouldn't. Curiosity and the spectre of danger propelled me forward. I picked up the paper and headed to the hotel restaurant.

After a large breakfast I went back to my room and went online to check the market and my e-mail. The one personal e-mail I had was short and sweet.

Watch your ass!
T. Elbert

I STARTED MY SEARCH at Le Alpi, an eastside Italian restaurant and a known hangout of Carlo Vincente. According to the FBI, Vincente owned a number of small Italian restaurants all over Manhattan. The guess was that he used them to launder money. The FBI had also learned that all the restaurants made money and that the food was surprisingly good. The maitre de at Le Alpi looked at me as if I had two heads when I asked if Carlo Vincente was around.

"Never heard of him," he said indignantly.

"If he should miraculously appear someday, give him this," I said, handing him my business card. On the back I had written "Marriott Marquis" and "*Where in the world is Joey Avanti?*"

By three o'clock I had covered El Roma, The Venice Palace, and The Gondola, and repeated the same inquiry with much the same result. I walked down Broadway to 28th Street and turned east. I had just crossed Fifth Avenue when I heard a car door slam behind me and then another. All of a sudden I was being shoved through a service entrance door of an office building on 28th. I spun to encounter a stocky, dark-complected, dark-haired thug in a blue suit, with a taller gray-suit version bringing up the rear. Blue suit was about to throw a punch aimed right at my jaws when I dropped him to his knees with a hard kick to his crotch. I quickly followed that up with a short hard right to the nose that I knew

I had broken as soon as I made contact. I loaded up with a left for gray suit and pulled up short when I found myself staring down the barrel of a 9mm Beretta. I knew the piece was a Beretta nine because I had one myself, although I had never looked down the barrel of it when it had a full clip.

"Easy," gray suit said.

"I'm cool," I said putting my hands halfway up, palms open.

Blue suit was still down with blood pouring from his broken nose. Gray suit threw him his handkerchief and looked back to me. "You shouldn't have hurt Gino," he said nonchalantly. "Now we will have to mess you up a bit."

"Sorry," I said with no conviction. "I'm not used to being mugged. It looked like Gino was about to hurt me."

Gino staggered to his feet holding the handkerchief in place on his bleeding nose. Gray suit handed him the Beretta. "Keep him covered while I give him a little New York welcome," he said. Like lightning he spun and hit me right in the mid-section. I had just enough time to brace for the impact before contact. Still, it was a formidable punch and nearly doubled me over. I made a mental note to do more stomach crunches. Gray suit was about to deliver another gut-buster when I heard two familiar sounds. One was the hammer of a .38 cocking and the other was a familiar voice saying, "I wouldn't do that if I were you."

Roy Husky had the barrel of his .38 tucked neatly underneath and behind Gino's left ear. "Put it away," he said to Gino in a soft icy whisper. Gino slipped the Beretta into his outside coat pocket. "Over there," Roy said, motioning with the .38 for gray suit to join Gino.

"Sorry, Frankie," Gino said. "I never saw him coming."

"You okay?" Roy asked, turning to me.

"I'd be a lot better if you had shown up a minute sooner." I groaned.

"Yeah, and a lot worse if I hadn't shown up at all."

"True," I said. "Watch your back. There may be a third one."

"Not to worry, Billy has that under control. Want to light this guy up a few times?" Roy asked pointing the .38 toward gray suit.

"Nah," I said, looking at Gino. "I think we're even."

Gino still had his head buried in the handkerchief so I turned my best detective stare on Frankie. "So what's the story?"

"What do you know about Joey Avanti?" Frankie asked in an accent that sounded like it was right out of HBO's *Sopranos*.

"Who wants to know?"

"I want to know," he said defiantly, and I believed him.

"Who else?"

"Carlo Vincente," he said almost meekly.

"Why can't Carlo ask for himself?" I queried. Of course, I knew the answer. He didn't want to be bothered and so he sent two of his thugs. Unfortunately for them, two of my thugs had shown up and now I had the upper hand.

Frankie looked at me as if I had "lunatic" tattooed on my forehead. "He's busy."

"Fine. Tell Mr. Vincente if he wants information on Joey Avanti that he can personally phone me at the Marriott Marquis."

I looked at Roy and nodded.

"Get the hell out of here," Roy growled at Gino and Frankie. They went like whipped puppies.

We followed them to the street. When he saw us coming, Billy got out of a black limo and slipped a hunting knife into a sheath attached to his belt near his lower back and hidden by his leather jacket. He evidently had just removed it from the throat of the limo driver. Gino and Frankie slid in and the limo roared away down 28th Street heading east to Madison. At the corner the limo turned north on Madison and disappeared.

I turned to Billy and Roy and asked nonchalantly, "So what brings you two to New York?"

Roy smiled. Billy never changed his expression.

"We thought you might need some help. You haven't been out of our sight since you got here," Roy said.

"Guardian angels?" I asked.

"Naw," said Roy. "Protecting the boss's investment."

Billy glared at me. "If you are not careful, you are going to end up dead."

Billy was stone-cold serious and at that moment I felt guilty that he was afraid for me. I was his best and almost only friend and I knew that if anything happened to me, Billy might never recover. The burden of that guilt also made me a little angry.

"You should have stayed home, Chief," I said staring hard back at him.

A barely perceptible smile curled at the corners of his mouth. "Not likely," he said.

WE WENT TO GALLAGER's for steak. I eat red meat maybe once a month and there was no better place to have my monthly treat. Roy and Billy were unusually talkative as they regaled me with the story of their conspiracy to keep tabs on me; it was male bonding of the highest order. In truth, I was not surprised. Billy was as overly protective as a mother hen. He had called Roy and proposed the New York undercover mission and Roy had jumped at the opportunity to do something exciting. I must admit that I hadn't sensed that I was being followed, but my experience in these situations is limited. I had just learned a valuable lesson: Watch your back.

"Where's Jake?" I asked Billy.

"Moto's."

Moto kept Jake on occasion when Billy and I were both away. Moto had a Siberian husky named Karate that Jake loved to play with. A large fenced area behind the gym served as a romper room for the two big dogs, and they eventually wore each other out and then came in for a nap in Moto's office. I sometimes took Jake with me to the gym so that he and Karate could work each other out. Big dogs need the exercise.

"What next?" Roy asked.

"Well, Vincente knows I'm here," I said. "I'll give him tomorrow to get in touch. If he doesn't, then we'll head home."

"You think he will get in touch?" Roy asked.

"He will unless he found Joey and killed him. He might anyway if he is curious about what I know. If I don't hear from him, then I think Joey and Sarah Ann are probably both dead."

18

The call came early. I had just returned from a workout in the Marriott's physical fitness center. I had spent an hour with the machines and aerobic equipment and sweat was still running freely. I was mopping my face with a towel when the phone rang.

"Mr. Youngblood?"

"Yes."

"Hold for Mr. Vincente, please."

I held. A few seconds passed.

"Mr. Youngblood, Carlo Vincente." The voice was a low, controlled growl that you might expect from a mafia boss. "I hear you want to talk to me, so talk."

"Face to face," I said.

"Why should I bother?"

"Because I have interesting news and I am fun to be with."

I detected a faint chuckle.

"My office," he said. "Six PM."

"Marriott Marquis," I answered, "Five PM for drinks under the big clock."

There was a long pause.

"Why not. See you at five."

I WAS TUCKED AWAY in a corner of the lounge under the big clock nursing a draft at exactly five PM. Billy and Roy were at separate tables across the lounge in case I needed help. I didn't expect to need help but it never hurts to have backup, especially if the backup is Billy and Roy.

At five past five a distinguished-looking man arrived and stood at the edge of the lounge and surveyed the clientele. He was, no doubt, Carlo Vincente. He had two recognizable companions, Frankie and Gino. Gino wore a strip of white tape over his nose. Frankie leaned and said something into Carlo's ear and nodded in my direction, then Vincente headed my way. His face was attractive without being handsome and the lines in it led me to guess he was in his late fifties or early sixties. He was about six feet, trim, with salt-and-pepper hair and very well dressed in a beautiful light-gray pinstriped suit. I didn't need to see the label to know it was expensive. I was glad I had worn my blue blazer and appropriate accompaniments.

The boys had gone to sit near Roy. Billy had disappeared but I knew he was close by. I stood up as Vincente approached. To my surprise, he offered his hand.

"Mr. Youngblood, Carlo Vincente. Nice to meet you," he said with a smile.

A bit dumbfounded, I returned the handshake and muttered, "Nice to meet you, too."

We sat and a waiter appeared instantly.

"What can I get you, Mr. Vincente?"

"Chivas on the rocks," Vincente responded.

"A pleasure, sir." The waiter slipped away.

Vincente looked at me and smiled. "You look younger than I expected," he said. "Why does a Wall Street whiz kid turn private detective?" Vincente had obviously checked up on me and wanted me to know it.

I shrugged. "Who knows, boredom maybe."

"But not anymore."

"No, not anymore."

"So," he paused. "You didn't come to New York just to spread your business cards around at all of my restaurants, and you obviously know that I would very much be interested in Joey Avanti. The question is how do you know so much?"

"Friends in high places," I smiled.

"Ah!" Vincente quietly exclaimed as his Chivas arrived. He picked it up. "Salute," he said and took a long drink. "You are well connected," he observed.

"I always say that it is not who you are but who you know."

"So true," Vincente chuckled. "Except, if you are me. Then it is also who you are."

"Good point," I agreed.

"You have a question?"

"Yes."

"Ask it."

"Did you find and hit Joey Avanti recently?" I held my breath as Carlo Vincente stared at me. "I'm not wired," I said. "And I really couldn't care less about Joey, but I am looking for someone who may have gotten caught in the crossfire."

Vincente continued to look at me as if he was deciding if I could be trusted. Or maybe he was trying to decide if I was brave or just plain stupid. I was wondering that myself. Then Vincente looked at his Chivas, swirled it and took a drink. I was counting on my directness and his ability to read people.

"Let me put it this way," Vincente said measuredly. "If some of my people found and eliminated a particular problem, no one would get caught in a crossfire. We are very focused and very efficient."

I believed him and so I asked my next question. "Have you had an employee go missing recently? Say four to five weeks ago?"

For a brief instant, I saw his face tighten and then it was gone. He sat in silence looking at his drink as he twirled the ice inside the glass. He looked up.

"And if I answer this question, what do I get in return?"

"The life and times of Joey Avanti over the last five years," I answered.

Vincente took another drink and contemplated my offer. He caught the waiter's eye and nodded toward his near-empty glass.

"Fair enough." he said. "About a month ago, more or less, I get a call from one of the boys, Frankie's younger brother Eddie, that thinks he has just seen Joey at LaGuardia airport. Eddie says this guy looks a lot like Joey, moves and acts exactly like Joey, and what do I want him to do. I say stay out of sight but stick with him and phone in and let me know what is going on. All my boys have cell phones now so reporting in shouldn't be a problem. That's it. I'm still waiting for the call. Frankie, of course, is going nuts. So we are at a dead end. Then you show up."

"Pretty big coincidence that Eddie spots Joey at LaGuardia, don't you think?" I was looking for a reaction. I did not get one. "What was Eddie doing at LaGuardia?"

"He was coming back from Miami from a business trip," said Vincente. "I know this because I sent him."

The question I could not answer was why was the alias Ronnie Fairchild in New York in the first place? I took another sip of my beer. Maybe it all tied together. Joey must have spotted Eddie and got rid of him. Maybe he got rid of him in New York. Maybe Eddie followed Joey to Tennessee and Joey got rid of him there. Joey would know exactly where to dump a body. It was probably at the bottom of a TVA lake. Maybe.

"So Joey spotted Eddie and disposed of him," I said.

"Looks like," Vincente said.

"Did you make inquiries?"

"We turned the town upside down. If Joey got rid of Eddie here, he was quiet about it. But I think it is the most likely scenario. Eddie said it looked like Joey was waiting for a flight but he didn't say to where. We checked passenger lists as best we could, but no Eddie. It is unlikely that Eddie would use a false ID at the last minute. That's one body that we'll never find."

"You interested in knowing where the deed was done?" I asked.

"You think you can find out for sure?"

"I do."

"How?"

"How is not important, but I'll find out."

"I'm interested," Vincente said.

"If Eddie had used a false ID, do you know what name he would have used?"

"No. I don't even know if he had a false ID. But some of my boys do in case of emergencies."

"Did you talk to Joey's father?"

"Joey's father is no longer in our employ," Vincente said quietly.

I felt a slight chill.

"Now, what can you tell me?" he asked.

I told him that Joey had assumed another identity and appeared to have had plastic surgery that slightly altered his appearance. I told him of a marriage into an influential Southern family and the likely murder of another Tennessee private investigator. I told him that Joey had disappeared about the time Eddie had disappeared. I told him of the missing wife. I didn't mention the name of Fairchild or Fleet or the town of Mountain Center. I told him that I had been hired to find Joey and the missing wife by the wealthy father of the wife and that the harder I looked, the more complex and sinister the case became.

"And you came here to make sure I hadn't found Joey and killed him," Vincente said.

"And to confirm a few of my suppositions."

We ordered another round. No matter who or what he was, Carlo Vincente was hard not to like. I am sure the devil, too, can be quite charming when he wants to be, I told myself. We sat silently with our thoughts as our drinks arrived. We raised our glasses and took a sip.

"Would he kill her or take her with him?" I asked.

"The Joey I knew would kill her in an instant if it served his purpose."

"That's what I figured."

"Where do you go from here?"

"Home. I have to somehow pick up his trail. It is probably the only way I am going to find out what happened to the wife."

"Be careful, he's smart," Vincente said. "And he is unpredictable, mean and charming. He could talk the panties off a nun. Forget local airports. He would drive a long distance if he were going to fly out of the country. Check major airports with international connections. And he sure as hell *is* using a phony ID."

"You really know how to instill confidence," I said. "Do you think he would have left the country?"

"Is he flush?" Vincente asked.

"Very."

"Then he probably left the country."

Vincente handed me a business card. It read:

WORLD WIDE IMPORTS
NEW YORK, NEW YORK
CARLO VINCENTE, PRESIDENT

On the back he had written a telephone number.

"My private number. I don't give it out to just anyone. If you need anything or have any questions, call me anytime. My advice is to forget it. Tell the girl's father that she is dead and go back to playing the stock market." He gave me a hard look, then continued. "My guess is you won't do that. So if you find Joey, let me know. Joey is my business and the girl is your business. I'll deal with Joey and he will tell me about the girl. I guarantee it."

I believed him. Vincente stood up and finished the last of his drink. He was letting me know the meeting was over. I stood.

"I would appreciate knowing about the girl if you find out anything," he said. "I have two daughters. It would be a terrible thing to lose one."

I nodded. We shook hands. It was a firm handshake on both ends.

"I hear you are pretty good with your fists," he smiled, and looked in the direction of Frankie and Gino.

"Much to my surprise," I smiled back.

Vincente walked away. Frankie and Gino followed.

Billy and Roy came over and sat down.

"How did that go?" Roy asked.

"Not bad, but he is a very scary guy. I may have nightmares. Tell me, did Ronnie go to out of town right before they disappeared?"

"Yes, he had just returned from Connecticut, or so he said. The day before, if I am not mistaken. I was surprised when they told Fleet they were leaving the next day for Florida."

I pondered that bit of information while I finished the rest of my beer. Ronnie had spotted Eddie at the airport, probably after he had checked in at the counter. Then one of two things happened. Eddie bought a ticket and followed Ronnie to Tennessee, or Ronnie somehow got rid of Eddie in New York. Either way, I was going to find out.

FROM MY ROOM AT THE MARRIOTT I called Scott Glass at his direct number in Washington.

"Glass," he answered in a cold, professional tone.

"Friendly," I teased. "Makes me want to tell the FBI everything."

"What are you doing in New York, Blood?"

"Very good, professor. Do you know my room number, too?"

"Give me a minute and I can get it in case you have forgotten."

"Ha, ha," I said slowly with emphasis. "I need a favor."

"Need I remind you that I am not your personal lackey?"

"Looked at your portfolio lately, Scottie?"

"You keep reminding me. You're not playing fair, Donnie. I might as well give up arguing with you," Scott said with mock exasperation. "Or find another financial consultant. What is it this time?"

"Last October third, Ronnie Fairchild flew out of LaGuardia on Delta to Tri-Cities. I need to know the names of any passengers who bought a last-minute ticket and how they paid for it, cash or credit card."

"Hold on. You're in New York. Did you track down Carlo Vincente?"

"I did. Very interesting fellow."

"I'll bet. So you are still digging into the whereabouts of Joey Avanti?"

"I am. And this is your way of helping. Now, how long do you think it will take?"

"It will probably cost me a dinner, but I should have something for you tomorrow. I'll call you on your cell phone."

"Is she good-looking?" I asked.

"Not bad," Scott laughed. "Not bad at all." He hung up before I could get in another smart remark.

19

The fire in the fireplace burned from the most realistic gas logs I could find on the market. I had my feet up with my VCR playing the latest episode of *Law & Order*, one of the few network TV shows I bothered to watch. Jake lay contentedly on his bed, exhausted from his time with Karate and no doubt glad to be home and back to his old routine. In front of me on the coffee table was a pepperoni pizza from Best Italian and two bottles of Michelob Amber Bock. I was a little exhausted myself.

Roy, Billy, and I had caught a half-filled early morning flight home. We barely spoke. Roy was reading the latest Carl Hiassen and every now and then laughed out loud. I was reading an Alex Cross novel by James Patterson. Billy was reading *Searching for Red Eagle* by Mary Ann Wells. He said it was a personal journey into the spirit world of native America. Billy was always searching for his Native American self. We landed and went our separate ways, with Roy promising to update Joseph Fleet and to start preparing him for the worst. Billy went to his studio to work on his latest painting of a Cherokee Indian village prior to the Trail of Tears.

I had just finished my show, half the pizza, and both beers when the phone rang. On the fourth ring I heard my rather generic message and then the beep.

"Mr. Youngblood, this is Chief McSwain. I need you to call me as soon as possible. The number . . ."

I cut off the recording by picking up the phone. I knew this had to be about Mary Sanders.

"How is Mary?" I asked immediately.

"She's okay. Improving," McSwain said. "But I need a favor and Mary needs help. I called Chief Wilson and he said you are the man for the job. Mary is ready to be released. Physically there is no reason for the hospital to keep her any longer. But we know Teddy Earl Elroy will seek revenge for the death of his brother. He is crazy-mean-white-trash scum. We know he is still in the area but he's one slippery son of a bitch with lots of low-life scum friends who are helping him avoid us. We want Mary out of town for a while, but she is not ready to be by herself. Can you help us out?"

"I have a case right now that is taking up most of my time," I said, although spending time with Mary Sanders was not unappealing.

"Same case you were working on when you talked to me?"

"Same one."

"Slow going?"

"Dead end."

"So take a break and maybe something will turn up," McSwain offered.

"Let me think about it. Give me a number I can reach you at tomorrow morning."

He did and we hung up.

I had just finished brushing my teeth when the phone rang again. My desire to get to bed early was apparently not shared by the rest of the world.

"Hello."

"Is this the famous private detective, Donald Youngblood?" Scott Glass asked, trying to disguise his voice.

"Don't quit your day job, Scott. Voice impersonation is not in the cards for you."

"Rats! And I practiced so hard."

"What have you got? Make it quick. I'm beat."

"Well, first of all Ronnie Fairchild did not fly into Tri-Cities. He flew into Knoxville on a flight arriving at 9:30 that evening."

"Knoxville? That doesn't make any sense." Another loose end.

"No, it doesn't, but does it make any difference?"

"Maybe," I said. "But I'll sort it out later. What else have you got?"

"Does the name Anthony Carbone mean anything to you?"

"Nothing."

"Well, Anthony paid cash for a last-minute ticket on the same flight that Ronnie Fairchild was on."

I dutifully wrote the name on the pad I keep by the telephone.

"Thanks, Professor. That's good to know. I'll talk to you later."

I was about to hang up when Scott said, "Know what else is interesting about Anthony Carbone?"

"No," I said yawning. "But I bet you are going to tell me."

"Anthony Carbone is dead."

I was a little more awake. "I'm listening."

"Know when he died?"

Scott loved to play these little games when he knew something that I didn't and he wanted to drag it out as long as possible. I played along.

"Soon after he landed in Tennessee?" I guessed.

"Wrong," Scott said making a game-show buzzer sound. "Anthony was a bit of a miracle. He died two years before he took the flight."

I was now wide awake and the wheels were turning.

"Let me guess," I said. "Anthony at one time was in the employ of Carlo Vincente."

"Very good, gumshoe. Now, can you tell me who was on that plane impersonating Anthony Carbone?"

"Yeah, according to Vincente it was one of his boys named Eddie who had spotted Joey Avanti then promptly disappeared. Joey spotted him and got rid of him, no doubt. That's why Joey took off so fast. Joey had no idea how much Carlo knew. Thanks, Professor. Now I really must get some sleep."

I hung up before Scott could ask any more questions, but I had one. *Why did Eddie use a false ID?* I went to bed without an answer.

20

November was fast approaching. I noticed that many stubborn autumn leaves remained clinging to various trees as I took Jake for his early-morning constitutional. The day was overcast with a cold mist in the air. A typical day in the mountains that signaled winter was approaching. I was in no particular hurry and neither was Jake. I needed time to think about my upcoming trip. I had called Mc-Swain and told him I would watch after Mary Sanders, but it had to be my way. He agreed, so it was a go. I had also called Roy and Billy and told them to meet me in the office later. I went over my plan in my head and decided I liked it. I went back to 5300 to pack. Jake tagged along knowing it was mealtime.

I packed what I thought I might need for a two-week trip. I unlocked the gun cabinet and stared at my collection of guns and holsters before choosing the Beretta nine and its speed holster, custom-made to fit on a belt at the small of my back.

IN THE OFFICE I MADE COFFEE and checked e-mail. Just junk; nothing from Sandy. It was my turn to write her. I checked the market. Down. Typical October. I was getting hurt a little but not much. I could not postpone the inevitable forever. I opened Sandy's old e-mail and clicked reply.

> Hey Sandy!
>
> Sorry I haven't written but things have been nuts and I have been traveling involved with a really unusual case. I am on the road again to-night. Sounds like everything is working out for you. I miss you and wish

you were here but I understand your position. I wish I could make the commitment you want but right now I cannot. Maybe time will change that. Write when you have time. I hope you will let me come visit. No matter what happens I always want to be your friend.

    Don

I looked at the screen and reread. I cared for Sandy but I had skillfully avoided using the "L" word with anyone. I still had not found *the one*. I reread it again. It was a little mixed up and rambling but it was honest. I clicked send and logged off just as I heard the outer door opening and shutting. Billy poked his head around my doorway, nodded, and disappeared back into the outer office.

I phoned Carlo Vincente at the number on the back of his card.

He answered himself. "Yes?"

"Mr. Vincente, Don Youngblood."

"Yes, Mr. Youngblood. You have information, I assume."

"The person we discussed definitely passed away in Tennessee."

"You're certain?"

"Positive."

"Is there anything else you wish to tell me?"

"Not at this time."

"Well, take care of yourself, Mr. Youngblood. And stay in touch."

Carlo Vincente hung up.

Later that afternoon I phoned Big Bob and told him I had agreed to play bodyguard for Mary Sanders. He made a crack about her body that I ignored and then I asked him for his help in executing my plan.

"Midnight?" he exclaimed.

"Midnight."

We hung up. I heard voices in the outer office.

"Roy's here," Billy stuck his head back in and growled.

"You two come on in here."

They came. I explained.

"You're trading one dangerous mess for an even more dangerous mess," Roy pointed out.

"Umm," agreed Billy.

Roy turned to Billy.

"I bet this Officer Sanders is a looker," he said.

"Umm," agreed Billy.

"Want some help?" Roy sneered at me.

"No," I said, straight-faced and professional. "I think I can handle this. I am just doing a favor for the Knoxville Chief of Police."

"Sure you are," Roy said. "What do you want us to do while you're off gallivanting around the countryside with Sanders?"

"Put your heads together and see if you can come up with a plan to uncover Joey Avanti's trail," I replied.

21

We were in the Wilson kitchen a few minutes past midnight. Sylvia was making coffee for our trip. I had just arrived at Big Bob's to implement phase one of my master plan to disappear with Mary Sanders. I would follow Big Bob to Knoxville in his car to a place we had picked out and we would switch cars and he would wait on me to return with Mary Sanders. We would switch cars again and part company. I did not want anyone who might be watching the hospital to see what I was driving or get its license plate number. And I wanted to make sure I was not being tailed. After the second switch, Big Bob would go home and Mary, Jake, and I would leave town. Only a trusted few would know where we were going or would be able to reach me by cell phone. Maybe I was being overly cautious but I had to assume Teddy Earl Elroy seriously wanted to kill Mary Sanders. McSwain had faxed me Teddy Earl's jacket. He was a real bad boy. He had been locked up twice on robbery convictions and was suspected of killing at least two people but without enough evidence to convict. Knoxville police suspected it was his bullet that had killed Officer Arnold E. Wiggins.

Big Bob appeared, wearing jeans, cowboy boots, and a cowboy hat with an Indian-style hatband, and a police jacket. He was armed with a pearl-handled .38 special Smith & Wesson nickel-plated long barrel.

"You expecting the shootout at the OK Corral?" I asked.

"You never know," he smiled.

"Jesus!" Sylvia exclaimed. "Is this dangerous, Don?"

"Nah, just precautions."

"You guys are nuts," she said.

"Probably," I answered.

Sylvia grabbed Big Bob by the jacket and looked him straight in the eye. She was a tall woman and didn't have to look up much at his six-foot-four-inch frame.

"You call me when you get there and when you leave there and on the way back," she ordered.

"Yes ma'am," he said as he kissed her.

FOLLOWING BIG BOB WAS LIKE chasing an F-16. We cruised down I-81 at ninety miles an hour and passed very few cars. Jake was asleep in the back of the Pathfinder. It never hurts to have a watchdog, besides I didn't have the heart to leave him again. We made Knoxville in one hour and five minutes, well ahead of my scheduled arrival time.

We parked in Tyson Park and switched cars. Tyson Park was a good choice for the switch from the standpoint of being able to see if you were being tailed. There were entrances at both ends. If someone was tailing me and I entered one way and exited the other, they could not get past Big Bob without being seen. Exactly how safe we were was open to debate. Tyson Park has the reputation as a retail drug mall. Drugs were bought and sold, people were stabbed, robbed or worse.

I leaned near the open passenger-side window of the Pathfinder.

"Watch your ass," I said. "This can be a mean place."

"Shit, Blood, nobody is going to fuck with me. I got Jake in the back as protection."

I looked at Jake. He was sound asleep.

"I see what you mean," I said.

"You better not let Sylvia hear such language," I added as I walked to his Lincoln. "Or you will need protection."

MARY SANDERS WAS IN room 414 at UT Medical. I parked in the lot near the front and went in through the main entrance. A security guard paid little attention to me. I passed the gift shop to the elevators and stepped into an open car. I pressed four and the door slowly shut and I waited impatiently as the car started its slow ascent. I was used to New York elevators that cover forty floors at mach one. I looked up at the floor indicator lights to see if we were really moving. Finally, the door opened. I turned right toward the hall that led to the hospital rooms on the fourth floor. An orderly, with his head down slowly pushing a crash cart, passed about ten feet in front of me as I headed toward the front desk. I looked at the signs for room location. Room 414 was to the left in the direction the orderly was going. I stood motionless staring at the room sign, trying to process something from a recent memory. Suddenly an alarm rang in the back of my mind. A picture flashed from earlier in the day.

I turned toward 414 and shouted, "Elroy!"

The orderly was at least thirty feet away and the instant I shouted, I saw him spin with a gun in his hand. I dove for the partially open doorway of room 402 as three shots rang out and plaster sprayed around me. I rolled to safety and pulled the Beretta in time to see Teddy Earl shoot the guard at Mary's door. The guard's gun had cleared the holster but he didn't have time to get off a shot. I fired three quick rounds at Teddy Earl to get his attention as he ducked behind the crash cart. If he had ducked a second later he would have been dead.

An instant after I fired, three more shots echoed from behind me. Teddy Earl had had enough. Luckily for him, he was next to an emergency exit door. He ducked through and was gone. I turned to see McSwain running toward me. I joined him as we ran toward the fallen guard who was alive and moving.

"Stay here and get him some help," McSwain ordered. "And check on Mary."

He disappeared through the emergency exit door.

The shots had drawn a crowd of patients and a few nurses. Two of the nurses were already attending to the wounded officer whose nameplate read "Brady." Brady had taken a bullet in his right shoulder. It appeared he would be okay.

I went into 414 as Mary Sanders was coming out of the bathroom. She was noticeably limping, walking with a hospital cane. She was wearing jeans, a Banana Republic T-shirt and Nike running shoes. I would not have recognized her. She was much thinner, pale, and her eyes were sunken and outlined by dark circles. The beauty was still there waiting to be revived, but at this particular moment Mary Sanders looked like part of the cast of *Night of the Living Dead*. She seemed disoriented. Medication probably.

"Oh, Mr. Youngblood," she said weakly. "Did I hear gunshots?"

"Yeah, a little excitement. Teddy Earl Elroy tried to pay you a visit but he had forgotten it was after visiting hours," I said trying to fight fear with humor.

"Oh, God," she said.

I thought she was going to collapse. I helped her to a chair.

"Did they catch him?"

"I don't know yet. McSwain went after him."

I went to the door. More cops were showing up. One was running down the hall toward me.

"You Youngblood?" he asked.

"Yeah."

"Good. I'm Farley. McSwain said to do what you said. How can we help?"

"Get an officer in here with Mary and one on the door. Search all floors above and below. I'm sure he's gone but let's not take any chances. Go in pairs and shoot to kill."

"I like your style," Farley said and immediately started barking orders. I headed for the elevators. McSwain was getting off the far elevator as I was about to get on the near elevator.

"No luck," he said. "Someone was probably waiting with a car. I never even got a glimpse."

"Damn!" was all I could say.

We walked toward the nurse's station. I told McSwain what I had asked Farley to do.

"Not bad," he said. "You should have been a cop. Good 3 you were early. You probably saved her life."

"You can thank Big Bob for that. He drives like a bat out of hell. Didn't you also have a guard in the room?"

"Yeah. He was downstairs getting coffee. Bad timing."

"I doubt it. Elroy was probably hiding out somewhere waiting for him to leave the room. You better check and make sure none of the hospital staff is missing."

"Good idea. I'll have someone get right on it."

We reached the nurses' station.

"How's Officer Brady?" McSwain asked the nurse at the desk.

"He is going to be okay," she said. "But I don't think he will be back in uniform for a while."

"I'm going to get Mary and get out of here," I said to McSwain.

"Another good idea. Call me when you get settled."

I started down the hall toward Mary's room.

"Hey, Youngblood," McSwain hollered. "How did you know it was Elroy?"

"The picture you faxed. I never really got a good look at him tonight but something in that picture triggered an alarm."

"Good thing," said McSwain.

IN TYSON PARK we made the switch and I told Big Bob about all the excitement.

"Shit," he said. "I should have been there."

"Yeah," I teased. "Probably would have got your ass shot off and Sylvia would have killed me."

He glared at me. "You had three shots at him and missed? And you are supposed to be a hotshot marksman?"

"It happened so fast," I argued. "Besides, if he doesn't duck at just the right moment, I blow his head off."

I got in the Pathfinder and handed Mary a blanket and a pillow.

"Try to get some sleep. It is going to be a long drive," I told her, then rolled down the driver's side window and spoke to Big Bob. "Follow me for a while to make sure I'm clear."

I went out Kingston Pike and stopped at a Dunkin' Donuts to get a large coffee for the road. It had been a long time since I had pulled an all-nighter and I did not expect any help with the driving. Mary was already asleep. So was Jake.

I made a right turn near Calhoun's Restaurant and drove to the I-40 interchange and headed south. As soon as I was on the Interstate, my cell phone rang.

"You're clear, Blood," Big Bob said. "Be careful and stay in touch."

"Will do. Try not to set any land-speed records on the way home. And thanks." I meant it, too.

TRAFFIC WAS NONEXISTENT. I set the cruise control on seventy-five and started sipping coffee and concentrating on staying awake. Daylight was still several hours away. At the I-40 and I-75 split, we took I-75. Chattanooga came and went quickly. Early Saturday morning traffic in Atlanta was light and dawn was just breaking.

I stopped at a rest area south of Atlanta. Mary and Jake were still dead to the world. I locked the car and went to the bathroom. The cold water on my face felt good and I was relieved that I had made it through the night. I got a cup of free coffee and went back to the Pathfinder. No movement from my passengers. We set out again. By mid-morning I crossed the Florida–Georgia line and continued down I-75 past Gainesville to the Sunshine State Parkway, where I stopped at the first rest area shortly past noon. When I shut down the engine, Mary stirred and opened her eyes.

"Where are we?" she asked.

"Florida."

She yawned. "I need to go to the bathroom and I would kill for a cup of coffee."

"Me, too. Let me help you and then I'll come back for Jake."

"Who's Jake?" she said, still not quite awake.

"My dog."

"You have a dog in here?"

At that moment Jake stood up in the back and yawned and yawled and shook himself.

"I hope you like dogs," I said.

"I love dogs," Mary said meekly as she turned to look at Jake. "He is beautiful. Hey, Jake."

With cane in hand, Mary got out of the Pathfinder. She did not want my help. She said it was good therapy for her to do it on her own if I didn't mind the fact that she would be slow. I said I didn't and for her to take her time. I took Jake to the dog run and walked him around while I enjoyed the beautiful Florida fall day. I was surprised at how good I felt. I knew that evening I would be totally exhausted.

When I returned to the Pathfinder, Mary was back inside. I put Jake in the back, went to the toilet and then inside the rest station for a bottle of water and some snacks. In a few minutes I had rejoined Jake and Mary and we were once again heading south on the turnpike toward Orlando.

"How much farther, Mr. Youngblood?"

"Call me Don," I said. "About four hours."

Mary smiled. "So we aren't going to Disney World?"

"Not today, maybe later."

We talked sporadically with long periods of silence in between. For Mary conversation seemed to be an effort and I let her know that it was all right to be quiet. She seemed relieved that she was not obligated to be social and she went back to sleep. I cruised with moderate traffic through Orlando and on into the wide open little populated spaces of central Florida as the traffic thinned.

By sunset we were safe on Rivera Beach inside Scott Glass's Singer Island condo at a complex called The Seagull. I had used Scott's condo on other occasions and had been instrumental in the purchase of it for a couple of reasons. First, I had helped Scott accumulate the wealth to make the purchase, and second, I knew the area. My parents had owned a unit at The Phoenix Towers. I had sold it when they were killed and bought a penthouse unit at The Seascape a mile north. The memories were just too painful for me to return to The Phoenix Towers. If Scott was curious as to why I was not staying at my own place, he kept it to himself. I really did not think that Teddy Earl Elroy had the resources to track me all the way to Singer Island, but I was not taking any chances.

I had made a stop at the local supermarket and purchased staples—coffee, beer, wine, cheese, crackers, salad mix and other food stuffs to make the stay more bearable. Luggage, groceries, and passengers were now secure. I showed Mary her room and gave her a tour of the elegant three-bedroom layout. I had given Mary the master bedroom with king bed and a huge bathroom that contained a Jacuzzi tub, a separate shower, and lots of countertop and mirrors. I would sleep in the guest bedroom with a queen bed and a smaller private bath with a shower. The third bedroom doubled as an office with a computer module. Each bedroom had a short hallway that led to the great room—a combination of living room, dining room, and kitchen. A balcony off the great room spectacularly overlooked the Atlantic. We were twenty floors up in one of the three penthouse condos.

I had asked Mary what she wanted for dinner and she said she really didn't care and wasn't very hungry. I decided to grill some boneless chicken teriyaki style and make a Caesar salad. As an afterthought I fixed some garlic bread. We sat at the dining room table staring into the night through the sliding glass doors that opened onto the balcony. A few ship lights twinkled far out on the Atlantic. Jake lay between us on alert for any nibble that might accidently tumble from the table. Crumb patrol, I called it. Mary was quiet but she seemed to be enjoying our dinner. She drank bottled water and I had a Michelob Amber Bock.

Mary smiled faintly and said, "It is really quite good. I wouldn't have figured you for a cook."

"I hate eating out all the time. So, it is either cook or starve. Actually, I like to cook."

"I appreciate what you are doing," she said.

"My pleasure."

Mary smiled weakly and continued to eat. She seemed as delicate as a newborn bird that had fallen out of the nest. This was not the same woman I had met a few weeks ago. Maybe being shot and almost killed gets you in touch with your own mortality. And maybe being so in touch leads to a depression that is hard to recover from. I didn't know. I was just speculating as I ate and watched Mary. I wanted to say it would be all right but I didn't know if it would be or not.

"Did you almost get shot last night?" she asked.

"Almost."

"I'm sorry."

"Not your fault."

We finished the rest of our meal in silence and Mary started to clear the table.

"Don't. I'll clean up later."

"Do you mind if I turn in? I'm really tired."

"Good idea. I'm beat. too."

Jake followed her through the master bedroom door; so much for loyalty. I would have called for him, but something told me that my dog had a sense of who needed him most and right then it was Mary. Never question the wisdom of animals. As she closed the door, I heard her say something to Jake that I couldn't make out.

I called Billy on his cell phone from my cell phone. Untraceable. I told him where we were. He would be the only one who knew and I knew he would die before he gave up the secret. I told him about the gunfight on floor four. I asked him to call Big Bob and let him know everything was OK for now.

"If you need to get in touch, call the cell phone or use e-mail," I said.

"All these precautions," he said. "Not like you."

"True. Then again, I have never been shot at before. And Teddy Earl was definitely trying to kill me."

I hung up with Billy, cleared the table, and went out on the balcony to sit down on the lounge and finish my second beer. Big mistake. The southerly breeze caressed me to sleep in minutes. When I awoke it was 3 AM. I went in, undressed, brushed my teeth, and went back to sleep for another six hours.

22

The first few days Mary fell into a routine that seemed a sure sign of depression. She slept a lot. She was still withdrawn and fragile and I did not want to push, and so I faded into the background hoping she would find her own way back.

I was up at daybreak to run while Mary slept late. I had to run early in Florida because the heat and humidity later in the day was a killer. Even after an early morning run, it took half an hour to cool down enough to take a shower. Mary would emerge around 10 AM looking for coffee and cereal. She would read and watch TV and we would occasionally talk about the island and restaurants and things to do. When I suggested we go out for breakfast or dinner or to a movie she would respond that it sounded like a good idea when she felt better. She would nibble at lunch, take an afternoon nap, get up and read or watch TV, nibble at dinner and go back to bed. By Tuesday night I wondered how long I should let this continue. I thought I might need to get her professional help.

But gradually Mary started to show signs of life. She started going to the pool and the beach after breakfast. She read more and quit watching TV except for the occasional movie I would rent from Blockbuster. She skipped her afternoon nap. Her appetite improved. Thursday I joined her at the pool and we actually had an in-depth conversation about growing up, our parents, and our lives in general. Friday we went out to breakfast and I asked her if she would let me help her rehabilitate her leg. She agreed.

We started the rehab program in the swimming pool that day. Walking in water is great therapy for leg injuries. Running in water would be our next goal. Mary was eager to please and worked hard. The harder she worked, the more animated she became, and the Mary Sanders that

I had first met in Knoxville was emerging.

Friday night we went out to dinner and Mary had her first glass of wine. We stayed up late talking. Saturday morning we took Jake for a long walk and I stopped by the local gym and joined for a month. The walk was slow and painful for Mary but she did not complain. She still needed the cane. We did more pool work Saturday afternoon. I was hoping the pool work would help her eliminate the cane, both physically and psychologically.

"You are a slave driver," Mary said that night.

We were eating dinner at the dining room table. I had grilled fresh Wahoo, baked potatoes, and made Caesar salad. Jake was in his usual position on crumb patrol.

"No pain, no gain," I smiled.

"Well, I must be gaining a lot," she smiled back.

"You sure look better that a week ago."

"Thanks. I think."

I WAS DEEP UNDER THE SURFACE of a peaceful sleep when a scream aroused me. I could feel myself rising from the depths and then I popped through like a breaching whale. As I sat up I heard another scream. Mary. I reached underneath the far pillow for the Beretta and tore out of my room, down the short hall into the great room and past the sliding glass doors to the master bedroom hall door. One thought ran through my mind—Teddy Earl Elroy. How? As I pushed through the hall door that led to the master, a light came on somewhere in the bedroom. I burst in low with the Beretta pointed and ready. Mary was sitting up like she had seen a ghost. I quickly scanned the room with the Beretta.

"It's okay," she said catching her breath. "Bad dream."

I lowered the Beretta and placed it on the nightstand by her bed and sat down on the edge next to her while she regained her composure.

"He was coming after me. I was trapped in my apartment and didn't have my sidearm."

"Teddy Earl?" I asked.

"No, Larry."

"Larry is dead."

"I know," she said emphatically. "Have you ever killed anybody?"

"No."

"I cannot get it out of my mind. I took a life. I dream about the shootout and I feel so guilty," she implored. "And now this nightmare."

She was still trying to catch her breath.

"I know it is easy for me to say, but you killed a very bad guy in self-defense while you were doing your job and protecting your community. You are a cop. You knew this could happen. If you are looking for absolution, fine. You're absolved. Guilt is for people who have done something wrong and you have done nothing wrong. End of speech."

She smiled.

"Thanks," she said. "I'll try to remember that. Will you stay here while I go back to sleep?"

"Sure," I said as I cut off the light.

I picked up the Beretta and sat in the comfortable rocker in the far corner of the room. I rocked and drifted off to sleep.

An hour later I was aroused by a slight creak at the window caused by a freshening breeze coming off the Atlantic. I crept out of the master bedroom, down the hall and into the great room, shutting the door behind me. I was now wide awake so I went online. I had an e-mail from T. Elbert saying everything was status quo in Mountain Center and to please keep him updated on my escapades. I also had an e-mail from Sandy.

Don,

I think it is obvious from your last e-mail that I cannot expect anything more from our relationship than what we already have had. As painful as it is for me I have to ask you if we could just be friends while I sort out my feelings. I am very much enjoying my job and the people here are great. Let's please stay in touch and please know that the last year for me was very special.

Love,

Sandy

So there it was, a burning bridge, and although I read Sandy's e-mail with a sense of sadness I realized I had no desire to put out the fire. I was beginning to feel that I could never make a marriage commitment to anyone and that revelation bothered me. Why had I turned into a selfish loner, unwilling to permanently share myself in a long-term relationship? It probably had something to do with the death of my parents.

I composed a poignant reply saying that we would be friends forever and that I was sorry that things did not turn out the way she wanted. And I was sorry, but I did not like ultimatums and I knew that—outside of death and Tennessee winning at least eight games a year in football—nothing was final. I signed off.

Outside the wind was blowing harder and making eerie noises and I felt a bit spooky. I checked the locks on the entrance door to the condo and returned to bed and a restless sleep.

23

As our second week unfolded, we continued Mary's rehab. By the time I returned from my morning jogs, she was up and ready to go to the pool. By Tuesday she was running in waist-deep water for a half an hour. In the afternoons we worked in the gym with light weights and when I wasn't helping her, I returned to my normal weight-training program. We were both feeling good about our progress. Mary Sanders was back.

"I think I'm ready to go jogging with you in the morning," she said on a beautiful clear Wednesday.

"Not yet," I said.

"Why not? I feel great."

"Your leg may feel great in the pool, but it could not stand pounding the pavement just yet. Our next goal for you is running on the beach."

"Yes, master," she teased and smiled flirtatiously.

I had a funny feeling in the pit of my stomach. I smiled my most timid smile. Not an easy task. I sensed trouble. Maybe I even wanted trouble. Mary Sanders was becoming more and more irresistible. I liked her immensely and her physical appearance was approaching goddess status. She had gained back some of the lost weight. Her body was tan and lean, revealing great muscle tone and her ample breasts did nothing to downplay her great figure. The sun had lightened parts of her hair into a natural frosted look of a whiter blond onto a golden blond. Her blue eyes sparkled. She was smart and witty and comfortable to be with, but I was determined that I would not make the first move toward intimacy. *I may have to start running twice a day*, I thought, *with two gym workouts, and maybe two cold showers.*

THAT NIGHT AFTER MARY had gone to bed, I went to the bedroom office and called McSwain on his cell phone. He seemed a little surprised to hear from me but he was anxious to hear about Mary's progress.

"It was touch and go for a while," I said, relating my frustration and fears of the first week. "But she slowly pulled out of it and now she is making great progress."

"She is a fine-looking woman," McSwain said in his unmistakable Irish brogue.

"I noticed."

He paused. "I wouldn't want her hurt any more than she already has been."

"Liam, I would never do anything to hurt Mary," I said firmly.

"No, of course not. I'm sorry. And I appreciate everything you are doing, Donald."

"She is a grown-up, Liam."

"Yes, of course she is."

"And I do not know where it will lead, but it has not led to anything yet, if you get my meaning."

"I do, I do," he blurted. "I should have kept my big Irish mouth shut."

"What about Elroy?"

"He has gone underground. We think that he is not even in this area right now."

"Do you think it is safe for Mary to come back?"

"No. There are people that would let him know and he would come back and try to kill her."

"Maybe we need to set a trap," I said.

"What kind of trap?"

"Let me think about that."

We talked another ten minutes. McSwain was very interested in my program for rehabbing Mary's leg.

After I said good-bye I signed onto AOL. I had e-mails from Scott and T. Elbert. Both wanted updates. I gave them the short version and went to bed.

24

Friday morning I wrapped Mary's leg in an Ace bandage. The stitches had dissolved and the scarring was minimal. Someone had done a fine sewing job, a male doctor, no doubt.

We went through the security gate to the beach and jogged lightly toward the Singer Island pump house. We were wearing bathing suits and T-shirts to absorb sweat. Mary perspired almost as much as I did. I liked that about her. She did not mind sweating. We kept to the soft sand that was harder work but less pounding on Mary's leg. It was daybreak and the beach was empty except for a few sleepers who had spent the night and a few early morning shell seekers. The breeze was warm and the newly rising sun was already heating up the day. When we reached the pump house, we went into the water to cool off, leaving the Ace bandage and our T-shirts abandoned on the beach.

"How is the leg holding up?"

"Fine. I can feel soreness but not sharp pain."

"That's good," I said.

"The Ace bandage was a good thought," Mary said. "I felt like I had extra support for the leg."

"That's the idea. You should wear one when you run until your leg is a hundred percent."

The water was cool, calm, and crystal clear. I could easily see the bottom where tiny fish swarmed around my legs. As I moved, they moved. I looked up and noticed Mary staring east toward the horizon of the ocean. Her expression was pensive and distance. We were about six feet apart.

"A penny," I said.

"I was thinking how beautiful it is here. I could just about leave everything behind and stay here forever."

"I have tried that on a couple of occasions. I can last about a month and then I am drawn back to the mountains and friends and the old routine."

"Yeah, I guess you're right. I just haven't had enough yet."

"Don't worry. We are not leaving any time soon. In fact, we are not leaving until you are ready."

"Good," Mary said. "I'm getting hungry. Let's head back."

"You are swimming back," I said, walking out of the water and picking up the T-shirts and the Ace bandage.

"What?"

"You heard me. Takes the place of your pool work. Take it slow and easy and I'll walk along beside you in the shallows."

"Okay, slave driver," she smiled.

I had that funny feeling again in the pit of my stomach. I was probably just hungry.

25

At the dawn of our third Sunday at Singer Island, I sat on one of the weathered wooden chairs on the beach and stared out at the Atlantic. As far as I knew, Mary and Jake were still asleep in the master bedroom. I needed to find Joey Avanti and Teddy Earl Elroy, and both would gladly kill me if they knew I was looking for them. I had no reason to think either did know, but I was not comforted by the thought.

My cell phone rang. "You are up early," Billy said.

"On the beach," I said. "Thinking."

"Come up with anything?"

"No, you?"

"My contact at Delta is searching for possibles but it is like hunting for one grain of sand on that beach you are on. Any suggestions?"

"Yeah. Narrow the search to single males that paid cash."

"Good thought. Will do. How is Mary?"

"She is doing fine."

"When will you be back?"

"Don't know. Whenever Mary wants to go back or whenever they catch Teddy Earl Elroy.

"You okay? You sound down."

"My hormones are trying to get in the way of my professionalism."

"Umm," Billy muttered. "Hard to control Mother Nature."

"You are a big help," I said.

At that moment Mary sat down next to me. She was drinking coffee from a styrofoam cup.

"Got to go, Chief," I said. "Mary just came down for our morning run."

"Remember, Blood, there are some things you cannot control," Billy said as we hung up.

That night I was reading in bed, the only light in the room from the bedside table lamp on my left. I felt a presence in the room and looked up to discover Mary standing at the foot of the bed watching me. I stared at her. She stared back with a slight smile. Seconds passed.

"Are you gay?" she asked.

"What?" I laughed.

"Well, are you?"

"NO!"

She pulled off her nightshirt to reveal the most gorgeous female body I had ever witnessed in person. All of a sudden I was having a hard time breathing.

"Well?" she said.

"Your scars are healing nicely."

"Goddamit, Don! Are you going to make love to me, or what?"

Since she put it that way, the only polite thing to do was to lift the covers so she could slide in beside me.

Billy was right. There are some things you can't control.

The next morning, I slept until noon. That happens when you stay up until four o'clock exploring every aspect of lovemaking you can think of. Mary was still sleeping when I slipped out and closed the bedroom door. I went to the kitchen and made fresh coffee knowing the smell would coax her out of bed. It did. She came meandering through the living area toward the kitchen wearing one of my T-shirts and a cat that ate the canary smile. She walked up to me and gave me a light kiss on the mouth.

"You are definitely not gay," she said.

"Good to know," I said. "And good morning to you, too."

We took our coffee and danish to the balcony overlooking the ocean and planned our day. Then we planned our week. All the plans included sex. I liked our plans.

26

Plans or no plans, the world is still out there. After three more weeks, I realized sadly that paradise was not all it was cracked up to be. We had loved well, slept well, played well, and eaten well, but loose ends dictated that we couldn't stay in paradise forever. We were both getting restless. I had kept in touch with Billy and McSwain almost daily but nothing had changed. Billy had no new leads and Roy had reported that Joseph Fleet was coming to grips with the fact that his daughter might be dead. McSwain was sure that Teddy Earl Elroy had left the Knoxville area. McSwain and Big Bob had worked out an exchange of officers that would allow Mary to work on the Mountain Center police force until Teddy Earl Elroy surfaced. How they had accomplished that I had no idea, but they were both smart and persuasive men and I was not surprised at their creativity.

In the dusk one evening Mary and I, with Jake between us, were sitting on our balcony overlooking the Atlantic enjoying our daily cocktail hour. Jake was abstaining. We were quiet with our own thoughts.

I looked over at Mary and she smiled. She was a goddess and I was smitten.

"It's time," she said. "Isn't it?"

It was a statement looking for confirmation rather than a question.

Mary was fully recovered physically from her wounds from the shoot-out and had a handle on the emotional end of it as well. Wounds to the psyche sometimes take years to heal and can be ripped back open later. I knew about those wounds. I carried a few.

"Yes," I said. "It is."

"When?"

"Whenever."

"Tomorrow."

"Then we should get to bed early."

Mary laughed that sexy laugh I had become so familiar with over the last few weeks. "It that all you men ever think about?"

"Are you complaining?"

"Not one bit."

WE ARRIVED BACK AT MY PLACE after a twelve-hour Sunday marathon drive from south Florida. Our luggage and other "stuff" was piled in the foyer and the living room. More of Mary's things were also in the living room, compliments of Billy who had made a midnight run to Mary's apartment in Knoxville. Hanging neatly in the foyer closet was a Mountain Center police uniform.

"I'm sleeping with you but I would like to take the guest room as mine so that I can have my own space," Mary said.

"No problem," I said. "That's your room at the top of the stairs."

We silently went about unpacking and in less than an hour we were on the living room couch with wine in hand and Jake sprawled in front of the fireplace. A low fire cast a romantic spell as the flames created a shadow dance on the nearby walls. The scene was mesmerizing and I felt the tiredness begin to engulf me. Mary looked as weary as I felt.

"Tired?" I asked.

"Beat."

"Ready for bed?"

"More than ready."

We left Jake alone with his dog dreams.

27

I returned to my office early on a cold gray Monday morning that was spitting snow and threatening more. Was it just a few days ago I was on the beach in Florida with the blond goddess? Mary and I had spent the weekend at the lake house, which she fell in love with, and she immediately commandeered one of the guest rooms as *her* room. No matter, she slept in my bed.

The next morning we woke, showered, and dressed early. Mary was in uniform as I dropped her at the police station a few minutes past six o'clock. The uniform disguised most of her considerable assets. Just as well, I mused. Now I was back to my early morning routine and happy for it. The market was in a typical December slump and I smiled as I recalled that I had turned most everything into cash in early September. In a few weeks I would go on a buying spree.

I heard noise in the outer office that I knew was Billy because Jake did not even flinch. I heard coffee being poured. A familiar frame filled the doorway.

"Welcome back, Blood," Billy said.

"Thanks, Chief. What's happening?"

"Not much, nothing new on our missing persons. It is hard to believe but there were no single males paying cash anywhere in the system on the days in question. Of course, that is only with Delta."

"Not surprising. Cash would attract more attention than a credit card. If our boy is as smart as Carlo Vincente says he is, I'll bet he had a clean credit card or a hidden bank account with a debit card."

"Yeah, but how?" Billy asked.

"Not hard, lots of ways. For instance, steal a pre-approved credit card application somewhere. Fill it out and rent an out-of-town post office box to use as the address for the alias. Make a few charges and pay them on time and all of a sudden you have a clean card with a good credit history. Or he might have opened a non-interest-bearing checking account somewhere using a phony social security number and maintained a balance of a few thousand dollars he could easily get to in case of emergency with an ATM or debit card. Not hard to keep that going. You can make all your deposits by mail and your statements can come to your post office box. And I would be willing to bet he has a phony driver's license and passport to match."

"Why non-interest bearing?" Billy asked.

"Nothing to report to the Feds that would red-flag the phony social security number."

"Um," Billy growled. "Not bad."

The phone rang.

"Youngblood," I answered.

"Well now, are we all rested and tanned and ready to get back to work?" Roy asked in a teasing singsong voice.

"I don't know about, you but I certainly am," I retorted.

"How was bodyguard duty?" he asked more seriously.

I thought about that for a few seconds as visions of the body I was guarding danced in my head. "It was pretty good duty."

"Where are you on our case?"

"At a standstill, but I have a few more ideas. I may need to talk to Fleet again."

"Can't you just talk to me? Mr. Fleet finds it hard to discuss his daughter."

"Not this time, Roy. I have to talk to the man and pick his brain. You can be there if you like."

"When?"

"I'll be in touch."

I hung up.

The phone rang again.

"Meet me out front," Big Bob ordered and hung up.

BIG BOB WAS WAITING in an unmarked car at the front entrance of my office building. I slid in the passenger-side door. He pulled away as I was closing the door. Big Bob was in a big hurry.

"What's up?" I asked.

"Just got a call from Jimmy Durham. Said some bass fisherman picked up something big on their fish finder this morning out on Cherokee Lake that looked like a vehicle. He sent some divers in and they found a white SUV.

"Oh hell no!" I gasped. "Did they get the make?"

"He didn't say. They are going to be pulling it out in a few minutes."

I watched the countryside zip by and prayed what they found was not a white Grand Cherokee, but I didn't like the odds. I tried not to watch the speedometer. My thoughts turned to Jimmy Durham. I had not seen Jimmy since I took the Fleet case. Jimmy was a friend from my high school days who went to a rival school. We still occasionally played pick-up basketball together as we did in high school. In those days we met twice a year in real basketball games when our teams played each other. Jimmy was a great athlete whose career was ended when he blew out a knee playing football in his senior year. These days he was county sheriff.

We arrived at the scene, a picnic area close to the edge of the lake with a few picnic tables and parking for four cars. Jimmy was watching two tow trucks set up their winches and put their cables in the water. I stood beside Jimmy and looked over the edge of the embankment into the dark water. Nothing was visible below the surface. The drop off was extreme and the water looked deep, a perfect place for someone to drive a car into the lake. Two divers were in the water with the other ends of the cables. They flipped and went under seconds after I looked their way.

"Hey, Blood," Jimmy drawled.

Jimmy had the rugged blond good looks and laid-back country boy manner that always attracted the ladies, and he had stayed in playing shape. We were among the few remaining bachelors of our era.

"Hey, Bull. How did you know to call us in on this?"

"Big Bob filled me in weeks ago. Told me to be on the lookout for a white SUV. Told me you were workin' a missin' persons case." He spat chewing tobacco over the edge, his most disgusting habit. Maybe the reason he was still single.

"Jesus, Jimmy. You still chewing that disgusting shit?"

He spit again. "Down to once a day. Gonna quit for the New Year and stay quit." Then he spit the whole wad into the water.

"Fish love it," he said as it sunk beneath the surface.

"Lord help us," I laughed.

We watched the divers surface and give a thumbs up that the cables were in place. The tow trucks were anchored and ready. The drivers in charge of each truck inched their lines tight then nodded to each other and at the same moment started the winches. The engines whined under the strain and the lines moved ever so slowly. Finally a white blur appeared beneath the surface and grew larger as the seconds crept by. The rear of the SUV finally surfaced and my heart sank—a white Jeep Grand Cherokee Limited. License tag number SAF 222—*three deuces down.*

"Goddamnit," I muttered.

The winches hit another gear as the weight of the Cherokee broke the surface. Slowly it crawled up the steep bank with water escaping the interior from the seams of the doors and the undercarriage. The windows were tinted and fogged up, making it impossible to see inside.

Jimmy, Big Bob and I walked toward the SUV as it crested the top of the embankment and came to a standstill. Big Bob took the lead and I gladly let him. He opened the driver's side door and looked in.

"Other side," he said.

Jimmy went around the back of the Cherokee to the passenger side and I followed. He opened the front door and a body fell out. I felt as if I had been punched in the stomach. The corpse was showing all the signs of weeks in the water but there was no doubt that it was a blond female. I had failed to find Sarah Ann Fleet. She had found me.

THE TOW TRUCKS WERE long gone. One truck was taking the Grand Cherokee to be impounded as evidence in an apparent murder. The other truck was off to answer another call. The emergency rescue ambulance was just leaving with the body bound for the county coroner's office. As it pulled out, I was by myself leaning against Big Bob's cruiser trying to figure out what I was feeling. I guess I was depressed. I had been looking for someone who had turned up dead. The search was over but there was no happy ending. Who would tell Joseph Fleet that his daughter was dead?

"Nothing more we can do here," Big Bob said walking toward me. "You know who did this, Blood?"

"Yeah, I know," I said softly. "I'll tell you the whole story on our way back to town if you promise to drive like a normal person."

"Get in the car," he said gently.

Big Bob drove like an ordinary citizen and I talked. I laid out the course of events as they had unfolded from the day that Roy Husky had walked into my office through his call to me this morning. I left nothing out.

"Want me to tell Fleet?" he asked.

"No," I said. "I want to talk to Roy first."

"Better do it soon. It will be all over the media in hours."

"You have time for a detour?"

Big Bob looked at me grimly and nodded.

I picked up my cell phone and dialed Roy's cell phone. I knew I had to make this call but I desperately did not want to.

"Roy here," he answered.

"Where are you?"

"At the mansion."

"Stay put. I'll meet you out front in ten minutes."

I broke the connection before Roy could respond.

ROY WAS WAITING as we pulled up. He wore a full-length camel's hair topcoat over his business suit. The temperature seemed to be dropping and the wind had picked up. The flurries had escalated to light snow. I hadn't heard the forecast, but we might be in for one.

I grabbed my ski jacket from the back seat. Big Bob stayed inside with the engine running.

"What's up?" Roy asked. He had a worried look on his face.

"Let's walk," I said as I headed toward Fleet's elaborate maze of a garden laying dormant, waiting for spring. Roy followed in silence and I knew that he knew.

"We found her."

Roy remained silent. He walked slowly beside me with his head bowed.

"Where?" he finally asked.

"We pulled the SUV out of Lake Cherokee. Sarah Ann was inside."

He took time to digest it.

"Dead before she hit the water?"

"I'm sure of it. I'll talk to the coroner later today to confirm. I'm sorry, Roy. Want me to tell Fleet?"

"No, I'll do it. It's going to damn near kill him."

He looked at me. Tears were forming and I couldn't tell if they were tears of sorrow or anger. Both I suspected. This was a hard man who had seen a lot in a hard life. He wouldn't be easily moved to tears. At that moment I was sure of what I had suspected for a long time. Roy Husky was in with love Sarah Ann Fleet.

"If it's the last thing I do in this life," he said softly through gritted teeth, "I will find that son-of-a-bitch and kill him."

"We'll find him," I said putting my hand on his shoulder. "We'll find him."

As Big Bob drove back to the office, I made another call, to the county coroner's office to talk with Wanda Jones. Wanda was my one true female friend. We had met at a cocktail party soon after I returned to Mountain Center. She was a tall slender brunette with a substantial chest and I was immediately attracted by the body and by a personality that was brutally direct. I tried to ask her out but Wanda was clear that she was not interested in a long-term relationship and that she basically thought all men were rats.

She said, "Give me your phone number and I'll call you sometime if I am interested."

I laughed and gave her my phone number. She called a week later. We went out to dinner. She made it clear that sex was out of the question. I saw Wanda about once a week in those days and we talked on the phone in between. Wanda was smart and interesting and we enjoyed each other's company. She told me her life story and I told her mine. Wanda had been married once to a professional baseball player. They were married at home plate in a minor-league ballpark before a game. The marriage lasted about a year. Wanda said she then turned her anger and energy toward medical school and received a medical degree from Eastern State University.

After a series of events proved that she wasn't much of a people person she accepted a job in the county coroner's office and five years later became the chief medical examiner when the incumbent ME died suddenly of a heart attack. Her first autopsy was on her old boss.

"I really loved cutting that SOB open," she had told me.

A few months into our friendship I asked Wanda if she was gay. She laughed and said she was nothing, but if she had a preference it just might be women. Late one night about six months into our friendship, she showed up at my condo and practically ordered me to make love to her. I obliged. It was spectacular.

When she left hours later, Wanda looked me directly in the eyes and said,

"I was never here."

I nodded. Dumbfound, I watched her leave. It was the one and only time that Wanda and I were ever physical. I had no idea what had happened and to this day I had not asked.

Despite her obsession with work and my many female companions, we had somehow maintained our friendship over the years. We usually talked once a week when I was in town.

"Long time no talk," Wanda said as she came on the line almost immediately. "Where have you been, stranger?"

"Out of town," I said.

"I hear you brought back a souvenir from Florida," she teased.

"I forget how small this town really is."

"You usually do not call me at work, Don. What's up?"

"There is a body heading your way. I need you to take a look and I'll be by later and we'll talk."

"Yeah, it just came in. I haven't looked at it yet. Know who it is?"

"Sarah Ann Fleet," I said.

"Oh, shit."

"Really."

BIG BOB DROPPED ME in front of my office building and I went up to the second floor in search of Billy. He was there with Jake laying nearby and paying no attention to either one of us.

"What happened?" he asked.

I told him in great detail everything that had happened since I left the office. He sat silently taking it all in, occasionally shaking his head and muttering under his breath. Finally I finished.

"Nothing we could have done," he said. "She was probably dead before we took the case."

"Probably."

"Roy pissed?"

"Extremely."

"Wouldn't want him pissed at me."

"Me either."

I LEFT BILLY AND JAKE at the office and went to see Wanda Jones. The county coroner's office was a fifteen-minute drive from downtown Mountain Center. Light snow was starting to accumulate on the ground. The roads were wet and snow-free, but the temperature was dropping and I knew the road conditions would only get worse. The macho side of me couldn't wait to put the Pathfinder in four-wheel drive. The practical side of me hoped the roads stayed clear. Icy roads in east Tennessee always led to numerous accidents.

I parked in visitor parking and went through the double glass doors to the receptionist's desk. A young slender redhead looked up and smiled. It was not flirtatious. At that moment I felt old.

"Mr. Youngblood?"

"That's me," I answered.

"Go on back. Miss Jones is expecting you, sir. She is in her office."

Sir? I went down the hall toward Wanda's office feeling even older and thinking that you cannot outrun time. Sooner or later your time runs out, as it had for all of the visitors who passed through the back door of this building for temporary residence in the county morgue. Sarah Ann Fleet was the latest visitor. Her time was up, cut short by a probable sociopath named Joey Avanti. Somewhere down the line someone would stop his clock. I hoped it was soon.

Wanda was at her computer working steadily at the keyboard. On the screen appeared what seemed to be an autopsy report. I tapped lightly on the doorframe. Wanda spun in her chair, caught my eye and smiled.

"Hi," she said as she rose and crossed the room to give me a quick peck on the lips. "You're looking fit."

"I should be. I almost killed myself in Florida helping a young lady rehab."

"You did a fine job, I hear," she smiled. "A female cop no less. Living with you, I hear."

"Is there anything you haven't heard?" I said faking annoyance. "Any blanks I need to fill in for you, Wanda?"

"Calm down, big guy, I was only busting your chops a little. On second thought you could tell me what happened to Sandy-what's-her-name."

I folded my arms and put on my best hard stare.

"Okay. I looked at the body. She didn't drown."

"I didn't think so," I said. "Twenty-two bullet in the left temple?"

"How did you know?"

"I'm a detective. Besides, our suspected killer used to be with the New York mob. It's their style and he would have been in the driver's side of the SUV she was killed in."

"Well, I'll be damned," Wanda said. "A murder victim. Don't get many of those in this sleepy little town."

MARY AND I WERE RELAXED on the Oriental rug in front of the fire with a bottle of red wine and a sausage pizza with extra cheese. Jake was lying nearby on crumb patrol. His chances did not look good. Outside the snow continued to fall and the weatherman promised two to four inches by daybreak. Every now and then you could hear the wind blowing. Inside by the fire, Mary was recounting her day and I was recounting mine. We talked a little, ate a little and drank a little as the night slipped away with the stresses of the day, at least my stress anyway.

"This is certainly not the crime center of the universe," Mary said. "If things do not pick up I will die of boredom. Everyone is nice enough but there just isn't much going on."

"Relax," I said. "It's your first day. And you are with me and you are safe."

"Good point," Mary said as she raised her wine glass and saluted me. "So what's next on the Fleet case?"

"As far as I'm concerned, I'm done. It's a police matter now."

"Speaking of police matters," she smiled as she rose to pull me toward the bedroom, "I'm taking you into custody."

We left Jake licking crumbs from the inside of an empty pizza box.

28

Cold temperatures combined with light powdery snow and a cutting wind made a brutal December Thursday. I know this because I was standing in the Center of Angels Cemetery on the outskirts of Mountain Center listening to the local Methodist minister deliver the graveside eulogy for Sarah Ann Fleet. There was a big turnout.

"We gather here to pay our last respects to a young woman whose life was tragically cut short . . ."

My mind wandered away from the words and my eyes to the face of Joseph Fleet. It was the first time I had seen him since he had hired me. Fleet did not look well. He stared at the ground with his head slightly bowed. His eyes had receded into their dark sockets, his skin was pale, and he seemed smaller than I remembered. I could imagine few things worse than the death of your own child, especially a murdered one. Roy Husky was standing next to Fleet, staring straight ahead, and did not look much better. At that moment I passionately hated Joey Avanti, and I could tell from Roy's expression that he felt the same emotion except more intently.

My resolve from last night that the case was no longer my problem was fading as I watched the burial. A tear escaped the corner of my left eye. I felt the same finality as when my parents were buried.

The service concluded and the attendees filed by Joseph Fleet to offer condolences. I waited until everyone had moved away from Fleet to approach him. He was staring at the coffin as I touched his arm. He turned and smiled a sad smile.

"I am truly sorry for your loss," I said. My voice nearly broke.

He nodded, "I appreciate that and everything you did."

"I didn't do much," I said.

Fleet gave me a serious look. "You did more than you know. You dug and dug and found out things that at least make some sense out of this hideous act. Ronnie used my daughter and me to hide, and when he was about to be discovered, he killed her and ran. If it were not for you, I would not know who he really is and why he killed my daughter. Roy kept me informed of your progress. I am really impressed how much you found out and how you went about it. I just wish you could find the bastard so I could kill him."

I didn't respond. Fleet had paused and was fighting back tears. Roy walked over and put a hand on his shoulder.

Fleet raised his head and looked at me through watery eyes.

"I want him dead," he hissed softly.

I looked at Roy. "That makes three of us," I said.

MY PARENTS' GRAVES were close by and I turned and walked toward them. I had not been to the cemetery since the day their bodies were buried there. My faith told me that their spirits were in another place and I saw no reason to visit their graves. I rationalized that today's visit was paying respect to their memories, and I lingered for some time, lost in thoughts of the past. I remembered growing up at the lake house and all the fun I had as a child. I remembered pets that had come and gone. I remembered all the good times I had with my father, the football games he took me to, the fishing on the weekends, the pride I saw in his eyes as I grew up. Memories flooded back like a video tape in fast forward. I remembered my father at my high school basketball games and how after every game he always had positive comments, whether I had played well or not. My father never criticized a thing I did on the court and—rare among fathers—he never missed a game home or away. I remembered my mother and her loving care of *her* men. Hers was a beautiful gentle spirit that was comfortable in the background supporting her husband but was the sole ruler of our lake home. I shed some long overdue tears. Then I sobbed. I felt empty. Sometime later, I realized I was alone in the cemetery and that darkness was closing in. I reluctantly turned and walked away from the graves of the two people I had loved most in this world.

I sat behind the wheel of the Pathfinder for a few more minutes to regain my composure. I finally buckled my seat belt, started the engine and drove out through the cemetery gates feeling a deep sense of loss.

29

The weekend after Sarah Ann's funeral, at Mary's insistence, we purchased and decorated a Christmas tree. Being an orphan for most of the last two decades, I had basically ignored Christmas. When I did think of the subject, I was generally sad. Mary, on the other hand, was getting excited and it was contagious. The two inches of snow on the ground added to the holiday enthusiasm. I knew exactly where to find the forgotten ornaments of my childhood, and memories flooded over me as I found a special place on the tree for my favorite ones. We drank eggnog and sang Christmas carols. I shook my head in disbelief. I felt like a kid.

Mary had asked if her kids, Susan and Jimmy, could join us for the holidays. Even though I thought it was a rhetorical question, I dutifully affirmed. I was glad she wanted them to meet me. I could not believe how important she was becoming in my life. I was a bit frightened by the idea. Mary was settling into the less-than-exciting life of a small-town cop. Drunk and disorderly, domestic violence, and traffic citations made up most of her day. But she said it was a nice change and that she enjoyed being with me.

As Christmas drew closer, I had put private detecting on the back burner and was paying closer attention to the stock market. There were bargains to be had and I was intent on having them. Roy had called a few days after the funeral saying that he and Fleet were going away for the holidays to Fleet's house on Amelia Island. He said Fleet wanted me to go back to work on the case after the first of the year. I asked what case and Roy said finding Ronnie Fairchild or whatever the hell his name is. I said I would think about.

THE MONDAY BEFORE CHRISTMAS, I was in the office when the phone rang. A female voice said, "Hold, please, for Carlo Vincente."

I held.

"What's happening with the case you are working on?" Carlo asked in his low growl.

"It's over. We found the girl's body a couple of weeks ago. I've been meaning to call you."

There was silence on the other end. Carlo was probably unhappy that I had not called.

"I am very sorry to hear that," Vincente said. He sounded sincere. "Such a pity."

"Yes, it is."

I waited through more silence.

"Are you going to continue to look for our friend?"

I was curious that he did not use Joey's name. Maybe he thought his phones were bugged. "I haven't decided," I said.

"The father wants you to, I assume," Vincente said.

"Yes."

"Then you will."

"What makes you think so?"

"I am a good judge of character," he said. "It's the reason I am still alive. You will keep looking and I am betting in the end you will find our friend. I would like to know when that happens."

"If that does happen, why should I tell you?" I cringed at my own brashness—easy to crack wise with the devil when he is eight hundred miles away.

"Two reasons," Vincente said calmly. "First, I am willing to extract the kind of justice that you are not, and second, I will owe you a big favor. Somewhere down the line you may need one. And meanwhile, if you need anything from my end, you've got it. Have a good holiday."

He hung up before I could get off a smart remark. Just as well. I didn't have one.

30

arly Christmas Eve Mary's kids arrived. Susan was a gorgeous younger version of Mary, maybe an inch shorter. Jimmy was a good-looking kid too. He must have taken after his father because he looked nothing like Mary. Jimmy had dark hair and dark eyes and I could not get over how big he was. He was taller than Big Bob and almost as tall as Billy, and they were the two tallest people I knew personally. I guessed he was six feet five and weighed around 230. Most experts picked Jimmy Sanders to go in the first round of the upcoming NFL draft. We were in the living room having cocktails before dinner. Everyone was drinking except Jimmy, who still had one game left on his football schedule, a bowl game, a rarity for Wake Forest.

Wake Forest had gone 8-3 during the regular season and had landed a New Year's Day bowl game in Jacksonville. Luckily for them they were not playing Tennessee. The Vols were undefeated and would be playing also-undefeated Oklahoma in the Fiesta Bowl for the national championship. I was hoping lightning could strike twice in the same place.

"You had a good year," I said to Jimmy. Mary and Susan were wrapped up in another conversation a few feet away.

"We did. We lost a couple of close ones and even gave Florida State a good game."

"Are you excited about playing pro ball?"

"I'm excited about the money," he replied. It was not the answer I expected. "Don't get me wrong, I love the game but it has gotten so physical that everyone takes a beating. That does take some of the fun out of it and it will only get worse in the pros. I'm planning to play five years and then pursue my career as an architect. I have a degree and I intend to use it."

I admired his attitude. He seemed mature for his age, twenty-three in April. "Sounds like a plan," I confirmed.

The fire was putting out comfortable warmth and a pleasant glow as we chatted and I got to know Mary's kids a little. They were nice young adults, which did not surprise me, though I was a little surprised at the maturity level and intelligence of both. They carried the conservation like seasoned adults.

We had a light dinner around the kitchen bar and afterward I stepped out on the deck off the living room to get some fresh air and watch the light snow falling. A few minutes later Jimmy came out. He looked into the night and took a deep breath and exhaled.

"I love snow," he said. "Winter is my favorite season."

"Me, too. Do you ski?"

"Not since high school but I loved it. Coach would kill me if I skied now and I can't risk injury with an NFL career on the line. Some day, though, I'll get back to it."

The night was still as the snow fell and we took it in wordlessly for a while. The flakes, made even more magical by the floodlights, were getting larger and descending slower like miniature helicopters coming in for a soft landing. The scene was mesmerizing.

"Mom likes you a lot," Jimmy said breaking the silence.

"I like her a lot," I said.

"I'm glad she found somebody. She hasn't had a lot of happiness in the last few years. She loves the job and it's all that has been keeping her going. It's good she has someone in her life."

"We are just taking it one day at a time," I said, not really knowing what to say. I felt like I was talking to Mary's father instead of her son.

Jimmy laughed. "Don't get me wrong. I approve. We approve. Susan and I talked. We like you. You and mom seem to be a good match. We just wanted you to know."

"What a relief," I feigned. "Seriously though, I appreciate hearing it."

Jimmy turned and leaned on the deck railing looking into the night. "I really do love snow," he said.

NEAR NOON ON CHRISTMAS I picked up T. Elbert to bring him to 5300 for our midday feast of turkey and as many go-withs as you could think of. He complained that it was too much trouble and that I shouldn't have, but I knew he was pleased. Besides, he was anxious to meet Mary. T. Elbert, obviously, had been briefed by Billy and Big Bob. Billy had joined Big Bob for Christmas.

"I hear this Mary is quite a looker," he said with a grin and a twinkle in his eye.

"Uh-huh."

"Tall, I hear."

"Uh-huh."

"Blond."

"That too," I said. "Just where do you get all this information?" I asked knowing full well where it came from.

"Confidential," he teased. "Now step on it. I'm hungry."

"Hungry, hell. You are just a nosy old coot."

"You are right about that," T. Elbert laughed. "You know I don't get out much."

I pulled into the parking lot and helped T. Elbert into his motorized chair. We took the elevator to the third floor. I had briefed everyone on what to expect from T. Elbert and filled them in on a little history. Mary greeted us as we came through the door. She looked gorgeous in faded jeans and a bright red long-sleeved Christmas T-shirt that showed off all her best assets.

"Hi, T. Elbert. I'm Mary."

As they shook hands T. Elbert looked over his shoulder at me and said, "Wow."

Mary bent over and kissed T. Elbert on the cheek.

"Thanks," she said. "And Merry Christmas."

"Wow again," T. Elbert said.

Everyone laughed. We were off to a great start.

31

New Year's eve, Mary and I were on the couch in front of a warm fire drinking Merlot and reliving all the fun we had during the holidays. Christmas dinner had been a riot with T. Elbert telling funny stories about his days in the TBI. We laughed so hard we could hardly eat. Jimmy and Susan were totally captured by the crusty old veteran, and T. Elbert was smitten by Mary.

"She's a keeper," he told me on the way back to his house. "I'd latch onto her like a bulldog on a bone."

I laughed out loud. "I'll keep that in mind," I told him.

As we relaxed and let the wine do its magic, I suddenly had a sensation that something was not right. Then a red dot appeared on the floor and moved up Mary's leg toward her chest. My brain sounded the warning and I pushed Mary off the couch and shouted, "Get down!" A millisecond later the glass shattered in the sliding glass door leading to the deck. A bullet thumped the couch where Mary had been sitting. I rolled toward the bedroom where my Beretta lay dormant in the night stand as another bullet shattered the glass coffee table. Mary sprang up and ran out of the line of fire to the foyer where her Glock .44 hung on a coat rack near the front door. She had grabbed the portable phone and was calling for backup. As I ducked into the dark bedroom, a third bullet ricocheted off the stone mantel above the fireplace. I picked the fully loaded Beretta from the nightstand and rolled across the king size bed to the sliding glass door of the master bedroom that also led to the deck. I pulled the curtain back slightly and slid the door open about a foot and peeked out looking up into the night for any signs of the malevolent red dot. I knew the shots had come from the hill overlooking the condo complex and I was scanning the area for any movement. Nothing. All was eerily quiet. I heard a motorcycle engine rev and roar off. The sound of the engine faded into the night. Then I heard sirens and I knew that, for now, it was over.

HALF OF MOUNTAIN CENTER's police cruisers were in our condo parking lot within a few minutes. The red and blue flashing lights reflected off the snow in an ironic glow of holiday color, but there was nothing festive about the occasion. Someone was trying to kill Mary and maybe me. It didn't take a brain surgeon to figure out that it was Teddy Earl Elroy or someone doing his bidding. Billy and Big Bob were inside the condo with an investigation team collecting evidence that amounted to three slugs from a high-powered rifle.

"Two of the slugs are of no use," Big Bob said. "But the one in the couch is in mint condition. If we find the rifle, there will be no problem matching it."

I watched Billy survey the damage as I talked with Big Bob. I could tell he was seething. He stared out through the shattered sliding glass door into the night, slowly shaking his head. He turned and walked toward us, stopping to look down at the glass from the coffee table.

Billy looked up at me. "The son of a bitch," he said. "This is going to stop." He walked past us through the front door and disappeared into the snowy night.

"That is one pissed-off Cherokee Indian," Big Bob said. "Teddy Earl Elroy better watch his ass."

I followed Billy out. "Billy," I said sternly. I never called him Billy unless it was something serious and he had come to know that as a signal. He stopped. "I don't know what you are planning, but I want Teddy Earl alive. Understand?"

Billy looked at me with no expression.

"Understand, Billy?"

"Sure, Blood. But I guarantee you I will find him."

He turned and walked down the stairs and I went back inside.

Later, Big Bob and I climbed the hill behind the condo to look for the shooter's hiding place. We were joined by Big Bob's little brother, Sean, who at six feet three inches tall wasn't so little. The climb was somewhat steep and required more effort than normal due to the wet heavy snow that was falling. Once we reached the top, it did not take long to find where the shooter had been.

"Good position," Big Bob commented offhandedly.

"I'll be sure to compliment Teddy Earl on that the next time I see him," I snarled.

"Bike tracks," Sean pointed out.

"Dangerous to ride a bike in weather like this," I said.

"Roads are wet but not that slick," Big Bob said.

Other than confirming the spot of the shooting and the fact the shooter was on a motorcycle, we did not find any other evidence. Slipping and sliding, we descended the hill back to the condo. Out front in the parking lot, the investigation team was packing up to leave. Sean climbed in his squad car and pulled out into the night. The investigation team was right behind him.

"We have to do something to protect Mary," I said.

"I've been thinking about that," Big Bob responded. "I'll team her up with Sean and put them in our SWAT cruiser. It has bulletproof glass and reinforced steel. Looks exactly like all the other cruisers. Very few people know about the extras, so keep it to yourself."

"Better not tell Mary or she'll complain about receiving special treatment."

"Let her complain. I'm the damn chief of police and what I say goes."

"Thanks," I said.

"Don't mention it. And watch your ass. Teddy Earl has a score to settle with you, too, after the hospital incident. He would love to kill you both."

"Don't worry about it. The hunter is about to become the hunted."

Big Bob grunted and walked to his SUV. The driver's side door read Mountain City Chief of Police. The four-wheel Toyota 4-Runner was the only SUV in the Mountain Center fleet. Rank has its privileges. He turned back and called to me as I was walking to the elevator.

"Blood," he hollered.

"Yeah," I shouted back across the distance between us.

"Happy New Year!"

32

The day after New Year's, I was alone with my thoughts and back in the office, trying in earnest to gear up for detective work and get back in touch with the market. I had done neither for more than two weeks. I had not given up on finding Joey Avanti, but my most pressing need was to find Teddy Earl Elroy. He was trying to kill Mary, and possibly me. Teddy Earl was mean but not that smart and I was convinced that he would not be that hard to find. Avanti, on the other hand, was mean and smart and he would be hard to find. I sat quietly at my desk. I concluded that Teddy Earl was probably still in east Tennessee and probably hanging out with other redneck hardcases. The people who knew where he was would roll on him for a few hundred dollars. I needed to find one of those low-lifes. The question was how. Then I had an idea. I needed to talk to Billy but I had not seen or heard from him since the shooting incident on New Year's Eve. I called his home. No answer. I called his cell phone, also no answer. I knew he was up to something. I just prayed he did not do anything dumb.

The door to the outer office opened and closed. Jake raised his head, sniffed, and returned to his nap. Someone familiar. Not Billy. Jake would have gone to greet Billy to receive the petting that Billy always gave him in the mornings. Seconds later, Roy walked in and sat down with a nod of his head.

"Morning," he said.

"Happy New Year."

"You, too."

"How was the trip?" I asked.

"As good as could be expected."

"How is Fleet?"

"Better," Roy said. "He's a fighter and he is fighting back, but it's hard for him. He misses Sarah Ann and he is very angry."

"How about you?"

He paused, as if to access how he was really feeling. It gave me the feeling that Roy wanted to be as truthful as possible. He stared off to some far and distant place and finally looked back to me.

"I want us to find this guy," he said in a chilling semi-whisper.

"We will, but right now I have a more pressing matter," I said.

He stared at me and waited, and I gave him the full story on Mary and Teddy Earl Elroy. I surprised myself by sharing it all, but in the short time I had known Roy I had developed a belief that I could trust him. He was a hard man and had known some hard times, but beneath that rough exterior I sensed a man of honor and fair play. Until he proved me wrong, he had my complete trust and loyalty, and only a few other men in the world had that.

He remained silent for some time after I had finished. He got up and started out of the office, then turned around in my doorway.

"We'll deal with your problem first," he said. "I'll get back to you."

That Friday night, Mary and I went to Moto's gym. We were ten minutes into our workout and beginning to work up a sweat. I had gotten Mary into a three-times-a-week gym routine in exchange for playing racquetball with her twice a week. She was one hell of a racquetball player but I was gaining on her. The other two days we ran together. I was in the best shape of my life because I had partnered with someone as fanatic as I was about trying to beat the aging process. Mary was on the exercise bike and I was on the stair stepper. There were eight other people working out which was a pretty good crowd for a Friday night. Mary attracted a lot of attention from the guys and I had to smile at the admiring covert peeks. She acted unaware but every now and then I caught a faint smile of appreciation.

We heard Moto's portable phone ring and then he came walking toward me with it. "Dumb Indian," he mumbled with a smile as he handed me the phone.

"Nice of you to call, Billy," I said into the phone. I only called him Billy when I was pissed at him or wanted to get his attention.

"I tried sending a smoke signal but you didn't answer," Billy replied. "I'm back in town. I know where Teddy Earl Elroy is. In fact, I saw him. I've mapped out the site. We are going to need some help."

"My place in an hour," I said and disconnected.

As I continued to climb on the stair stepper, I turned to Mary. I didn't want to say too much until I knew more details, so I just casually told her, "Billy may have found Teddy Earl."

33

As it turned out, when Billy left us on New Year's Eve he went straight home to get his old Harley in running condition. After two days of work, he drove into Cherokee to get a line on Devil's Code, an old biker gang he used to run with. He was acting on a hunch based on the motorcycle tire tracks in the snow, but Billy's hunches were often eerily accurate. Two days later he hooked up with two of the current members of Devil's Code, and after hanging out with them for two more days, they took him to what they called Camp Code. At the camp he met two bikers he had run with in the old days, a good thing because Billy was not eagerly received by the majority of the estimated twenty bikers in the camp. The morning of the second day Teddy Earl Elroy had appeared. He was called "Zeke" and was pretty much a loner, but Billy said there was no mistake that it was Teddy Earl.

Billy said the days at Camp Code were pretty much the same. Most of the bikers drank, played cards, got in fights and abused their women, but "Zeke" kept to himself. After spending three days at the camp and covertly taking pictures with a tiny camera and getting the lay of the land, Billy quietly walked his bike out before sunrise on the fourth day.

Camp Code was hidden in the mountainous deep woods of Unicoi County near the North Carolina border. I knew the area. As Billy described how to get to the biker camp and told how he'd accomplished his brilliant detective work, I was having fond flashbacks of when I was small and my father used to take me into those woods to cut a Christmas tree. Not that we couldn't afford a store-bought Christmas tree. It was the thrill of the hunt and the male bonding between father and son that made the trip a necessity.

And now, Billy and I were standing at my dining room table looking at a drawing of the camp Billy had created from memory. Mary wasn't there; it had frustrated her to no end to have to, but she'd gone to work a partial second shift because someone on the force had the flu.

I studied Billy's drawing and his sneak photos. The camp was in a valley clearing, surrounded by trees with a dirt, single-track trail leading into it. The camp was inaccessible to four-wheel vehicles of any kind. In the center was an old but functioning well. Ten cabins were scattered back from the well about fifty feet in all directions. Set back and above all of this was a main building with a large front deck. Billy said this building had a kitchen and a large great room with an oversize fireplace and large round tables with chairs and a wide-screen TV. There was no electricity in the cabins but there was a generator for the main building. On the roof was a satellite dish. There was no plumbing anywhere but cold-water showers were supplied by rain barrels and supplemented with well water.

AFTER BILLY LEFT, I stayed up past midnight waiting for Mary to get home and watching the Tennessee Volunteers win the national championship and thinking about Teddy Earl Elroy. Thanks to the latter, sleep had come at the expense of tossing and turning for two hours until an exasperated Mary took it upon herself to *relax* me. I should toss and turn more often.

Early the next morning, I was having a leisurely breakfast at my usual table in the back of the Mountain Center Diner, while continuing to mull over how to extract Elroy from Camp Code. I had avoided telling Mary very much because as a cop she might have to spoil any particularly, shall we say, creative plans. The trick was to get Elroy out without anyone being hurt or killed. Except maybe him.

Doris had just delivered my feta cheese omelet with home fries and rye toast. Thanks to me, the Mountain Center Diner might be the only one in east Tennessee to serve feta cheese omelets. I had mentioned to Doris one day how much I missed them since returning home and instantly feta cheese omelets were on the menu and very popular, according to Doris.

By the time I was halfway through my second cup of coffee, I thought I had a plan. I picked up my cell phone to dial Raul Rivera in Miami. Raul was another of the many unique people I had met at UConn. Raul was captain of UConn's tennis team in his senior year and had risen into the top ten rankings in the NCAA as a singles player. He was gifted and competitive and had absolutely no desire to turn pro. With his handsome good looks, easygoing manner and slight Spanish accent, Raul was an instant lady-killer the day he arrived on campus. The girls could not get enough of Raul, which possibly explained why he was still unattached two decades later.

Raul was from a powerful Columbian family that was into a variety of businesses in the south Florida area, one of which was an import-export company. Whether they were all legitimate was another story.

Raul and I had stayed in touch through the years, and while Mary and I were lying low in south Florida I asked him to join us for dinner at Max & Eddie's Restaurant on Singer Island. He and Mary hit it off instantly and the evening flowed from drinks to food to dessert with the fellowship of shared stories and mingled histories. As the evening drew to an end, I realized how much I had missed seeing Raul on a daily basis and Mary realized that she had made a new friend.

Now, I saw a chance for Raul to help his old and new friends, and I knew he could be counted on.

Every time I called, Raul always had a good story to share. When he was finished with one of his tall tales I would always say, "is that the truth" and Raul would always say with a laugh, "almost all of it."

I rang Raul's cell phone.

"Hello."

"How goes life in paradise?" Always my opening line when I phoned Raul.

"Life in paradise is good, my friend." Always Raul's response. "Donnie, my friend, how are the lovely mountains of Tennessee? And how is the lovely Mary?"

"Both as beautiful as ever, Raul."

Raul never called me Don or Donald or Blood, always Donnie. He said it because I was like a brother to him and it was an expression of affection.

Coming from Raul, it sounded perfectly logical.

"I haven't heard from you in a while, Donnie. Are you up to something?"

"I am, Raul. I am up to a couple of things and I need your help."

"Remember, Donnie, I am a lover not a fighter."

"That's not the way I remember it that night in Riley's Pub when we were in school, Raul," I said. Some loudmouth had insulted a girl Raul was dating and Raul had taught him a lesson in manners. It did not matter that he was giving away a couple of inches and twenty-five pounds. Raul was quick and efficient with his hands, and the one-sided fight ended with an apology from the offender and drinks all around from Raul. It was Raul's nature never to stay angry and never to hold a grudge. His philosophy was that life was too short to waste energy on such things.

"Sometimes one must go against one's nature in order to uphold one's honor," Raul said philosophically.

"Well, remind me never to insult your honor, Raul," I laughed. "Anyway, you don't have to do any fighting. I have a unique shopping list I need filled and you are the man for the job."

"Shopping lists are right up my alley, Donnie. If I cannot get it, I will import it."

I read my list. When I finished, Raul gave a low whistle.

"Exactly what are you up to, Donnie?"

"Probably better that you do not know, Raul. Mary has a problem that I am going to take care of. When it is all over, I'll come down to the condo for a few days and we will get together at Max & Eddie's for dinner and I will tell you all about it. I'll need some expert help with the dosage for the darts."

"Not a problem, my friend. We are a full-service supplier."

"I hate to ask but the need is urgent."

"I'll ship it next day air tomorrow to your office."

"Thanks, Raul. I owe you one," I said.

"You owe me nothing, my friend. And Donnie," Raul said in an urgent tone before he disconnected, "be careful."

THE BREAKFAST CROWD was thinning as Doris removed my half-finished cup of coffee and replaced it with a new one. It did not matter if I was finished drinking coffee or not. As soon as my current cup got cold there was a fresh one on the table. No one else received this special treatment. Once or twice I had mentioned it was not necessary. "You let me decide what is necessary in my place," I was good-naturedly told. I did not protest again.

"Thanks for that generous Christmas gift, Mr. Youngblood," Doris said.

"My pleasure, Doris. You take as good of care of me as my own mother."

"Why, Mr. Youngblood," a flustered Doris responded. "What a nice thing to say. Your mother, God rest her soul, was a wonderful woman. Oh my," she muttered as she turned and went into the kitchen. Doris was blushing.

I smiled to myself. The thoughtful private detective, that's me, a happy accident that made my day as much as it did hers. My cell phone rang and snapped me back to reality.

"Hello."

"I think I may have a line on your problem," Roy said.

"Let me guess," I responded. "A place called Camp Code where a lot of renegade redneck white supremacist biker types hang out."

"Shit. You really are a detective. How did you know?"

"Billy recently vacationed with them. We are going to hit them in a few days and invite Teddy Earl to leave with us for the more comfortable confines of the Mountain Center Jail. Want to come?"

"Oh hell, yes! What's the plan?"

"Meet me in the office around six tomorrow night and bring a gym bag. I'll have some things for you to carry home."

"Mysterious fellow, you are," Roy said. "I'll be there."

Then I called T. Elbert to tell him I'd be dropping by tomorrow.

34

The next morning was cold with low clouds that made for a dark start as I picked up coffee and bagels at Dunkin' Donuts and drove to T. Elbert's. He was waiting in his rocking chair on the porch.

"Aren't you cold?" I said as I came up the walk.

"Heck no. These overhead heaters I put in make it just right. Fresh mountain air, now that's the ticket."

The excitement in his voice said *I am glad to be alive.* I handed him a black coffee and sat down and took the lid off mine.

T. Elbert took a drink. "Thanks, Donald. I just love this coffee."

"So you've told me about a thousand times," I teased.

T. Elbert sneered at my cup. "Cream and sugar," he snorted. "Sissy coffee. When are you going to grow up?"

We'd had this conversation before. "I told you that's what happens when you start drinking coffee at age six. It was too bitter without sugar and my mother made me add cream. So there you go."

"What's this I read in the paper that someone threw a rock through your picture window or something like that?"

"Cover story," I said. "Someone, probably Teddy Earl Elroy, was trying to use Mary and me for target practice."

T. Elbert raised up straight in his chair. "What?"

I told him all about the New Year's Eve excitement.

"So what are you going to do?"

"Billy found Teddy Earl holed up in a biker camp in Unicoi County. We're going in to get him late tomorrow night."

"Just how are you going to accomplish that?"

I told him my plan.

"Might work," he said. "Damn, I'd give anything to be in on that."

We didn't say anything else. We sat and watched the traffic go by and drank our coffee and ate bagels. But T. Elbert's words had struck a chord. Wheelchair-bound, T. Elbert was out of the action that he had enjoyed for so long a time. I knew he missed it like an athlete with a career-ending injury. Playing one day, history the next. *Damn, I'd give anything to be in on that.* I played those words over in my head and then a thought popped to the surface. T. Elbert had a black Hummer2. The black beauty, he called it. All hand controls and a special lift to help him get inside—state of the art technology.

"Want to drive?" I asked nonchalantly, an invitation that would later look like a stroke of genius.

"What?"

"Tomorrow night. Want to drive? Be our driver?"

"You serious?" he whispered. "Hell yes, I want to drive, but not because you feel sorry for me," he said indignantly.

I ignored that remark and continued.

"Ever had the Hummer off road?"

"Of course. I've had that damn thing places you wouldn't believe," he grinned.

"Still got a carry permit?"

"I do."

"Welcome to the team."

T. Elbert didn't say anything else, but when I left there was a big smile on his face.

"See you here around six-thirty tonight for a planning session," I hollered as I got into the Pathfinder.

"I'll be here," he said, still smiling.

THE PACKAGE ARRIVED later that morning at the office. I went through it item by item to be sure everything was there. No surprise, everything was. Typical of Raul, there was also a note with some instructions and helpful hints.

Billy arrived a little after nine o'clock and sat down in front of my desk. He looked in the box and then looked at me. He didn't say a word, just nodded and smiled slightly as if to say it might work. The phone rang at Billy's desk and he went to answer it and I booted up my computer and went online. The market was in a mild January rally and I was checking the status of various stocks I had been following when Billy stuck his head through my office door.

"Fire out at the lake last night. Might have been arson. Durham wants me to take some pictures. What's our schedule?"

"Meet here at six," I said.

Billy nodded and disappeared.

I spent part of the day familiarizing myself with the contents of Raul's box and the rest of the day going over the portfolios of my clients. My client list was exclusive and growing. My charge for my services was a bargain because I didn't need the money. Consequently, I only handled portfolios of people I liked or owed a favor or who might one day do me a favor. The list included, among others, my best friends, the owner of the local diner, several well-known sports figures who had attended college at either Tennessee or Connecticut, an FBI agent, a U.S. senator, several entrepreneurs of dubious character, a fitness center owner, a couple of ex-girlfriends, and myself. It was too many portfolios to watch for someone not motivated by money. However, I had not lost my touch and the list was thriving and no one was complaining. To me it was a game, and I love to win no matter what the game is.

By late afternoon I was waiting for Billy and Roy. I had called Big Bob earlier and told him to bring Mary to T. Elbert's at six-thirty. Mary was due to get off at six and I did not want to face her by myself when she found out what was going on. I knew we were about to have our first fight and I wanted her boss there as a buffer. My plans for Teddy Earl did not include Mary and she was not going to like it.

Roy and Billy arrived minutes apart and we piled in the Pathfinder and drove to T. Elbert's. My box of goodies was in the cargo area. Everyone was quiet on this cold, gray January day, and darkness had claimed the light as we pulled into T. Elbert's driveway. Big Bob's unmarked cruiser was parked on the street in front of T. Elbert's house. I retrieved the box and followed Roy and Billy up the stairs to the porch and through the front door. We did not knock. We knew we were expected.

The front door led to the living room and from there straight to the dining room. To the right of the living room was a den that T. Elbert had converted to his computer room. The kitchen was beyond the dining room, a common design for a house built in the early twentieth century. Mary, Big Bob, and T. Elbert were gathered around the dining room table drinking coffee. Mary gave me a *What are you up to?* look. I nodded at Billy and he pulled out his drawing of Camp Code and spread it on the dining room table.

Mary looked at me and snarled sarcastically, "So now I am going to find out the rest of the story?"

"Yes, Paul Harvey, you are." I smiled my most ingratiating smile.

Billy pointed to the map. "This is a drawing of a camp site in the mountains of Unicoi County. There is a main road here on the other side of this mountain ridge. There is a secondary road here that is not used that loops back to the main road. Off the secondary road here is an old one-lane trail that used to be a logging road."

Billy looked at T. Elbert. "You get us as far as you can in the Hummer and we will have to hike the rest. Two-hour hike."

Billy looked at me. "Your turn."

I opened my box and started passing out presents. To Roy and Billy I gave the most expensive night ops wardrobe money can buy: a wool toboggan, a heavy wool sweater with leather shoulder and elbow pads, gloves with leather palms and wool backing, wool pants with leather knee pads that tapered and velcroed tight at the ankle, a belt, long john tops and bottoms, socks, and hiking boots. Everything was black including the belt buckle, nothing to reflect light. My identical outfit remained in the box.

"Nice stuff," Roy said as he inspected it carefully. "How did you know my size?"

I arched an eyebrow in his direction.

"Right," he said. "You're a detective."

I reached into my magic box once again and pulled out small black backpacks and toys for each of us. "First," I said. "Night-vision goggles. They turn on here and fit over the face like this." I demonstrated. "Go ahead and adjust the strap now and try them on. Big Bob, if you would flip those lights off."

"Damn," said Roy as he looked into the darkness with his goggles on. "Not bad."

"Lights on, please," I said. "Billy, you might not need those but just in case." Billy had terrific night vision but the goggles let you see into shadows that no human eye could.

Billy nodded.

"Next, night vision binoculars. Turn them on here and adjust to you own eyes here." Again I demonstrated. I raised the blinds on T. Elbert's dining room window and flipped off the lights. "Look out the window and down the street."

"Incredible," Roy said.

"Unbelievable," I said as I looked through my night vision binoculars. Raul had spared no expense in getting us state-of-the-art equipment. I knew because I had seen the bill. At the bottom of the invoice Raul had written *no charge*. Raul was another client for whom I had made lots of money, and I mean *lots* of money. Raul was by far my richest client.

Next out of the box were walkie-talkies. Except these were hi-tech headphones with flexible mouthpieces. Raul's note said they were the latest and greatest. Not yet on the market. They were lightweight and comfortable with great range and forty channels. The left ear remained uncovered for outside noise while the right ear was covered to listen. The controls were just above the right ear. I had set them all to channel 39.

"These turn on here and the volume is here," I pointed. "Our channel is 39."

Then I pulled out the tranquilizer pistols. The pistols were matte black and resembled an old CO2 pellet pistol that Crossman used to make when I was a boy. Surprisingly lightweight, the pistol delivered a 15mm dart cartridge effectively up to a maximum of fifty yards. The cartridges had been drug-loaded for Raul by an expert to render a two hundred pound man unconscious in five seconds. Each pistol was accompanied by a case of six darts. I demonstrated how to load and unlock the safety.

"Eighteen darts," Roy said. "Are we going to put the whole camp to sleep?"

"Never hurts to be prepared." I said. "The plan by now must be pretty obvious. T. Elbert drives us as far in as he can and we hike the rest of it. We go in real quiet around two AM, locate Teddy Earl, tranquilize him and bring him out. If anyone else presents a problem or if there is anyone up and about, we will also tranquilize them. Rule number one: Do not leave any darts behind unless it is absolutely necessary."

"Are we going to carry him out?" Roy asked.

"No problem," said Billy.

Roy smiled. "Okay then."

I handed out handcuffs, rope, duct tape, knives with cases, and a black double shoulder holster that would hold the tranquilizer gun and another handgun of our personal choice. All black, of course.

"I think you can figure these out," I said. "Any more questions?"

"Yes, I have one," Mary said.

I braced myself.

"I would like to know why I have been left out of this little party." Mary's tone was razor sharp.

I looked at Big Bob. He had remained silent through the whole planning session and demonstrations. I prayed that he followed my reasoning. I shouldn't have worried.

"Because you are a police officer," Big Bob said.

"What?" Mary said as if that could not possibly be a reason.

"A police officer, Mary," Big Bob said sternly and precisely. "You work for the town of Mountain Center. That's your and my jurisdiction. Unicoi County is *not* our jurisdiction. If we were to know that a wanted murderer was hiding in Unicoi County, as police officers we would be obligated to pass this information to the Unicoi County Sheriff's Department. Therefore, we were not here. Do you understand me?"

Mary digested that bit of logic as we all stared at her waiting for a response. I could tell she knew she had been trapped. She knew she could not go now even if she wanted to.

She looked at me coldly. "Think you're smart, don't you?"

I knew my next response was crucial. I had visions of sleeping by myself for a month. I had a vision of Mary returning to Knoxville. I didn't like either vision.

"I love you," I heard myself say in front of God and everybody. "And for that reason I do not want you anywhere near Teddy Earl Elroy."

I must have shocked the room. I know I shocked myself. More surprising, I realized I was telling the truth. I couldn't hear a sound in T. Elbert's dining room, not even breathing. I was standing next to the window. Mary got up and walked slowly to me and took my arms and wrapped them around her and laid her head on my shoulder. She had tears in her eyes.

"I love you too," she said. "You be damn careful out there."

She sniffed and turned toward Roy and Billy. "Anything happens to him and you two better not come back."

"Not a problem," Roy said looking at Billy.

"Not a problem," Billy said looking back at Mary.

After a few uncomfortable seconds of silence, T. Elbert said, "What's wrong with going tonight? Why wait?"

We looked at each other as if to say why not.

"Good cloud cover tonight," Billy said.

"Let's do it," I said, feeling the excitement of a bold quick decision.

"We'd better change quickly," T. Elbert said. "Time's a wastin'. You guys can change upstairs."

There was a hall off the dining room and to the left was a staircase that led to an upstairs hall with railings on each side of the staircase that created separate hallways to the two upstairs bedrooms. The bedrooms were connected by a shared bathroom. At the top of the stairs Billy and I went left and Roy went right.

"I'm surprise you didn't hand out black shoe polish for our faces," Roy teased from the other bedroom.

"I left it in the box," I said.

"You're kidding."

"No, I'm not. Only it's called face black and it washes off with water like it was never there. At least that's what I am told."

"You seem to know a lot about this stuff for a Wall Street guy," Roy said.

I glanced at Billy. "Long story," I said.

"Like to hear it sometime," Roy said as we continued to change.

My only reply to that was silence. Some things were best kept secret. Ten minutes later we were reassembled in the dining room. I smiled to myself when I saw T. Elbert. He was dressed all in black.

"Mary and I will wait at the station," Big Bob said. "Keep us updated on the cell phone."

"Okay," I said. "Let's roll."

35

I estimated that we had about an hour's drive. I was in the front seat of the Hummer2 and Billy and Roy were in the back. Fifteen minutes after we left I was dozing. I did that when I was anxious. In high school before games I used to doze off and everyone thought I was so cool because I never showed signs of being nervous. In truth it was the exact opposite.

As we drove I was semi-aware of Roy and Billy talking in the background. I could hear light jazz playing softly on the radio. I was in between being fully awake and fully asleep, a half sleep. Time moves differently in this realm, a combination of real time and double time. It seemed only a few minutes before I was bumped awake. We were turning off the secondary road onto the old logging trail.

"Stop a minute," I said to T. Elbert as I snapped fully awake. "Billy, hand me your night-vision goggles."

I took the goggles from Billy and switched them on. I handed them to T. Elbert. "Try these on."

He switched off the Hummer's headlights and took a minute or so to get the goggles adjusted to his head and focused. "Hot damn," he said. "These are much better than the first generation."

"They should be," I said. "Now get moving and take it slow and easy."

The Hummer crawled up the old logging road. We bounced through ruts, drove through a small stream and over tree branches. Fifteen minutes in we abruptly stopped in front of a stone wall.

"I think that's all she wrote," T. Elbert said. "You guys will have to hoof it from here."

We unloaded.

"Double check your packs," I ordered. "Tran gun, binocs, goggles, rope, cuffs, duct tape, and walkie-talkies. Put the knife on your belt."

We put on the shoulder holsters and strapped in our tranquilizer guns and our personal weapons. Roy had a Glock 9mm and I had my Beretta 9mm. Billy did not carry a handgun. He hated guns of all kinds. He had unsnapped the second holster and left it in the Hummer. I knew somewhere on his person was probably a second knife. I handed a walkie-talkie headphone to T. Elbert. There had been four in the box even though I had only ordered three. Perhaps Raul was thinking ahead of me or perhaps they came in pairs. No matter, the fourth one would be useful.

"Maintain radio silence," I told him as I put on my headphones and adjusted my mouthpiece. "We will contact you. Only call me if it is an emergency."

"Will do," T. Elbert said. "You want to use code names on these thing just in case?"

I smiled. T. Elbert was really getting into it. "Why not." I said. "You are base and I am eagle one, Billy is eagle two and Roy is eagle three.

"Got it," T. Elbert said.

"Jesus," Roy said as he slipped on his headphones and adjusted his mouthpiece.

I looked at Billy as he put on his headphones. "Can you hear me?" He nodded. "You have the point. Say something."

"Why am I not eagle one if I have the point?" Billy said over the headphones. I knew he was teasing me.

"Shut up and lead," I teased.

We started up the mountain in single file. Billy, then Roy, then me.

"Eagle three, can you hear me?" I asked.

"Loud and clear, oh mighty eagle one," Roy said.

"Funny," I said. "Now you can shut up."

"Base, can you hear me?" I queried as we started up the mountain

"Loud and clear," said T. Elbert.

THE NIGHT WAS cold and still. The absence of wind was as much of a blessing as was the cloud cover. There was enough natural light for me to see Billy in front of Roy. We did not have a problem following Billy up the mountain. Billy moved quietly and effortlessly. Roy and I followed. We were on a narrow path, maybe an animal trail. We made very little noise. We crested the ridge and turned north. I could feel the drop in temperature at the top of the ridge.

I marked a tree with my knife. I knew Billy might want to come back ahead of us, and just in case I wanted some markers to guide me back. The hike was warming. My hands were no longer cold and I was on the verge of breaking a sweat.

"Chief," I said through my mouthpiece.

Billy stopped and Roy and I joined him.

"Let's take five," I said. "I don't want to break a sweat."

"Good idea," Roy said.

Billy nodded and sat down, Indian style. The power of genetics, I mused. Roy and I found separate trees to lean on. I knew the ground was cold and probably wet and I wanted no part of that. Roy seemed to be thinking the same thing. Billy was impervious to cold or wet.

When I was just about to get cold again, I stood. "Slow and easy," I said to Billy. "We are ahead of schedule. It's not even midnight yet."

We resumed our hike toward Camp Code. Billy slowed the pace and the effort was considerably less since we were hiking almost level ground across the ridge top. I marked a few trees. Forty-five minutes later we stopped.

Billy pointed down the west slope. "The camp is down in that valley about half an hour away."

"It's twelve-thirty now," I said to Billy. "What time do you think would be safe for us to go in?"

"Things start to quiet down after midnight. Let's wait an hour, then go."

We sat and waited. To pass the time, I hailed T. Elbert.

"Eagle one to base," I said softly.

"Base here."

"Everything okay?"

"Everything's just dandy here, eagle one."

"The eagles are roosting for an hour before flying in."

WAITING IS NOT one of my strong suits, and on top of that I was getting colder. I got up and moved around. I walked in place and did some stretches against a full-grown poplar. Roy was moving around also, flailing his arms and stomping his feet. Every now and then he took his gloves off and blew on his hands. Billy sat and didn't move or speak. He wasn't asleep but his eyes were almost closed. Finally, he opened his eyes and looked upward. "It's time," he said.

I looked at my watch. It read one-thirty. I have seen this display of Billy's sense of time so often that I no longer question it, but I still marvel at it. I looked up expecting to see stars. None. The cloud cover was holding.

We started our descent down the western slope toward the camp. About fifteen minutes later as we were moving slowly and quietly down the mountains, we heard a crash above us. Movement. Branches breaking. I reached for my night vision binoculars and Roy did the same.

Billy spotted it first. "Bear at ten o'clock and moving our way," he said.

I spotted it, a black bear. A very big black bear moving slowly down the mountain. January was in the middle of the hibernation period for black bears. Although unusual, male black bears will come out of hibernation looking for food. My guess was this bear had a den close by and had gotten a whiff of some kind of food from Camp Code and was going to pay the camp a visit.

I put on my night-vision goggles and unholstered my tranquilizer pistol. Roy followed suit. "We cannot let that animal reach the camp," I said softly as we took cover behind a giant hemlock. "He could wake up the whole place."

"These loads are set for a two hundred-pound human," Roy whispered. "How many is it going to take to bring that thing down?"

"Probably one from each of us," I said, keeping my voice low.

From the left side of the huge hemlock, Billy was peering back up the mountain as he too unholstered his tranquilizer pistol. "One minute," Billy said.

I knelt and peeked out from the right side of the giant tree. Roy was looking over my shoulder. I could see a large dark form starting to materialize out of the shadows. I wanted him to get as close as possible before we took our shots. The bear was moving slowly and unaware approximately one hundred feet away and heading directly for us. I took aim and waited. He kept coming, now only about fifty feet away. Then he stopped and sniffed the air and I knew he had sensed our presence. He started to turn away.

"Now," I said softly as I heard the hiss of my gas-operated gun unleash my dart. The sounds of Roy and Billy firing were almost simultaneous with mine. The bear turned and ran back up the mountain. I traced his movements through my goggles and wondered if we had hit him. Then I saw him topple over. I turned and started to say something to Billy but he had vanished.

I scanned the surrounding area and finally picked up Billy standing over the bear. He put his hands on the bear's chest and then made a picking motion. He stood and walked back down to us. In his hand were three darts. He opened up his pack and dropped them in. I took off my night-vision goggles and dropped them back into my pack. Roy did the same.

"Pretty good shooting," Billy said.

"How is the bear?" I asked.

"Sleeping and breathing normally," Billy said. "Hard to tell how long he will be out, so we better get moving."

Fifteen minutes later we came to a clearing just above the camp. The main building was down about a hundred yards to our left. Cabins of various sizes were scattered below the main building to the left and right, but most of them were to the right. I took my night-vision goggles out of my pack, put them back on and had a look around. All was quiet, nothing moved.

"Elroy's cabin is at one o'clock, closest to the woods on the other side," Billy said softly. "We had better go around and come out of the woods behind it."

I turned to Roy. He also had put his night vision-goggles back on. "Stay here and keep watch for any movement. Keep your walkie-talkie on but keep your voice low."

I followed Billy north staying on the edge of the forest and circling slowly to the west and then south until we were behind the cabin that we hoped housed Teddy Earl Elroy.

"Eagle three, we are in position," I said.

"Acknowledged, eagle one. All quiet."

"Now what, eagle two?"

"I'm going in," Billy said softly as he moved into the shadows at the back of the cabin. I watched in the misty green light of the night-vision goggles as Billy disappeared around the left side of the cabin. Less than a minute later, he was back at my side.

"He is not in there," Billy said. "There's a woman in there in a double bed. It looks as if she might have been with someone earlier."

I started to say something when I heard the creak of a door further off in the distance to my left.

"Hear that?" I whispered.

"Latrine," Billy said.

"Someone's coming this way." I said.

The figure with head bent moved slowly toward us from about fifty yards away being careful in the dark not to fall. As the figure came closer, I could not believe our luck. Coming slowly into focus in my night vision goggles was none other than Teddy Earl Elroy. He was just as I remembered him: long, narrow face, a scraggly goatee, about six feet tall with a slight frame. I would guess that he did not weigh over one hundred and fifty pounds. Billy recognized him too and raised his tranquilizer gun to fire, but I put my hand out and lowered his pistol. I wanted this shot for myself. When Teddy Earl was about ten yards away, I fired my dart. The CO_2-propelled dart tracked straight to the right thigh of Teddy Earl. He yelped and grabbed at the dart and pulled it out, looking at it with a quizzical look on his face. That's all he had time to do before the drug took effect. He groaned as he took one more step forward and collapsed into the waiting arms of Billy Two-Feathers, who slung him over his shoulder like a sack of potatoes. At that moment the cabin door creaked and the female inside came out and down the one step from the porch to see what was going on. I started to fire my gun when I realized I had not had time to reload.

"What's going on out here?" she asked in a slightly raised voice.

I had visions of the entire camp waking up. Billy did not hesitate. I heard the sound of his gun as his dart released. I heard the woman squeal and saw her reach for her hip. I watched as she staggered backwards and sat down on the porch and fell over.

"I've got her." I said.

I scooped her up and carried her back into the cabin, lay her on the bed and removed the dart. Thank God she was a small woman and not heavy. I covered her up.

"Sweet dreams," I said.

I was about to leave the cabin when I caught a glimpse of a rifle with a scope propped up in a corner near the left side of the bed. I took the rifle with me.

"Eagle one, what the hell is going on down there?" Roy demanded.

"Stay alert, eagle three. A few complications but we have the package," I said as I exited the cabin with the rifle and returned to Billy, who had withdrawn back into the bordering woods.

"Can you find your way back?" Billy asked.

"I think so."

"I'll see you at base," Billy said. He moved away quickly carrying Teddy Earl as if he didn't weigh more than a blanket.

"Eagle three," I said. "I will come to you. Any signs of life?"

"None."

I made my way quickly back the way we had come in, circling north, then east, then south to Roy's position. I knelt beside Roy to catch my breath and removed my goggles. The cloud cover was breaking up and some moonlight was peeking through. I put my night vision-goggles in my backpack.

"That was pretty slick," he said. "What were the complications?"

"Tell you later. I don't think you'll need those goggles."

Roy removed his goggles and looked around and nodded.

"Your friend is out ahead of us carrying the package?" Roy asked.

"Affirmative."

"Remind me never to fuck with him," Roy said as he covered his mouthpiece.

"Let's get out of here," I said.

I moved back up the mountain with the rifle in hand at a much faster pace than when we came down. I did not care whether I broke a sweat or not, I wanted out of there. We reached the ridge in twenty minutes and headed south keeping a lively pace. A half hour later we reached our five-minute break spot and just beyond was the tree in which I had left a location mark. I turned east down the mountain on the narrow path and Roy followed.

"Base to eagle one," T. Elbert said through my headphones.

"Eagle one."

"The package has arrived."

"Put bracelets on the package and store it in the rear," I said.

"Ten four, eagle one. Your ETA?"

"Fifteen minutes tops," I responded.

"Copy that. We'll be ready to roll. Base out."

I didn't respond. I thought T. Elbert had had enough fun with the covert ops speak. I had to admit that the idea was sound. The odds that someone would be listening in on our channel were remote, but why risk it? Anyone listening would certainly be entertained by our cloak and dagger linguistics, but they would have one hell of a time trying to decipher what we were talking about.

Roy and I moved swiftly down the mountain and I soon saw the red taillights of the Hummer and could hear the soft purr of the engine. T. Elbert had turned it around and was ready to head down the mountain.

"We're here," I said into my mouthpiece.

We reached the Hummer and I looked through the back window for Teddy Earl. I could not see a thing. The windows of the Hummer obviously had a very dark tint. Why did that not surprise me? Roy and I removed our backpacks, took off our headphones, and dropped them in the packs. I opened the front passenger's side door and slipped in, placing my backpack in the floor at my feet as Roy took the rifle from me and climbed in the back. Struck by the warmth of the Hummer, I realized how cold it had been on the mountain.

I looked at Billy.

"No problems," he said.

We were already moving down the mountain. T. Elbert still had on his night-vision goggles and the headlights of the Hummer were still off. When we reached the secondary road, T. Elbert stopped briefly and removed his goggles and turned on the headlights. The clock on the dashboard read 3:05. In fifteen minutes we were making a right turn onto a main highway. I had missed the drive on the way up because of my nervous dozing but now I was wide awake and taking in everything, even the flashing red lights in my passenger-side mirror, undoubtably a county sheriff's deputy.

"Shit," Roy said. *My sentiments exactly.*

"Relax," said T. Elbert, as he pulled over. He lowered the driver's side window and held out some sort of identification. "TBI," he shouted out the window. The deputy approached with a flashlight. The beam swept past the rear windows to T. Elbert's ID. The deputy took the ID and then handed it back to T. Elbert. He partially leaned in the driver-side window, shining his flashlight from face to face. Luckily his beam did not reach to Teddy Earl sleeping blissfully in the rear of the Hummer. At that point I was glad we had not used the face black and thankful for T. Elbert's tinted windows.

"What are you boys doing out this late?" the young deputy asked.

"Training exercise," T. Elbert said.

"What kind of training exercise?"

"A Tennessee Bureau of Investigation training exercise," T. Elbert said. He emphasized Tennessee Bureau of Investigation with enough annoyance as if to say he did not want to hear any more questions.

"Yes, sir," the deputy said as he turned off his flashlight. I knew we were okay. T. Elbert had established his authority.

"If you feel you need to wake someone up to check this out," T. Elbert said with the same tone, "then get to it. We're running behind schedule and I would hate to have to blame the Unicoi County Sheriff's Department."

"No, sir. Sorry to bother you, sir," the deputy said. "Carry on."

The young deputy turned and hastily returned to his cruiser. Seconds later the flashing red lights went out.

"Kids," T. Elbert sneered. Roy and I let out joint sighs of relief. T. Elbert chuckled. There was no response from Billy. From all appearances, he was asleep.

"You still have an active ID with the TBI?" I asked as we drove away.

"Yes. I do some computer work and some online research for the TBI," T. Elbert said. "On their computers, I am listed as a special agent. That also allows me to carry a government plate on the Hummer, which probably did not hurt our cause, and to carry a piece."

HALF AN HOUR LATER, when I had a good signal on my cell phone I called the Mountain Center police station.

"Mountain Center Police Department." Mary's voice.

"It's your friendly gumshoe," I said.

"Where the hell are you?"

"Such language. And from a police officer no less."

"Don . . ." Mary started with a lot of agitation in her voice.

"Okay, okay," I said. "Everything went according to plan with a couple or three interesting sidelights. We are probably about an hour from dropping off Mr. Teddy Earl Elroy. We are going to swing by T. Elbert's and pick up the Pathfinder and then come to the station."

I stayed on the phone with Mary another half hour, recounting in detail the adventures of this night. T. Elbert drove through the night, humming softly as I talked to Mary. I could swear it was the scarecrow's song from *The Wizard of Oz,* "If I Only Had a Brain." I wondered what that meant. Roy had joined Billy in apparent peaceful sleep.

As we ended our conversation, Mary said, "I love you."

"Me too you," I said. "See you soon."

T. Elbert stopped humming. "She's the one, Donald."

"Imagine that," I said.

"No sense fighting it. Mary won't take no for an answer and she has staked her claim on you. You couldn't find a better woman for you if you searched the world over."

"Enough," I said. "My head is spinning. Drive to your place so I can pick up the Pathfinder."

We drove to T. Elbert's in silence. When we arrived, I turned toward the back seat and woke up our sleeping passengers. I gave Roy my keys.

"Go back to the office and get your cars. Lock the Pathfinder and give the keys to Billy. He can pick me up at the station."

Men of few words, Roy nodded, Billy nodded, they got out, and T. Elbert and I drove off to the Mountain Center police station. The dashboard clock glowed 4:59. Sean Wilson was waiting for us when we pulled into the parking lot and turned right toward the police station. Straight ahead would have put us in front of the courthouse. A left turn would have taken us to the jail that served both city and county. A moan emanated from the back of the Hummer.

"The monster awakes," I said.

"It sure ain't sleepin' beauty," T. Elbert replied.

I got out and met Sean at the rear of the Hummer. We lifted the tailgate and half dragged, half pulled a groggy Teddy Earl Elroy to the pavement.

"On your feet, asshole," Sean growled.

"Who, what, huh, mmm . . ." Teddy Earl mumbled incoherently.

Sean pulled a stumbling, still handcuffed Teddy Earl up three steps and through the front door of the Mountain Center police station. I watched them go and turned and walked to the driver's side window of the Hummer. The darkened window quietly descended to reveal a smiling T. Elbert Brown.

"A good night's work," he said.

"I could not have done it without you, T. Elbert."

"Horse hockey. But thanks for sayin' it."

"Seriously, you made a big difference. I mean it. I'm glad you were part of the team."

"Donald," T. Elbert said as the window started its ascent, "I wouldn't have missed it for the world." The Hummer drove off into the early dawn

as I turned and climbed the stairs and entered the Mountain Center
police station.

THE STATION HOUSE was one large open room with offices in the rear
and partitions scattered about in no apparent pattern. To the right I
saw Mary rise from her desk and move hurriedly my way. To the left
Sean had seated Teddy Earl near a holding cell while Sean answered a
phone call. A dispatcher near me was also on the phone, but the place
was generally quiet.

Mary reached me and gave me a quick kiss on the lips.

"Good work. Glad you are all right," she said. "I knew you would be,
but I was worried anyway."

"Nice to know you were worried."

She smiled. "Are you ready to go home and get some sleep?"

"In a minute. I want to see Big Bob."

"Take your time, I have some paperwork I need to finish."

Mary turned and walked back to her desk while I watched and fan-
tasized about what she looked like without the uniform. Then I snapped
myself out of my daydream and walked back to Big Bob's office. I leaned
my back against the door jam so that I was halfway in and halfway out
of Big Bob's office. I glanced over toward Mary who had her head down
busy in paperwork, and I turned back toward Big Bob. The tiredness
was beginning to take hold.

"Good work tonight," Big Bob said.

"I had help."

"Yeah, but it was your show."

I nodded and turned my head to look at Teddy Earl. Sean had the apparently still groggy Teddy Earl on his feet and was leading him toward
the holding cell. He stopped to take off the cuffs. As the handcuffs came
off, my world took a weird turn on its axis. All movement became slow
motion. Teddy Earl sprang to life and shoved Sean Wilson across the
nearest desk, at the same time ripping Sean's Glock .44 from its holster.

I could feel myself push away from the door jam as my hand went to the small of my back for the Beretta. The hand that held the Glock was rising and aiming across the room toward Mary as my Beretta cleared my holster and came around toward Teddy Earl.

"Die, bitch," Teddy Earl screamed and fired three shots.

The Beretta exploded in my hand and a tiny red dot appeared on Teddy Earl's forehead as one very large hunting knife appeared in his chest. The lifeless body of Teddy Earl Elroy went crashing backwards over the nearest desk and lay motionless on the station house floor.

I spun toward Mary who was nowhere in sight. My heart stopped. I couldn't breathe. My knees nearly buckled. Time had stopped.

"Mary," I shouted.

"I'm okay," came a shouted response. A blond head popped up from behind Mary's desk. It was the most beautiful and welcomed blond head that I had ever seen. My world righted itself. Time started again. So did my heart. I let out a long breath and gulped for air. The whole thing had taken no more than five seconds.

I saw Billy from the front door of the police station. It was his knife that protruded from the chest of the most recent Mountain City corpse. Billy had made a very accurate and deadly throw from the station house front door. Mary came quickly across the room to my side.

"Are you all right? You look rather pale."

"I thought I had lost you," I said softly.

We held each other silently. I felt Big Bob go past us as he started barking orders. We let go of each other and followed Big Bob over to the body.

"Sean, tape this area off and no one touch anything," Big Bob said loud enough for people in the next block to hear. "Billy, get your camera and take some shots of the body from all angles. Get some close-ups." Billy turned and went through the front door. "Somebody has to call Wanda and get her down here now."

Big Bob looked at me when he said call Wanda. I shook my head.

Wanda was notorious for ripping people's heads off who called her when she was asleep.

"Come on, Blood, I have to deal with the press and write all these goddamn reports. It's the least you can do."

"Okay, you coward. I'll do it," I said recovering some of my composure.

We looked down at the body of Teddy Earl. The shift was changing and we were gathering a crowd of about a dozen officers, the ones just arriving and the ones that had not left. I was surprised that I felt no remorse. I had never killed anyone. I felt only relief that this animal would not be stalking Mary. Teddy Earl looked very dead with a bullet hole in his forehead and a knife in or near his heart.

"Now that's what you call overkill," Big Bob said standing right next to me.

"Don, I'm real sorry," Sean said. "I was careless. I thought he was still out of it."

"It's all right, Sean." I could tell he was really shaken.

"Like hell it is," Big Bob interrupted.

I turned and touched Big Bob's arm. Big Bob glanced at me and I shook my head slightly as if to say not now. He let it slide. I heard the whirring sound of a camera taking pictures. Billy was back and moving around with his 35mm, the camera singing as he rapid-fired from all directions.

"Show's over," Big Bob growled. "Get to where you are supposed to be. Now!"

The area cleared as officers scattered. Mary and I walked back to her desk.

"I need to make one phone call and then we are out of here," I said.

I picked up the phone and called Wanda at home.

"Didn't even have to look that one up, did we?" Mary asked in mock annoyance.

I was too exhausted for verbal jousting, even if it was meant to lighten the moment. Mary was certainly dealing with the whole episode better than I was. I listened to the phone ring, and ring, and ring. I heard Wanda pick up.

"Somebody better be dead," she said groggily.

"Somebody is," I said.

"Donnie! Are you okay?" Wanda exclaimed, obviously now wide-awake.

"I'm fine, Wanda, but we need you at the police station right now. Thanks to me, there is a fresh one on the station house floor. Or should I say, thanks to Billy and me."

"Donnie, you are not making any sense. What do you mean thanks to Billy and me?"

"You'll see when you get here, Wanda. Get moving. Please!"

"On my way." The line went dead and I hung up the phone.

"She is coming right over," I said to Mary. "Let's go."

"In a few minutes," Mary said slowly with a barely perceptible knowing smile. "Relax."

I sat for a minute or two as Mary worked on a call report and then the light went on.

"You want to check out Wanda," I said waiting for the mock denial.

"Never hurts to check out the competition," Mary said slyly.

"Believe me, Wanda is not the competition. You have no competition."

"How sweet," she said sarcastically. "Now, just sit and be quiet while I finish. I'll only be a minute."

Women, I thought to myself. How could the male of the species ever expect to figure them out? I—her man—had been on my greatest adventure, risking life and limb to capture a scumbag intent on killing her, and she had been shot at no more than a few minutes ago, and now all she was worried about was checking out the competition. *Could somebody please explain this to me?*

Then Wanda arrived. She couldn't have looked sexier if she tried.

She came through the front door wearing tight faded jeans, an opened leather jacket, and a white T-shirt that revealed way too much. Her light brown hair had just the right bedroom look, and every guy in the station stopped to take a long hard look at her, including me. I took a quick look at Mary who was staring hard at me. Her right eyebrow arched.

Wanda headed straight for the body and I followed with Mary a step behind. Big Bob had seen Wanda and was coming out of his office. Wanda went under the police tape and knelt by Teddy Earl. She shook her head and looked up at me.

"I see what you mean. You shot him and Billy knifed him."

"Almost simultaneously," I said.

"Billy has taken pictures from all angles," Big Bob said.

"Okay," Wanda said. "Give me a few minutes here."

Wanda looked back up at me, then to Mary and stood up. "You have to be Mary," she said extending her hand that Mary accepted. "I'm Wanda Jones. Nice to meet you."

"Nice to meet you, too," Mary said. She sounded sincere.

Wanda leaned in between us and said just loud enough for only the two of us to hear. "Good thing you saw her first, Donnie." She winked at Mary and Mary laughed out loud.

"Thank you," Mary said.

"Can we go now?" I pleaded.

"Yes, dear, we can go now," Mary said, winking at Wanda.

"Men," Wanda said as she turned and knelt beside the body of Teddy Earl Elroy.

Women, I thought. I'll never figure them out.

36

I was dead tired but I knew I had to tough it out and stay up until at least early evening or my whole sleep pattern would be screwed up. Mary agreed with my thinking and so at a little past six AM we found ourselves at the Mountain City Diner. Doris always opened at six. I knew a substantial breakfast would wake me up and get me through most of the day. After traipsing around the cold East Tennessee Mountains for most of the night, I was beginning to realize just how hungry I was.

The early morning regulars were spread out around the diner and my table in the rear was ready and waiting. Before we could even get seated, Doris was pouring coffee for us.

"Heard there was some excitement at the police station," Doris said. "I sure am glad you two are okay."

I looked at Mary dumbfounded. She only smiled.

"And exactly where did you hear that, Doris?" I asked in mock annoyance.

"Word gets around fast in this town, Mr. Youngblood. You should know that."

"I guess I forgot. Can we order?"

"Sure."

And we did.

THE BREAKFAST AND sporadic cups of coffee kept me awake into the late afternoon. I did my usual online stock market routine, reviewed portfolios of all my accounts, played a running game of solitaire and pondered a new problem.

By killing Teddy Earl Elroy, I may have inadvertently killed my relationship with Mary. Mary was supposed to stay on the Mountain Center police force only until Teddy Earl was safely behind bars. Now Teddy Earl was safely dead. Mary, at times, had expressed boredom with the small-town scene but I had not heard any complaints in a while. It was true that Knoxville was only an hour and a half away, but I now found myself wanting this relationship full-time. Selfishly, I did not want to move to Knoxville. I had done the big-city thing, the real big-city thing. I had that out of my system. I was now a small-town guy. I realized I loved Mary, but could our relationship survive if one of us wasn't happy? I knew I would have to face this problem soon.

The phone rang.

"Why didn't you just shoot him at the camp and save Billy the trouble of carrying him out?" Roy asked.

"If I had known what was going to happen, I would have."

"You okay?"

"Yeah, why?"

"Ever killed anyone before?"

"No, have you?"

"I was in Nam before I ran afoul of the law. I killed plenty."

"You would think I would feel at least a little guilt, but I don't feel anything."

"You shouldn't. Teddy Earl was a scumbag. You did the world a favor. Forget about it and move on."

"I intend on doing just that," I said.

"Speaking of which, do you have any more ideas as to finding Joey Avanti?"

"Now that Teddy Earl is not occupying all of my time, I'll see what I can come up with. My first priority is to go home and get some sleep. Call me in a few days."

"Will do."

The clock seemed to be in slow motion as it crept past four PM. I picked up the phone to call Wanda.

"County Coroner's Office. This is Stacy."

"Hello, Stacy. Don Youngblood calling for Wanda," I said.

"Hello, Mr. Youngblood. One moment, I'll tell her you are on the line."

Elevator music replaced Stacy's voice.

"Hey, Donnie. How are you doing?"

"I'm doing fine, Wanda. Have you done the autopsy on Teddy Earl yet?"

"No, just the prelims. But I can tell you he died of a bullet wound to the head, or a knife to the heart. Take your pick."

"The chest wound would have killed him?"

"Deader than a doornail."

"How are you going to list the cause of death?"

"I was thinking multiple wounds to head and chest. What do you think?"

"Sounds good to me. Thanks, Wanda." Billy and I would share in the taking of the life of Teddy Earl Elroy. I would not bear that burden alone. For Billy, that would not be a problem. I was not so sure about myself.

"You shouldn't feel guilty about this, Donnie."

"Yeah, I've been hearing a lot of that."

"I like your lady," Wanda said, abruptly changing the subject.

"Thanks, I kind of like her, too."

"I think this is the one for you, Donnie."

"Yeah, I've been hearing a lot of that, too."

"Get some rest, Donnie. And stay in touch, you hear?"

"Sure, Wanda. I'll talk to you soon."

I HAD ONE more call to make before I went back to the condo and crashed. I dialed T. Elbert.

"Did you hear the news?"

"Just heard it on the four o'clock report. What in the hell happened?"

I told it slowly and with great detail the way I remembered it. The retelling of this scary tale was more unsettling that I could imagine. I kept thinking of what could have happened if I had not turned and looked at Teddy Earl the moment I did. But then, of course, Billy was there. But what if Billy had not come through the front door when he did? The what-ifs were unnerving me. How do you distinguish between luck and divine intervention?

"Damn, I wish I had been there," T. Elbert said. "I would have put an extra bullet in him myself just to make it final. I'm glad everyone is okay. Feeling any guilt?"

"None."

"Good. If you start to and want to talk, let me know. I had to have counseling after my first kill."

"I'll remember that," I said. "I'm going home and get some rest. I just wanted you to get the straight facts from me."

"Go get some rest. I'll see you Wednesday mornin.'"

I HAD JUST started my shut-down routine of two computers, the coffee maker, three desk lights, two sets of indirect wall lights, and one calculator when the phone rang. "Cherokee Investigations."

"Donald Youngblood, please," said the completely recognizable voice on the other end of the phone.

"Hello, Liam."

"That's you, is it Donald?' asked Liam McSwain.

"Tis!" I said.

"Nice work with Teddy Earl. Too bad you had to kill him. I mourned for maybe two seconds."

"Well, that's two seconds longer than me."

"No doubt. How is Mary?"

"Finer than frog hair," I said.

"Come again?"

"An old Southern expression that loosely interpreted means perfect."

"I'll have to remember that one," McSwain laughed. I smiled trying to imagine McSwain saying *finer than frog hair* with his thick Irish brogue.

"You have another question, Liam?" I, of course, knew that he did.

"I was wondering if Mary is coming back to the Knoxville police force."

"It's a little soon to be asking, don't you think?"

"Of course it is, but I have my reasons. I wanted you to know that Big Bob and I have agreed to make this arrangement permanent if that is what Mary wants. The man Big Bob sent down very much wants to stay, and he is a good man from all I hear, so that would make it a simple swap."

"I would like nothing better," I said. "I'll talk to Mary about it in the next day or two and let you know. Send a little of that fabled Irish luck my way."

"Will do, Donald. And again, nice work."

"Thanks, Liam. Talk to you soon."

I sat and pondered my strategy on approaching Mary about staying. My normal modus operandi would be to let her go and move on, but I had to agree with everyone who was telling me *this one is a keeper.* Okay then, where and how? Under the sheets, no, that would be cheating. Candlelight dinner? Better, but still cheating. In the gym? Not bad. Certainly not cheating but during an endorphin high. Might work.

MARY AND I SAT ON OPPOSITE SIDES of the bar in the kitchen with drinks in hand. I had a Moretti, an Italian beer, and Mary had a glass of Ecco Domani Pinot Grigio. We were both mentally and physically exhausted. We were silent for a long time, comfortable in that silence, knowing instinctively what the other was thinking as we recounted the events of the day.

"Thanks," Mary said, breaking the silence.

"My pleasure."

"Don't feel guilty," she said.

"I don't."

"You might later."

"I doubt it. Besides, I would only feel half guilty. According to Wanda, it was a shared kill."

We finished our drinks in silence and poured two more. I had learned early on that I could not keep up with Mary in alcohol consumption. She could drink a whole bottle of wine and show no effect from it. I, on the other hand, would fall asleep if I had more than two or three beers. I was on my second beer and feeling very tired.

"By the way," Mary said nonchalantly, "I've decided to sign on permanent with your sleepy little police force."

My mouth fell open as my planning went up in smoke. Mary smiled wickedly.

"You sure?"

"Positive."

"Well," I said, "I'm glad we got that settled."

"Me too. I love you and I am going to bed."

"I love you too. I'll be in soon."

It was seven PM.

Soon turned into later. I sat at the kitchen bar cleaning the Beretta and thinking about taking a life. Every time I tried to feel guilt, the image of Elroy lying on the station house floor popped into my mind and all I felt was relief. I didn't even feel guilty about not feeling guilty. Maybe it was a character flaw. I looked down the barrel of the Beretta and saw the light reflecting through the smooth clean inside. It reminded me of the openings of all those James Bond movies. I put away the Beretta and the cleaning kit and went to the bathroom and prepared for bed.

I slipped in beside Mary and fell into a deep sleep.

37

Twelve hours sleep made me feel almost human again. I had a dull headache, which I treated with coffee and a large breakfast at the diner before I went to the office. I pushed the memories of the last twenty-four hours to the back room of my consciousness and slammed the door. They would always be there residing with a few others that I did not care to confront. It would take some effort not to let any of them escape.

There was still the unfinished business with Joey Avanti and the murder of Sarah Ann Fairchild. Scott Glass and Carlos Vincente had been right: I was not going to stop looking. I needed another avenue to explore. Where would Joey go? Better yet, where would I go? Someplace I always wanted to go. Someplace that offered something I was interested in. Someplace where I knew someone. I called Roy.

"Yeah?"

"Real friendly. Must have known it was me."

"Ever heard of caller ID? What do you need?"

"I need to know everything you can tell me about Ronnie Fairchild."

"I'll have to give that some thought," Roy said.

"Make some notes. I need to know what he did in his free time. Did he have hobbies? Did he travel anywhere? Where did they take vacations? What did he do at work? Anything."

"I get the idea."

"Meet me tomorrow morning at the diner and let's go over it. There is something somewhere that will give us a lead."

"What time?"

"Your call. I'm up early."

"Six-thirty?"

"I'll be there. Table in the back."

At six the next morning I was at the Mountain Center Diner with two old friends, *USA Today* and a cup of steaming hot coffee. I was looking over the NCAA basketball conference records for all division one schools to see who was doing what. When it came to football, I basically was loyal only to the Tennessee Volunteers. With basketball I was more of a Connecticut Husky fan. I also rooted for Tennessee and nearby East Tennessee State University. All my teams were having good years and all were ranked in the top twenty-five, even ETSU.

"You can actually read," I heard Roy say somewhere in the background of my consciousness.

I surfaced from the depths of the sports pages and saw Roy staring down. "Amazing, isn't it," I smiled.

Doris appeared as if she had been beamed to our table. We ordered as if it were our last meal. For Roy, a western omelet with sausage patties, wheat toast and a side of home fries. I asked for my favorite: a feta cheese omelet, bacon, rye toast, and home fries.

"Did you come up with anything?" I asked.

Roy smiled. "Shouldn't you have asked me this a long time ago?"

"I've been busy trying to protect my lady love," I protested. "Besides, I am new at finding people."

"Well, you may not have found anyone but you have certainly unraveled quite a mystery."

"I'm like a barnyard chicken. I scratch around and scratch around and sometimes I uncover stuff. Sometimes it is stuff I am looking for and other times not. Today I'm scratching some more. Tell me what you can about Ronnie."

Roy took a deep breath. "Well, I didn't like the son of a bitch at all. I think you knew that. So I stayed away from him and never got to know him. He spent a lot of time with Sarah Ann and a lot of time at the office. Fleet put him over the sales division and he seemed to be good at it. Whenever I saw him at the office he was always on the computer and he had a small computer room at the mansion. So I guess he knew computers pretty well. He stayed in shape and worked out three or four times a week. He and Sarah Ann traveled some. Fleet has a mountain house near Gatlinburg and a million-dollar-plus condo at Amelia Island and a lake house. Ronnie and Sarah Ann spent a lot of time at the lake house. They had a boat and water-skied and fished. That's all I know. I wasn't around him much."

"You said he worked out. Does Fleet have a gym at the mansion?"

"Yes, a small one. Most of the time Ronnie worked out downtown at that gym the Japanese guy owns."

"Moto's?"

Roy could see my surprise. "Yeah, you know it?"

"Sure, I work out there quite a bit myself with Billy, and I do not recall ever seeing Ronnie Fairchild. I'll have to talk to Moto. Also, tell Fleet not to let anyone touch Ronnie's computers. I want you to bring me the hard drives from his computers as soon as you can. If Ronnie planned his escape in advance, there may be a clue there somewhere."

"Wouldn't he have erased everything before taking off?" Roy asked.

"Probably, but there are ways to recapture the information if you know how."

"And you know how?"

"No, but I know someone who does."

We sat in silence for a time and finished our breakfast. The diner had begun to buzz with the arrival of the morning regulars and only a few tables and booths remained unoccupied. Dishes clinked, coffee was poured, and greetings were exchanged as a new day dawned full of anticipation and hope.

"And one other thing," Roy said. "They played golf together. They were members of the Mountain Center Country Club. I understand they were both pretty good. Sarah Ann was the ladies club champion a couple of times."

"I remember she played in high school. So that makes sense."

Roy drained his coffee cup and stood to leave. I could tell talking about Sarah Ann and the man who killed her had opened old wounds.

"I need to go. I am driving Fleet to Knoxville for a meeting. I'll get those hard drives to you tomorrow, and if I think of anything else, I'll call." He didn't wait for me to acknowledge his leaving. He just turned and walked away.

Doris poured a fresh cup of coffee for me and remained silent as she did it, which was unusual. She must have sensed that I was working something out in my mind and she did not want to break my train of thought. I had picked up one or two more avenues to explore, but I knew I was going to need a major break to have any chance of tracking down the alias Ronnie Fairchild.

MOTO WAS BEHIND the front desk when I opened the glass door of the gym and walked in. He looked up in surprise. I never worked out in the morning. I was a lunchtime or later person. I could not get prepared mentally for a morning workout. Mary, on the other hand, preferred mornings. She would be at the gym while I was still sleeping.

"Wrong time for you to be here," he said. "Have never seen you work out in morning."

"I'm not here to work out, Moto. I need to ask you a few questions."

"So ask," Moto snapped. Japanese personality.

"Did you know Ronnie Fairchild?"

"Sure. He worked out here. Morning person."

"Did you ever talk to him? Get to know him a little?"

"Never. Quiet person. Wouldn't talk to anyone."

"Anything else you can tell me?" I asked.

Moto paused for effect. "Strong man," he said. "And quick. Would not want to mess with him. Also, cold man, mean, I think. Could see it in his eyes."

Well, that sure made me feel a lot better. I thanked Moto for his time and left.

38

Stanley Johns lived just south of downtown in a quiet older section known as the Tree District. All the streets were named for trees: Oak, Poplar, Pine, Locust, Maple, Walnut, Beech and more. Stanley lived at 418 West Locust Street in the modest two-story house his grandparents had built and he had grown up in. He was an odd little man whom I had known in high school. Short and round with dark curly hair and a raspy high voice, Stanley may have been the original geek. He was shy and sensitive with the innocence of a small child. In high school Stanley did not always make good grades. He was indifferent to English, literature, health, geography, psychology, and social studies. In these areas he barely managed passing grades and that drove our teachers crazy since Stanley was a whiz in the sciences and math. It was not surprising that Stanley turned out to be a computer genius.

In high school Stanley was almost invisible with few or no friends until an incident in my junior year changed his life forever. Big Bob and I were in the hall near our lockers a few minutes after our final class of the day when we heard a commotion down the hall. A couple of punks with the reputation for being tough were harassing Stanley. We could hear Stanley pleading for them to stop and to leave him alone, but they were having too much fun with their cruelty. I normally avoided fights but every now and then something set me off, and this was one of those times. Down the hall I went. I was within feet of confronting one of the offenders when Big Bob shoved past me, grabbed the largest punk by the front of his shirt and slammed him against the locker. Big Bob's eyes were on fire. I had never seen him so wild. A look came over the larger punk's face as if he knew he was.near death. The smaller of the two harassers stood motionless with his mouth open. I stared hard at him, doing my best to look intimidating. For a few seconds our little group of five was in a vacuum.

"Stanley is our friend," Big Bob said in a low growl between his teeth. "Anyone touches Stanley, they answer to us. You'll spread the word, right?"

"Yes sir, I will," said the wide-eyed punk. Big Bob released him. "Now get out of here."

They left as if the building were on fire.

From that day forward, the word was out that we were looking out for Stanley. Stanley responded with the appropriate hero worship, especially for Big Bob. He sought us out just to say hello. At first it was embarrassing. Jocks did not want geeks hanging out with them. But word filtered back from our classmates that we had done a good and noble thing, and soon the whole junior class had taken Stanley under its wing. From that day forward, Stanley was a kind of a mascot of the junior class. It did not change after graduation. Our class would always look after Stanley and I had learned a valuable lesson: Good and noble deeds were infectious.

After high school Stanley enrolled at East Tennessee State University in the infant computer sciences program. Four years later he graduated. His overall GPA was unspectacular but his grades in his math, science, and computer courses were straight A's.

I didn't lose touch with Stanley after high school graduation because Stanley would not allow it. Stanley never left Mountain Center but he made it one of his life's works to know where almost everyone in our graduating class was. From time to time I would get phone calls from Stanley checking up on me. He would always delight on filling me in on all the local happenings and gossip. I didn't need the *Mountain Center Press*. I had Stanley.

After Mike Brown graduated from Duke, he went to work for Computec International. At that time computer technology was still in its infancy and Mike realized the opportunities were limitless. Then he went to work for IBM. Ten years later Mike started his own company, Software Unlimited. One of his first hires was Stanley Johns. Since Stanley was shy and did not really want to interact with other employees, Mike let Stanley work from home. Stanley's basement office was something to behold. Langley would have been proud. Stanley's early career was spent writing software for various accounting and financial management programs. They made a fortune for Mike and Stanley.

I had handled Stanley's finances since I was on Wall Street and had negotiated with Mike for a percentage of sales for Stanley on all the programs he authored. Stanley was now a very rich man who cared absolutely nothing about money. We gave Stanley's money away by the thousands to various charities. When I questioned any of the charities that Stanley wanted to give money to, he always told me with the seriousness of a priest in the confessional that it was a worthy cause. I gave up long ago trying to reason with him.

Ironically, the money manager program Stanley had written years ago was the one I used for Stanley to pay his monthly bills.

With the advent of the Internet, Stanley had a whole new world to explore. Had he wanted to, Stanley could have been a world-class hacker. Instead he turned his considerable talents toward writing anti-virus programs, and Mike and Stanley made another fortune. They created another company, SJ Anti-Virus Software, Inc., one of the leaders in the market segment. Stanley was the superhero of the Internet. Anti-Virus Man. Whenever a new virus was wreaking havoc with computer systems, Stanley quickly came up with a countermeasure. In his computer domain, this, shy sensitive, naïve soul was king.

I drove to 418 West Locust with the two hard drives Roy had delivered to my office early that morning. One came from Ronnie's Fleet Industries office and the other from his office at the Fleet Mansion. I expected any clues to come from the latter. Keeping secrets at work is never easy.

I pulled in behind Stanley's Chevy Malibu. Stanley had enough money to buy half the town and he drove a used Chevy Malibu. When I teased him about it, he would only smile and say it was all he needed.

I went to the basement door, the entrance to Stanley's computer world. I knew going to the front door would prove futile. Stanley rarely was upstairs to answer the front door. I pushed the buzzer on the back door and waited, staring at the small, yet tasteful, sign that read Software Unlimited. Mike, of course, had provided the sign. Stanley would never have bothered.

Since Stanley was expecting me, I knew he would eventually answer the door. I had called him earlier that morning to let him know I was coming. A few minutes later the back door opened.

"Don," Stanley said with the exuberance of a child, "come in, come in."

I entered into a kind of waiting area much like the reception area in a doctor's office. It was expensively decorated, compliments of Mike Brown. Directly opposite the back door was the entrance to Stanley's computer domain.

A sign on the door read *Oz*. It was appropriate. When it came to computers, Stanley was the wizard. Stanley used a remote control opener to unlock the door to his computer world and we went in. I was always amazed anytime I visited. Monitors were everywhere. There must have been two dozen in the twenty-by twenty-five foot room. Hard drives, scanners, printers, a few desks and chairs, book shelves, work tables and a huge mainframe computer occupied the rest of the space. The lighting was subdued and peaceful and soft jazz played through multiple speakers.

"Where do you want this?" I asked Stanley, referring to the hard drive.

He pointed. "Put it on that table over there."

I placed the hard drive on the table that Stanley had pointed to and started toward the door to get the second hard drive from the Pathfinder.

"Come with me to the car, Stanley. I need to get the other hard drive and you could use some fresh air and sunshine."

I could tell he wanted to protest but I was still his hero and all he said was, "Okay."

We walked to the front and I retrieved the other hard drive. Stanley was looking around as if he had not seen sunlight or smelled fresh air in some time.

"You need to get out more, Stanley."

"I know," he said sheepishly. "But there are so many viruses that I need solutions for."

"You can't save the computer world all by yourself Stanley."

"I know," he said, without much conviction. I could tell he was anxious to get back to his inner sanctum.

"Let's go back inside, Stanley, and I'll tell you why I am here."

Stanley darted in front of me and hurried back down the walkway to the rear of the house. I had never seen him move so fast. Once we were back inside his world, Stanley seemed to relax and take command of the situation.

"Now, Don," he said very business-like. "Tell me what you need."

"These hard drives belonged to a very bad man, Stanley," I began. "He hurt someone and then he disappeared. I have been hired to find him. I have not had much luck so far. These hard drives have been wiped clean. I know sometimes you can recover information that has been erased, and I want you to see what you can recover. I am looking for any clue that might tell me where he has gone. Understand?"

"You mean you're looking for Ronnie Fairchild and these are his hard drives."

It wasn't a question, it was a statement and I should have known that nothing escapes Stanley when it comes to the comings and goings of Mountain Center. The question that I could never answer was, how does someone who rarely leaves his house know so much about what goes on?

"So you know about that?"

"Of course."

"Do you think you can help me?"

"I don't know, Don, but I will do my best," Stanley said earnestly.

39

Mountain Center Country Club was not in town. The drive from Stanley's house would take twenty minutes. The sprawling and exclusive private club was situated in an underdeveloped area northeast of the city. For the avid golfer, the club offered an eighteen-hole championship course, a top-caliber par-three course, three putting greens, and two driving ranges. The club also offered tennis, platform tennis, croquet, swimming, skeet shooting, archery, racquetball, and a fitness center. A full-time masseuse, saunas, whirlpools, and steam baths were available to soothe aching muscles. There was a first-class restaurant with a chef who was a graduate of Johnson & Wales College in Providence, Rhode Island.

The club was for the well-to-do, at least by east Tennessee standards. Initiation fees were $50,000 in the form of a stock purchase. Annual membership was $12,000 per year plus another $3,600 in food allowance, billable whether you used it or not. Big Bob's father had sponsored my membership; no one would dare blackball a prospective member sponsored by B. Franklin Wilson. There were no female members, but there were a few black members. Wives of members had full privileges with the exception of golf (they could play only on ladies day or with a male member on other days) and the men's grill. The women did have their own grill (off limits to men) and their own pro shop, and men could not golf on ladies day.

Over the years I had taken advantage of almost all the club had to offer, with the exception of golf. There was something about the frustration of chasing a little white ball all over the countryside and trying to corral it in a round cup that I just did not get.

Besides, I liked sweaty games.

The cost was insignificant to me, but I had joined the club for a very dumb reason—to play racquetball during the winter. Still, it would have been cheaper to build my own racquetball court or to pay Moto to build one, but Moto did not have the room. Club rules stated that in any activity you could bring a guest only twice a month. Since the racquetball ball courts were not in high demand, the rule was not enforced for racquetball. Billy and I played racquetball two or three times a week in the winter and now Mary and I were also playing. Sometimes Big Bob joined Billy and me for a game of cutthroat. Big Bob had a membership, compliments of his father.

I drove though the iron gates at the club entrance and stopped at the guardhouse. Guards were on duty 24/7, and over the years I had gotten to know all the guards. Theirs was a sought-after job with good pay and benefits, and guards rarely quit. Once, a guard was fired for drinking on the job and another was fired for having a woman in the guardhouse.

"Hello, Jerome," I said to the middle-aged black man on duty.

"Good morning, Mr. Youngblood. I haven't seen you in a while."

"I don't come out this way much during the day, Jerome. How's the family?"

"Oh, they're good, Mr. Youngblood. And I hear there is a new lady in your life. Serious, everyone says," Jerome chuckled.

"Has Big Bob been running his mouth again?"

"I don't really recall," Jerome grinned, knowing full well that it was indeed Big Bob. "Word gets around."

"Especially in Mountain Center. See you later, Jerome."

I drove through the gate and along the winding tree-lined road and parked in the lot nearest the golf pro shop. I walked past one of the putting greens and up the few steps to the pro shop entrance. Large, glass double doors slid noiselessly open. The pro shop rivaled any expensive men's store. Not only did it have anything you could want in the way of golf and tennis ware but it was fully stocked in an exclusive line of men's clothing from suits and shirts right down to underwear. A full-time tailor was on duty. The Mountain Center Country Club pro shop was a classic, successful model of good marketing.

"Good morning, Mr. Youngblood," said a familiar looking young man from behind the counter near the cash register. His greeting surprised me. I visited the golf pro shop about as often as a total eclipse of the sun. I sneaked a quick peek at his name tag.

"Good morning, Bobby," I said. "How do you know me?"

"I'm Bobby Black, Doris Black's son. I've seen you at the diner and mom talks about you all the time."

"I thought you looked familiar. Say, congratulations on that golf scholarship to UT. Your mom is so proud she can't stand it."

Bobby beamed. "Thanks, Mr. Youngblood. Can I help you with something?"

"I'm looking for Tony."

"Believe it or not, he's on the west driving range."

"A little cold for practice, isn't it?"

"Not for Tony," Bobby said.

"Thanks, Bobby. Nice meeting you, good luck at UT."

"Thanks, Mr. Youngblood."

The west driving range was a half mile from the pro shop near the first tee of the par-three course. There were no other cars in the lot. A lone golfer near an empty golf cart teed up another ball and drove it far past the 250-yard marker. He glanced over his shoulder toward my car, gave a tiny wave, teed up another ball and hit it very nearly identical to the previous one.

I sat in the car and watched. I did not play golf but I did enjoy watching the major championships on TV, and I admired anyone who could play the game well. I was watching a pro at work. I watched another drive rocket off into the distance with a slight draw at the end, a thing of beauty. About 280 yards, I calculated.

Tony Price grew up in a rival town and had played basketball for a rival high school. I met Tony at a UT basketball camp in my junior year of high school and we had casually stayed in touch. Tony was a good basketball player but a great golfer. He won a scholarship to Wake Forest and then went on tour. A few years later Tony won the New Orleans Open and finished eighth on the money list. Endorsements followed and the money came rolling in. Tony asked me to handle his finances. He was one of my first private clients when I was just getting started, and I had been grateful that he had given me the opportunity.

When the Mountain Center Country Club's golf pro retired six years ago, the executive board contacted Tony and asked if he was interested. By this time Tony's golf career was past its peak, and he decided the time was right to say good-bye to the rigors of tour life and settle down. From time to time, Tony and I had dinner and on occasion played some tennis. He was a pro golfer, but an average tennis player.

Tony waved me out of the car and I walked toward the practice tee.

"Looking good. But don't you think it's a little cold to be hitting golf balls?"

"How are you, Don?"

"I'm good, Tony. And yourself?"

"I'm fine. And to answer your question, this is a perfect day for hitting golf balls . . . a little cold maybe, but no wind and no people. I rarely get time alone on the practice tee."

Tony teed up another ball and drove it beyond and to the right of the 250-yard marker. He turned back to me. "You've been in the news lately. I read about the shooting at the police station but the paper didn't give a lot of details. Rumor has it that you and Billy were involved in that."

"Don't believe everything you hear," I said, trying to deflect his comment. "For that matter, don't believe everything you read." Tony turned and hit another ball. "I was hoping I could ask you some questions pertaining to my investigation of Sarah Ann Fairchild's murder."

"You investigating that? Terrible thing," Tony said, putting his driver back into his golf bag. "Let's go sit in your SUV. I could use some warming up."

We walked to the Pathfinder, got in and I started up the engine.

"I saw you at the funeral but I didn't get a chance to talk to you," Tony began. "Huge crowd. How can I help you?"

"I understand that Sarah Ann and Ronnie played golf. I need you to tell me anything you can think of that might give me a clue to tracking down Ronnie."

"You think he killed her?" Tony asked wide-eyed.

"I do."

"Damn." He paused. "Okay. Well, at one time or another I gave lessons to Ronnie and Sarah Ann. Sarah Ann played in high school and was pretty good. She kept improving after I gave her lessons and won the Ladies Club Championship a couple of times. She routinely shot in the mid-to-high seventies from the ladies' tees. She didn't talk much and she seemed happy. Ronnie was about your size and very athletic and in great shape. He had never played golf and that was great from my standpoint because I could build his game from the ground up. I think he originally took lessons to please Sarah Ann, but he was soon hooked and made great strides in a short time. I gave him lessons three times a week and took him out on the course to play eighteen once a week, and he practiced a lot. In a year, he was scoring as well as Sarah Ann and they played together a couple of times a week."

"What did you and Ronnie talk about during all this time?"

"Golf mostly. Small talk. You know, weather, how is work, and such. Toward the end of my giving him lessons he did talk about playing some of the great courses like Augusta National, Pebble Beach, and St. Andrews, but all golfers talk about that. And he did say he was going to Ireland someday and play the links courses. I know he watched a lot of golf on TV after he got hooked on the game. We used to talk on Monday mornings about the latest tournament."

"When he talked about Ireland and St. Andrew's did he talk about taking Sarah Ann?"

"Now that you mention it, no. I remember thinking about that but it wasn't my place to ask, and Ronnie never pretended that we were friends. I was just someone he had hired to give him golf lessons. I just assumed he might be going with some of the guys from the club. Some of the club members organize trips to Ireland or Scotland every now and then."

"Anything else you can think of?"

"Not really."

"Okay, Tony. Thanks. If you think of anything else, give me a call."

"Will do. I hope you find the son of a bitch. I really liked Sarah Ann," he said, shutting the door firmly as he got out.

He was walking back to the practice tee when another thought hit me. I slid down the window. "Hey, Tony." He stopped and turned around. "Did Ronnie store his clubs here?"

"Sure."

"Can you find out if they are still here?"

"Sure. I'll check later and give you a call."

I nodded and Tony continued to the practice tee and pulled a long iron out of his bag. I watched as he kicked some balls around the tee and then began pounding long, low rockets toward the 250-yard marker. There was anger in his swing. I watched a few more swings and then I slowly drove back toward the main gate. Ireland or Scotland, I thought. Were they real clues or idle talk?

40

Three days later I was hoping for snow, but the thermometer refused to dip below thirty-eight degrees and my imagined snow was replaced by a bone-chilling rain. I was at my desk looking out the picture window from my second-story perch onto Main Street, which was deserted except for a lone familiar figure walking toward my building from a black Lincoln Town Car parked across the street. Roy Husky wore a raincoat fully buttoned with the collar pulled up and a Dick Tracy-style hat pulled low. He carried a Dunkin' Donuts bag. Ever since the capture of Teddy Earl Elroy, Roy would show up about once a week with coffee and bagels and we would sit and talk. Sometimes about the case and other times about sports or anything that came to mind.

I waited. I was alone with Jake, who was snoozing on his bed. Billy had been called out to take pictures of an accident. He was often called out when the weather was bad. Billy usually joined us but he didn't like Dunkin' Donuts coffee, so Roy never brought him any. I heard the outer door open and shut. Jake raised his head, sniffed, and went back to snoozing, his dog radar fully functional.

Roy walked in.

"Great watchdog you have there," he smiled.

"If he didn't know you, he would tear you limb from limb," I said. "You look more like a private detective than I do in that getup. Nice hat."

Roy ignored me, tossed the hat and coat on a nearby chair, and dove into the Dunkin' Donuts bag. Two medium coffees, mine with cream and sugar, a toasted everything-bagel for Roy and a toasted poppyseed bagel for me. Both bagels had ample cream cheese. Oh, joy. We began devouring the bounty.

"Thanks," I said.

"Don't mention it. Anything new?"

"Nothing concrete, but I am working on a few angles. I need to go to the mansion later today and look around if it is okay with Fleet."

"Don't see why not. I'll see him later this morning. I'll call you sometime after lunch."

We sat in silence for a few minutes and ate the bagels and drank the coffee and watched the rain. Jake whimpered and let out a tiny bark. His back legs jerked.

"What's with him?" Roy asked.

"Dog dreams. Probably has a rabbit on the run."

More silence, more bites, more sips.

"Heard anything from your computer guy?"

"Not yet. I can't push Stanley. He is too busy protecting the world against evil hackers. Which reminds me, did Ronnie have an Internet account?"

"Sure. We all have AOL accounts."

"Would you happen to know his user name?"

"It was RFairchild1. Fleet signed us all up with individual accounts. Fleet is JFleet1, Sarah Ann was SAFairchild1 and I am RRHusky1. What are you thinking?"

"Just brainstorming. If it comes to anything, I'll let you know. What's the other R stand for?"

"None of your business," Roy said sharply. Touchy.

Roy stayed a few more minutes. We talked a little NFL football and made our predictions on who would make it to the Super Bowl. I liked the Titans and the Redskins. Roy liked the Colts and the Redskins. The Redskins would play the Bucs on Saturday for the NFC title and the Titans would play the Colts on Sunday for the AFC title. Roy left the office and I went online to check the market and play a little solitaire.

I met Roy at the Fleet mansion that afternoon. Fleet had given me full access to his three-story home. I was to snoop to my heart's content. Anything was permitted in tracking down the alias Ronnie Fairchild.

Ronnie and Sarah Ann had adjoining separate bedrooms. I didn't bother to ask Roy why. *The rich.* I went to hers first and spent a half an hour rummaging around. Nothing. Then I went to Ronnie's bedroom. Something under the nightstand on the right side of the bed caught my eye. I picked it up and slipped it into a satchel I had brought with me. I spent a few more minutes in Ronnie's bedroom without finding anything else.

MARY AND I WERE CURLED UP in bed later that evening. I was reading *Golfing in Ireland* by Rob Armstrong, a book published by Pelican Publishing Company in Gretna, Louisiana. I really wasn't interested in golf in Ireland but apparently Ronnie Fairchild was. I was hoping the book from Ronnie's bedside nightstand would yield a new path to follow. In the here and now, all I was looking at were dead ends. Certain courses in the book like Lahinch and Ballybunion had been highlighted in yellow. I found it hard to comprehend that Ronnie Fairchild would plan to kill his wife and then go on a golfing trip. Still, he was a stone-cold killer, a probable sociopath, and therefore unpredictable. And it was a clue of sorts and I had very few at this point.

Mary turned off the light on her nightstand, rolled toward me, kissed me, and rolled back over. "Good night, my love," she whispered.

Something electrical swept through my body. "Good night," I replied.

Five minutes later my light was off and I was sound asleep, dreaming of running on a beach with a beautiful blond goddess and still feeling an unexplained sensation running through my body.

THE NEXT MORNING, returning from breakfast at the diner, I opened the office door to discover Billy reviewing photos of the accident he had photographed the day before. Not pretty. Jake got up and wandered over to snuggle against my leg and solicited a few rubs and scratches. With his nose pointed toward the ceiling, I scratched under his chin. He would have stayed that way all day.

"Enough," I finally said to him, and he wandered back into my office and plopped down on his dog bed. The bed had his name on it, just in case he forgot who he was.

"How can you continue to do that?" I asked Billy. "It's not as if you really need the money."

"It's part of what I do. I'm good at it and I do not allow myself to get emotionally involved. People depend on me to do it. Death is not the end, Blood, it is the beginning."

Billy sometimes thought he was a Cherokee Confucius. I headed for my desk, picked up the phone and called Stanley. It rang a long time.

"Hello!" said what seemed to be an annoyed voice.

"Hello, Stanley."

"Oh, hello, Don. I've been trying to figure out a fix to a new virus and I haven't really had time to look at those hard drives." Stanley obviously knew why I was calling and was taking the offensive.

"Stanley, this is important. There will always be new viruses and a few hours are not going to make a difference. I am coming over tonight. I need to find out if the AOL software is still on the office hard drive. Should I pick up a pizza from Best Italian?"

Stanley perked up. He was a sucker for our infamous local pizza house. "That sounds real good, Don. Half pepperoni and half chicken and pesto, okay?"

"You got it, Stanley. What time?"

There was a pause. "Six-thirty," Stanley said. "Got to go, Don, bye." Stanley hung up leaving me staring into my receiver.

I smiled. Pizza bribery always worked with Stanley.

"THIS IS SO GOOD," Stanley said as he started on another piece of pizza. "I'm going to save the rest for tomorrow night."

I had finished two large slices and my salad and washed them down with two bottles of Michelob Amber Bock. Stanley had finished his salad and was working on his third piece of pizza and drinking Diet Coke. Stanley did not drink alcohol. He said it clouded his creativity.

"No problem," I said. "I'm done."

"I had a chance to look at those hard drives," Stanley said mumbling between chews. "The home one is perfectly clean. Nothing recoverable. I used a new program that I developed that I call Resurrection. I found a few fragments but nothing I could piece together. It is almost as if the hard drive had been removed and replaced with a new one. The office one has some business files on it but nothing I would call a clue. It does, however, still have the AOL software and the User ID was saved but not the password."

"That's good news. It means I can look at his address book and favorite places."

"I have it hooked up to that Compaq monitor over in the corner. See what you can come up with. I'll get back to work."

I booted up the machine and then clicked the AOL icon and the AOL sign on screen appeared. I pulled down the address book and scanned through it. There were lots of names but none that I recognized. I pulled down favorite places and found airlines, hotels chains, sports web sites and other miscellaneous sites that meant nothing to me. I did notice Orbitz was on the lists. That was one site I would like to have a look at.

I started trying passwords. I tried *Joey* and *Avanti* and every combination of Joey Avanti I could think of. I didn't think he would be stupid enough to use his old name but I had to rule it out. Then I tried every combination of every New York sports team I could think of. Then I just sat and stared at the screen trying to come up with another angle. Scott Glass told me that a confidential FBI study showed that people rarely use random passwords for anything. It is always something they associate with.

I was sifting through the back of my mind for all the information that I had amassed on Ronnie Fairchild when something Roy said popped to the surface. I looked at my watch. 8:30.

I dialed Roy's beeper. A few minutes later my cell phone rang.

"Hope I didn't interrupt anything," I said.

"A little later on maybe, but not yet," he said.

"Good to hear. A quick question. You said that Ronnie and Sarah Ann had a boat at the lake. What was the name of the boat?"

"What's a boat name got to do with anything?"

"I am trying to crack Ronnie's AOL password and I'm grasping at straws."

"Let me think. Something to do with golf." There was a pause on the other line. I stayed quiet. "Birdie two, that's it," Roy said. "The number 2, not spelled out."

"Hang on." I typed in Birdie2. "Bingo," I said. "Thanks. Now go have some fun."

I signed on as Ronnie Fairchild and went immediately to Orbitz. I signed in using Ronnie's AOL e-mail address and Birdie2 and was welcomed as Ronnie Fairchild. I clicked My Stuff and another screen appeared showing current reservations, past trips and canceled trips. Nothing. Wiped clean.

I went to Marriott and accessed his honored guest account. Ronnie's last stay at a Marriott Hotel was Marco Island, Florida, in April of 2003,

probably a vacation with Sarah Ann. I was at another dead end. *Think,
Youngblood.*

I looked at my watch. 9:30. I looked at Stanley. He was alternately
pecking away on two keyboards no doubt finding the key to eradicating
the latest virus. It was going to be a long night. I swiveled in my chair
and looked around the office and found what I was looking for. The
Gevalia coffee maker and canister I had given Stanley were on a small
table next to a mini-fridge. I opened the canister. It was half full. Coffee
filters and bottled water were beneath the table. I checked the fridge.
Stanley had half-and-half. My hero.

"I'm going to make some coffee, Stanley. Do you want some?"

"Sounds great, Don. Thank you," Stanley said, not missing a beat at
the keyboards.

While I waited for the process to complete, I called Mary on our
condo phone.

"Hello, my love," she answered. *Ain't caller ID just grand?*

"Hello, yourself. I'm going to be late. I'm with Stanley in the land of
Oz trying to come up with another lead on Ronnie Fairchild."

"Any luck?"

"Not yet. Don't wait up."

"I'm in bed already. Reading and starting to fade. By the way, all I
have on is one of your T-shirts."

"Talk like that might force me to wake you up in the middle of the
night," I teased.

"Be my guest, big boy," Mary said in a Marilyn Monroe voice.
"Bye."

I poured mugs of black coffee for Stanley and me. I added half-and-
half and sugar to both and went and sat beside Stanley.

"Here, Stanley. Take a break."

Stanley turned away from his keyboard, picked up the mug and
took a sip.

"You make the best coffee Don."

"Have you noticed," I asked, "that coffee usually tastes better when someone else makes it?"

"Maybe so, but you still make good coffee."

"When do you usually go to bed, Stanley?"

"Around midnight," he responded casually. He gestured around the room. "This is my life. In a way, I am just like you, a private investigator. You investigate people and I investigate viruses."

"Yeah, but I have a life outside work, Stanley. You work too hard and don't have enough fun."

"That's where you're wrong, Don. I am having fun. I love what I am doing. I find it exciting and challenging. And I know what I am doing is important."

Stanley was getting fired up.

"I stand corrected," I said. "And I do know what you are doing is important."

STANLEY FINISHED HIS COFFEE and turned back to his keyboard. I went back to my workstation and stared at the Orbitz screen. If Ronnie left the country he did so under another identity. If he was as smart as Carlo Vincente said he was, he had one or two identities ready to go. Then a wild idea hit me.

Using my cell phone, I called Carlo Vincente on his private number. It rang a few times, then I heard a click and it rang again. Call forwarding.

"Hello," said a female voice.

"Donald Youngblood for Carlo Vincente, please," I said in my most cultured non-Southern tone.

"Mr. Vincente does not want to be disturbed, Mr. Youngblood."

I heard a mumble on the other end and then Carlo Vincente was on the phone. "Mr. Youngblood, for you anytime. What can I do for you this fine evening?"

Vincente sounded in a good mood. I had a vision of a scantily clad young playmate, a bedroom with a fire going in the hearth, a bottle of champagne, and two half-filled glasses.

"Sorry to call so late. I hope I am not interrupting anything."

"Nothing that cannot wait a few more minutes." I heard a giggle in the background. "You have a question or something to tell me?"

"A question. What was Frankie's brother's last name?"

"Romano. Why?"

"Did he look anything like Joey?"

"Similar, yes. You know, all we Italians look alike," Vincente chuckled. He paused. "Ah, I see, very smart. You think maybe Joey used Eddie's ID. Those driver's license photos are never very good. He might get away with it."

"Or he could have altered it," I said. "All you need is a Polaroid camera, an Exacto knife, and a laminator."

"Good point."

"Did Eddie carry a passport when he traveled inside the U.S.?"

"I do not know, but I can ask Frankie. I'll get back to you."

FOR THE TIME BEING I had used up my favors with Scott Glass. I needed to get Stanley to do some harmless hacking. I knew Stanley would not want to do it. Before he went to work for Mike Brown, Stanley hacked into every system imaginable, including some highly classified government sites. He was never malicious, never downloaded or printed anything, and never shared his secrets. He did it for fun and the challenge and for a few other reasons that I am sure only a clinical psychologist could explain. But now Stanley was on the other side. It would be like trying to get a reformed smoker to sit in the smoking section. I walked over to Stanley's workstation and sat down.

"Stanley, I need a favor."

"Sure, Don, what is it?"

"I need for you to do some innocent hacking." Stanley's eyes went wide. I thought he went a little pale.

"You know I can't do that, Don. It's not right. I don't do that any-more."

"Look, Stanley, I am trying to catch a killer and I need your help. I'm not asking you to do any damage, just look at some records."

"What kind of records?"

"Airline records."

"Airline records?" Stanley paused. "Fine, tell me what you need."

That caught me by surprise but I tried not to show it. I had expected more resistance, so I moved quickly before he had a chance to change his mind.

"Okay, starting with October fourth, look for a passenger named Eddie or Edward Romano flying internationally from the United States. If you find anything, I need to know if he paid by cash or a credit card. I'm sure it would be cash but I just need it confirmed. If you need to narrow your search, try Ireland and England first."

"What airlines?"

"Try Delta first and then anyone who flies to Ireland or England."

"This will take a while and I do not like to be watched," Stanley said, turning back to his console and keyboard.

I went back to my workstation. The Orbitz screen was still active. I downloaded and printed a list of airport codes. Then I began plugging in U.S. cities in the eastern region and cities in Ireland to see which airlines serviced those areas.

"Delta is the only airline that flies nonstop out of Atlanta," I said to Stanley.

"Right."

"No nonstops out of Dulles or Washington Reagan."

"Okay," Stanley said. He was pecking away on his keyboard and scrolling down screen after screen.

I was working on the premise that Joey Avanti would not fly out of New York for fear of being recognized. Why he had been at LaGuardia Airport in the first place was still a question I didn't have an answer to.

It was a loose end that I wanted to tie up. Suddenly I had a disturbing thought. Did Carlo Vincente know Joey was in the New York area? Did they have something going on between them? Maybe Carlo tipped Joey that he had been spotted and Joey got rid of Eddie. My head was spinning. I had to be careful about what I told Carlo Vincente. I could be a pawn in a deadly game. I was beginning to develop a headache. Maybe I was being paranoid. I turned my attention back to the premise I was working on and then an idea struck. I keyed in BOS to SNN, plugged in a bogus date and found a nonstop flight on Aer Lingus from Boston to Shannon, Ireland.

"I'm finished with Delta," Stanley said. "No luck."

"Try Aer Lingus out of Boston."

"That's going to take a while. You might as well go home and get some sleep. Call me in the morning."

"Why would Aer Lingus take longer than Delta?"

"Delta is a customer of SJ Anti-Virus so I have top access to all their computers. Aer Lingus is not a customer of ours. The screens that I will be looking for are not high-security areas so I should eventually get in but it might take a few hours. There is nothing else you can do here, Don, so go home."

Stanley was basically a loner and had obviously had enough of my companionship for one night, so I took his advice and left Oz with the wizard pecking away at his keyboard.

I MOVED QUIETLY through the front door of 5300 and closed it slowly behind me. I set the security alarm that I had installed soon after Teddy Earl Elroy tried to kill us, and tiptoed toward the bedroom. A light was on but Mary was sleeping soundly, propped up in bed with a book on her chest. I gently lifted the book and placed it on the nightstand and removed one of the pillows from beneath her head. She rolled over and smiled with her eyes half open.

"Thank you," she said.

I kissed her cheek. "Go back to sleep," I said as I switched her light off. "We'll talk in the morning."

"Um," she cooed. "Good night, my love."

I slipped into my side of the bed, the left side. *Good night, my love* echoed in my head. I tried to recall the first time Mary had said those words to me as we turned out the lights to go to sleep for the night. Ever since, those were always her last words to me at evening's end. *Good night, my love.* I smiled and drifted off.

41

The next day I visited Joseph Fleet. He looked marginally better than at the funeral, but he had little to say that helped me. He wasn't aware of any talk between Ronnie and Sarah Ann about visiting Ireland or Scotland. He recalled that Ronnie had mentioned taking Sarah Ann to South America, where Ronnie said he knew people, but Sarah Ann had been uninterested.

"Why was Ronnie up north the day before he and Sarah Ann disappeared?" I asked.

"Business. I sent him there to nail down a parts contract with Sikorsky," Fleet said, his anger rising. "We did a conference call that day and he flew home that night. He wasn't all that happy about going, I can tell you that. Now I think I understand why."

"Why did he fly out of Knoxville?"

"Ronnie hated to fly. When he flew he always looked for direct flights. There is a direct flight out of Knoxville to LaGuardia but not from Tri-Cities to LaGuardia. He would drive to Nashville to avoid making connections."

Fleet's explanation made sense and I could tell he blamed himself for Sarah Ann's death. Had he not sent Ronnie to Connecticut, Sarah Ann might still be alive. That had to hurt.

"Thanks for your time," I said as I rose to leave. "And do not blame yourself for what happened to Sarah Ann. You didn't kill her. Someone else did."

Joseph Fleet started to say something but it died in his throat. He turned back to the fire and seemed to slump a bit. I left the big man alone with his private torment.

MEANWHILE, I HAD LEARNED from Carlo Vincente that Eddie Romano did have a passport, which I was betting Joey Avanti now had. And then Stanley Johns hit paydirt. He called to ask me to drop by, and when I got there he handed me a print-out.

"An Edward Romano took an Aer Lingus flight out of Boston to Shannon, Ireland, on November 3." Stanley said. "He flew into Boston from Rutland, Vermont. He paid cash for a round-trip ticket and was supposed to return on November 17, but there is no record that he made the flight."

"That's got to be our boy, Stanley. You did real well."

"I searched every flight out of Ireland after he arrived, up to and including yesterday. If he left Ireland, he did not use the name Edward Romano."

"Good work, Stanley. That really helps."

Stanley beamed.

THE FOLLOWING MORNING I was in the office having coffee and bagels with Roy and Billy. Roy and I were enjoying our Dunkin' Donuts coffee and Billy was drinking his own special brew that resembled heated cough syrup. I brought them both up to date on my brilliant detective work. If they were impressed, they were practicing restraint.

"So now what?" Roy asked.

"I guess I am going to Ireland," I said.

"Not alone you're not," Billy said. The way he said it let me know there was no arguing.

"Fine. Which one of you wants to go with me?"

Roy and Billy looked at each other. "I'll go," Roy said. Billy nodded.

"Fine," I said. "I'll make the reservations. I want to leave tomorrow. You okay with that?"

"As far as Mr. Fleet is concerned and as long as I am with you tracking Ronnie, I could leave right now," Roy said. "Mr. Fleet's private jet can take us to New York to hook up with a commercial flight if you want."

"Well, if you can do that," I said, "we might as well go out of Boston. We would need to be there around six o'clock tomorrow night."

"I'll set it up and give you a call. Plan on me picking you up. I'll drive and leave the car in the hangar."

The rich. Must be nice.

"You two be careful," Billy growled.

"Relax, Chief," I said. "No way Fairchild is still in Ireland. The best I can hope for is to pick up his trail."

"Maybe," was Billy's reply.

Maybe, indeed. Having Roy Husky as backup was a comforting thought.

I SPENT THE REST OF THE DAY planning the trip. I even called Liam McSwain for some tips. As darkness fell outside my office window, street lamps lit the recently restored Mountain Center downtown district. Trees had been planted, a parking garage built, and store fronts renovated. Businesses that had fled to shopping centers on the outskirts of town were moving back thanks to some nice incentives from local government. Downtown was alive again and attracting people. I found that comforting, as if someone had turned back the clock to my childhood. Jake snoozed in the corner as I put the finishing touches on two round trip-tickets from Boston to Shannon, Ireland. It was a long way to go on a wild goose chase, but it was the only lead I had.

Then I went home and faced Mary.

"Ireland!"

"Uh-huh," I grunted nonchalantly.

Mary and I were sitting opposite each other at the kitchen bar on bar height swivel chairs. I was drinking an Amber Bock and Mary was having her usual glass of wine—or two. I had just informed her of my impending trip and the announcement had been received like the prediction of an eighteen-inch snowstorm.

"Can I come?"

"No."

"Why not?"

"It is a business trip, not a pleasure trip."

She made an indistinguishable noise that I took to mean she was not happy with my answer. I was beginning to feel married. It was an uncomfortable feeling I was not used to. I plowed on.

"Do I ask you to take me to work and ride around in your squad car?"

"I get the point." Mary said with a glare. "That would probably be okay with Big Bob, though." She smiled. "Relax, I understand. Okay?"

"Okay."

Her send-off the next morning made me wonder if I shouldn't travel more often if it earned that treatment.

42

R oy and I were booked on an 8:10 PM Aer Lingus flight that arrived at 7:00 AM the next day, taking into account the five-hour time difference. So we needed to be at Boston Logan by six and Roy graced the doorway to my office around noon. He stood there with a smirk on his face wearing a white turtleneck, an obviously expensive dark blue blazer, charcoal gray slacks, and black dress boots. He was almost posing.

I laughed. "You clean up pretty good."

"You, too. Interesting we both chose turtlenecks and blazers," Roy said.

I was wearing a dark green turtleneck, a Brooks Brothers camel's hair blazer, Oleg Cansini dark brown wool slacks, and dark brown Florsheim dress boots with belt to match. I had dressed to suit a private jet, I guess.

When we got to Fleet's hangar at Tri-Cities Airport, a Lear Jet 60 sat on the tarmac outside and a man in a shirt, tie, and pilot's cap was inspecting the gleaming aircraft. It looked brand-new. Fleet Industries was emblazoned on the tail in maroon lettering. The outboard edges of the wings were tipped up at almost a ninety-degree angle, a beautiful bird.

Roy popped the trunk on the black Lincoln Town Car and we retrieved our bags—the person who invented wheels for luggage should get a Nobel Prize. We stopped at the bottom of the pull-down stairs. "Leave your bag here," Roy said. "Jim will store it in the cargo hold."

The pilot, Jim Doak, came over to greet us and Roy introduced me. Then we climbed the stairs and entered the Lear Jet. It smelled of new leather and privilege. There were four large, light gray leather chairs, a couch that would seat two, several small tables, and lots of blond wood trim. We chose the first section of seats and sat facing each other across a small dining-height table.

"You didn't bring your laptop?" Roy asked

"I can do without e-mail for a week," I said. "Anyone who needs to know has been alerted that I will be out of the country."

"You packing?"

"No, are you?"

"No. What'll we do if things get dicey?"

"I know an Irish cop in Knoxville. He said to call him if we got in a jam and he could help us out."

"Handy," Roy said.

The twin engines on either side of the fuselage came to life. As we taxied, Doak's voice came over the intercom and asked us to buckle up as we had been cleared for takeoff. The high-pitched rev of the jets preceded the thrust I felt as my back was pinned against my seat, and we began hurtling down the runway. Seconds later we gently lifted off and I watched the ground diminish as we steadily climbed. About twenty minutes later, we heard from Doak again, telling us we were cruising at forty-one thousand feet and five hundred miles per hour and could move about the cabin.

"Want a drink?" Roy asked.

"Too early for me."

"Look around if you want. She's quite a bird."

I unbuckled and walked to the rear where I found the door to the lavatory and a small galley outfitted with a fridge, microwave oven, coffee maker, plates, glasses, and a wide variety of beverages. The lavatory was compact but well-appointed, much nicer than a commercial airliner. It all gave a whole new meaning to the term going first class.

An hour and a half later we landed at Hanscom Field just north of Boston. Roy had arranged for a limo to meet us and we were quickly on our way to Boston's Logan International Airport. The ride to Logan was uneventful and by five o'clock we had checked luggage, cleared security, and were in the Aer Lingus concourse. I called and left a message for Mary.

"Want something to eat?" Roy asked.

"No, let's wait. We'll get dinner on the plane and Aer Lingus has a reputation for pretty good food."

Roy nodded. We settled into an empty waiting area to read and wait for our flight to be called. I had brought *The Thin Man* to reread; Roy had the *Boston Globe*.

Mary called around seven thirty.

"I miss you already," she said.

"Absence makes the heart grow fonder," I said.

"Or out of sight, out of mind."

"You could never be out of my mind."

"How sweet. Now tell me about your flight up to Boston."

Fueled by time to kill and enjoying talking to her, I gave a detailed account of our flight, our pilot, and the Fleet Industries Lear Jet. Mary listened and asked questions in the right places. She recounted a boring day on the Mountain Center police force and gave me an update on Jake the dog, whom she had taken to the gym to play with Karate. We said good-bye when the flight was called.

The in-flight meal turned out to be very good—chicken cordon bleu, new potatoes, mixed veggies, rolls, wine, and dessert. The flight was only two-thirds full. After dinner, the cabin lights were turned off and a movie started that I did not want to see, so I settled in with my book. Nick Charles getting shot was the last thing I remembered before waking up as we started descending toward Shannon airport.

43

I had been to Ireland once before. At the end of my junior year in college, Scott Glass and I had a grand time hitchhiking around the Emerald Isle, from hostel to hostel and bar to bar. The Shannon airport had built a new terminal since then, but it was still a small airport considering the international traffic it hosted. We went through customs, retrieved our luggage, purchased international cell phones, and headed for the Hertz counter. We rented two cars so we could split up later and cover twice the ground.

Within an hour we were on route N18 to Ennis, a medium-sized town about halfway to our destination of Doolin, a small town on the west coast in County Clare. I was driving a silver Toyota Corolla and Roy was following in a maroon version of the same model. In Ireland these were full-size cars. Driving on the left side of the road was quite a challenge. Keeping alert was an even greater challenge. Ireland time was eight in the morning, five hours ahead of Eastern Standard Time. I was tired but alert thanks to an adrenaline rush brought on by the thrill of the hunt. I knew it would be tough staying awake the first day, but necessary to reset our internal clocks.

In Ennis we stopped for breakfast in a quaint little restaurant called The Hen's Nest.

We had the full Irish breakfast but skipped the blood pudding. By ten o'clock we were on the road again. We took N85 to Ennistymon. The roads narrowed as we inched closer to the coast. Irish roads were not built for speed. Irish speed limits are in kilometers and on the good roads are the equivalent of fifty-five to sixty miles per hour. The Irish definition of a major highway is a two-lane road, called a single carriageway, with a painted dividing line in the center. These types of roads made up no more than twenty per cent of the Irish road system. Some four-lane highways, called dual carriageways, could be found around the major cities but there were very few of them. Many secondary roads are so narrow that when cars meet both have to slow down and use part of the dirt shoulder to pass. Meeting a bus or truck has made many a foreigner give up driving in Ireland. Stone walls are so close to some secondary roads that broken passenger-side mirrors are a common occurrence in Irish rental cars.

Our final destination was a cottage in Doolin that I had booked on-line. I had chosen Doolin because it was close to the town of Lahinch, which contained one of the most revered golf courses in the Republic of Ireland. The cottage was a small, single-floor house consisting of two bedrooms, one bath, a living room, and a kitchen. The web site said that the cottage was only thirty-seven miles from the Shannon airport. It was the longest thirty-seven miles I had ever driven.

The proprietor, Anne Frawley, greeted us in the parking lot as we pulled in. Anne was a slender woman with short dark hair. "You're Mr. Youngblood, are you? Welcome to Doolin. The Geraldine cottage is ready for you."

"This is my associate, Roy Husky," I said. "And please call me Don."

"Don it is. Hello, Mr. Husky."

"Roy," said Roy.

"Okay, then, we are all on a first-name basis. Please call me Anne. This is your cottage over here, gentlemen. Come with me and I'll show you the particulars."

In her beautiful Irish lilt, she gave instructions on how to use the stove, oven, microwave, toaster, coffee maker, dishwasher, washer and dryer, and, most important, the shower. When she was finished, we followed her outside and she pointed out a graveled parking area on the right side of the cottage.

"Would you like for me to take care of the bill now?" I asked.

"Heavens no. Nobody has stiffed me yet. We'll settle up before you leave. If you want to use the phone, come to the main house and we will put it on your bill."

"Thanks, but we picked up cell phones at the airport."

"That's grand, then. Just let me know if you need anything."

WE UNPACKED AND got situated in our bedrooms and and changed into less dressy clothes. Around noon I made coffee. We were starting to fade. The weather was overcast and misty with the temperature hovering around fifty degrees. There was a stiff breeze. A *soft day,* as the locals would say.

"My ass is dragging," Roy said. We had an Ireland road map spread out on the kitchen table. I had purchased three, one for each car and one for the house.

"We need to occupy the rest of our day," I said, trying to stifle a yawn. "I think I will take a run over to the golf course at Lahinch. If Ronnie came over to play golf, he would gone there. Why don't we make a grocery list and you can go shopping?"

"Sounds like a plan," Roy said. "If I sit around here, I'll fall asleep."

We figured we didn't need much because we planned to eat our meals out. But we decided we needed cereal, muffins, toast, juice, and coffee. Then we added cold cuts and bread in case we wanted a sandwich. And cheese, crackers, beer, and wine in case we wanted to have a cocktail hour before dinner. By the time we finished, the list was significant.

Outside the breeze had freshened. I pulled my baseball cap down snugly on my head. Roy was hatless and his thick salt and pepper hair was being rearranged by the wind. Anne Frawley came out of one of the larger cottages. I called to her.

"Roy needs directions to a supermarket and I need directions to the golf course at Lahinch."

Anne turned to Roy. He had the driver's side door to the car opened and looked anxious to get in out of the wind. "Go back the way you came in and take N85 back into Ennis. When you get to the roundabout for

N18, take your first right and go down that road and you will see a large supermarket on your right. You can't miss it."

"Thanks," Roy said. "I'll find it. I'll see you back here later," he said, looking at me. "I'm going to take my time. I'll plan to be back here around five."

"Now," Anne said, "you want the golf course at Lahinch. Go right out of the drive way and left at the first intersection. The road is a little narrow but it's a short cut with no traffic at all. Follow that road until it ends and then go left. The golf course is a few kilometers down the road on the right. You can't miss it."

"Thanks."

"You are going to play some golf, are you? A little brisk for that I should think."

"No golf today," I said. "I just wanted to see the course."

I followed Anne's directions and took a left at the first intersection. The road was indeed narrow and also rough. I felt like I was in somebody's driveway. Free-roaming sheep grazing near the road paid no attention to me. A dog lying in his driveway chased my car. I bumped along and crested the hill and started down the other side. In the distance I could see the sea and the quaint little town of Lahinch. The road became smoother and wider as I descended the hill and came to a T intersection. I turned left onto a wider road. About a half mile down I was paralleling one of the fairways of the golf course. At the end of the fairway was a green. Further beyond were buildings and then a sign that read Lahinch Golf Club. I turned right into a parking lot that surrounded a putting green. I got out of my car and took a breath of fresh Irish air. The wind was making my jacket dance.

I walked up the stairs that led to a clubhouse on the left and a pro shop on the right. A tall man with white hair and a white mustache came out of the pro shop. He had on a Lahinch jacket and cap. Possibly an employee, I thought. "Excuse me, sir." I said. "Could you tell me who to see about tee times?"

"Certainly, sir," he answered. "You can see me. Follow me. Let's get out of this wind."

I followed him into the clubhouse to a large table bearing a lamp, large ledger, scorecards, and brochures.

"Have a seat," he said, opening the ledger. "Now, when would you like to play?"

"I did not come for a tee time. I wanted to ask you a few questions. I am looking for someone who might have played here in the first couple of weeks of November. This man," I said as I slid a picture of Joey Avanti across the table.

"Why are you looking for this man?" my host asked cautiously. He had a stern and serious look on his face.

I removed my private investigator's license from my inside jacket pocket and slid it toward him. "He is a fugitive from justice and I have been hired to find him."

He picked up my license, looked at it, and then at me, and handed it back. He sat silently as if trying to decide whether to talk to me.

"Mind if I ask what he did?"

"Killed his wife," I said straightforwardly. "Her father has hired me to find him."

"Oh, dear," he said. "Well, of course I'll try to help. Do you want to take a look at the book?" He turned it around and slid it toward me.

"Thanks. That would be helpful."

He got up and came around the table and pulled up a chair beside me. He thumbed back through the book to November.

"Here we go. November starts here. My name is James, Mr. Young-blood. I'll be back in a few minutes."

The tee times in November started at nine in the morning in ten-minute intervals and ended at three in the afternoon. Only last names were listed with two, three, or four golfers per tee time. I looked with no success for Romano, Avanti or Fairchild. I looked for any other recognizable name. Nothing popped out.

There were notations in the margins with names and numbers. I needed to find out what those meant. James returned a few minute later carrying a mug.

"Would you like a cup of tea?" he asked.

"No thanks. What are these notations in the margins?"

James leaned over my shoulder. "Probably players trying to be worked in. I don't keep the book ordinarily. Mary Kathryn is our regular scheduler. She is off on holiday for a few days. Back day after tomorrow, I think. Maybe you should come back and talk to her. She might remember your man."

"Thanks, maybe I will."

I said good-bye to James and went back outside past the first tee towards the stairs. I stopped and looked up the first fairway, an uphill par four. In the distance I saw the flag on the first green bending in the wind. You would have to be crazy to play on a day like this, I thought. I went down the stairs to the warmth of my rental car. I sat there a few minutes thinking how nice it would be just to lay my head back and grab a few winks. I was fighting a battle with fatigue, but I was determined to stay awake until nine o'clock.

I drove into Lahinch and parked in a lot near the beach. In Ireland, parking lots are called car parks. For the next three hours I walked around the town going in and out of shops and exchanging small talk with locals. In a jewelry shop I purchased a beautiful sterling silver Celtic cross on a sterling silver chain. On each tip of the cross were small but exquisite, emeralds. The cross was the most expensive gift I had ever purchased for anyone and yet I never gave that a second thought. Around four o'clock I had a Harp on draft at Old Tom Frawley's Pub and chatted with more locals. I left the pub as it was getting dark and retaced my route to Doolin. I was just putting the key in the cottage door when Roy pulled in.

We carried the goods into the kitchen. The temperature outside was dropping and the wind was picking up. Inside it was cool and damp. I decided to build a fire. The Irish do not burn wood in fireplaces because of the scarcity of trees. Instead they burn peat, which closely resembles dried manure. There were fire starter sticks, a small jar of kerosene, and a bucket of peat bricks beside the fireplace, but I took the easy way and used a fire log Roy had purchased at the market. I would add peat later. We put the groceries away and then I prepared a plate of cheese and crackers that we took to the living room with a couple of beers. I put the plate on a small table between two chairs in front of the fireplace. We sat down with sighs too deep for words.

"Nice preparation," Roy said.

"I aim to please."

We ate and drank in silence. I added peat to the fire and in no time the chill had left the room and we were enjoying the warmth and watching the flames dance.

"Want to go out?" I asked.

"I don't even want to move," Roy said.

"Same here. Why don't I grill a couple of turkey and swiss sandwiches and fix some of those oven fries and we'll call it dinner? We will eat by the fire and then turn in."

"My hero," Roy said.

We finished our beers and I brought out two more.

"Any luck today?" Roy asked

"Not much. The best person to see at Lahinch wasn't there. I did get a look at the schedule book for tee times. No clues there that I could see."

"What's next?" Roy asked.

"We eat, we sleep, and over coffee in the morning we plan the day."

"Sounds good to me, O wise one."

EARLY NEXT MORNING over coffee I started searching out and circling area golf courses on the map. Operating on the premise that anyone who came to Ireland to play golf would certainly play Lahinch and Ballybunion, I began to circle courses within an hour or so drive of those courses. By the time I had finished breakfast I had circled a dozen.

"I'm going to Ballybunion," I told Roy, pointing to the map. "It's here. On the way I am going to check out Kilrush and Kilkee. Here and here. Should take all day. I want you to check out the clubs at Ennis, Dromoland, and Shannon. They are here, here, and here."

Roy nodded.

"Talk to starters, caddies, pro shop employees, and restaurant personnel. They are probably going to be on a skeleton staff since it's January. Not exactly high golf season, but do what you can."

"Will do," Roy said, taking another swallow of black coffee. "How do you feel?"

"Good. You?"

"Human."

We left at first light. I took N67 down the coast. I spent an hour talking to everyone I could find at Kilkee Golf Club. It was mid-week and not many players were out and the staff was limited. I did not go into all the details that I had with James. If Joey was still around, I did not want word to get back to him that a private investigator was looking for him. My cover story was that he was a friend of mine who was supposed to be in Ireland playing golf but we had not run into each other yet. Nobody recognized the photo.

I drove to Kilrush and repeated the process with the same results. No one recognized the photo but some of the people who had been working in November were on holiday, and some just worked high season.

I mushed on. At Killimer I took the ferry across the Shannon River to Tarbert. From there I drove to Ballybunion. The starter thought he recognized Joey but he could not be sure.

"November, you said? Could be him."

"Did he take a caddie?"

"Probably. Can't remember."

He took Joey's picture to the caddie master who showed it around to the few caddies who were there with no positive results. After I had finished I walked around inside the clubhouse and looked at the restaurant and pro shop. Plush. High prices. Lahinch was more bare bones. Ballybunion had all the bells and whistles. I had lunch in the restaurant. The food was good. No surprise that it was overpriced.

When I finished lunch I walked out the front door toward the parking lot. To my left was the famous first tee and in the distance down the right side of the first fairway, the famous ancient town graveyard which supposedly held more golf balls than permanent residences. I almost wished I played golf. Almost.

AT THE END of day two, Roy and I sat in the kitchen of our rental cottage drinking tea . . . *when in Ireland*. Though it was only a little after four o'clock, the setting sun was disappearing outside the window next to the kitchen table. Another peat fire was killing the chill in the living room.

"Any luck?" Roy asked.

"Not much. You?"

"A lot of nos and a few maybes. Nothing positive."

"A lot of that going around," I said.

"What's next?"

"Dinner at a pub down in Doolin called McGann's."

"Sounds like a plan."

THE LITTLE VILLAGE of Doolin had one small food market and three pubs. *Now, here is a town that has their priorities straight*, I thought. The pubs were McDermott's, McGann's, and O'Connor's. Each had its own following but most locals frequented all three. If you wanted to start a heated argument among the locals, just ask which pub had the best food, or the best music, or the best anything, for that matter.

Roy and I sat in a back corner booth at McGann's away from the bar and the cigarette smoke. Ireland had a recent new antismoking law for pubs and restaurants, but the owners of most small village establishments like McGann's looked the other way when a local decided to have a cigarette or smoke a pipe at the bar. I had noticed a couple of elderly gents at the bar with pipes going when we came in the front door. The smell of a good pipe tobacco is not that unpleasant and brought back bittersweet memories of my dad smoking his pipe after dinner on the front porch of the lake house.

The pub was less than half full. Roy and I were the only customers in the back section of booths. The waitress brought a pint of Guinness for Roy and a pint of Harp for me. Both were on tap. I did not like Harp in a bottle but on tap it was just fine. Soon after the drafts arrived our food arrived. We had both ordered lamb stew, which turned out surprisingly good.

"Nice little pub," Roy said. "Been here before?"

"Many years ago," I said. "Hasn't changed a bit."

"That Dromoland golf course is a beauty," Roy said. "Of course, I don't play that sissy game, but if I did I think I would like to play there. There is a castle behind the eighteenth green. A waitress at the restaurant thought *maybe* she recognized Ronnie."

"So real men don't play golf. Is that what you're saying?"

Roy grinned. "You play?"

"No."

"Well, there you go."

"I don't play, but I have a real respect for those who can play well. It's the hardest game that I know," I said with conviction.

"Are we having our first fight?" Roy teased.

I laughed. "For a minute there you had me going."

"I tried golf when I was a kid," Roy said. "I swiped some golf clubs from the local country club, took them out in a field behind my house and practiced. Thought I was pretty good, so late one day I sneaked onto the local public course to play. I thought I played pretty well, so I started sneaking on a few days a week. Then I got caught. A grounds keeper called the cops to come and run me off. They were about to just shoo me away when they noticed the nice clubs I was playing with. One thing led to another, I ended up in juvvy court and my golfing career was over. Never touched another club."

"Roy, you are just full of surprises. Ever thought about trying it again?"

"Naw, it's a stupid game."

44

The smell of hot coffee brought me from a dream I was having about running with Mary on the beach at Singer Island. I had had the same dream on a few other occasions and wondered if it meant anything. I rolled over and looked at the clock on my bedside table; the clock glowed 6:03. *Early to bed, early to rise, Roy's a regular Ben Franklin. Either that or we now have a maid.*

I felt the early morning chill as I left the warmth of the bed. I quickly put on jeans, socks, sneakers and a long-sleeved T-shirt. I went down the hall to the bathroom. I emptied my bladder, gargled and combed my hair. I was ready for that first cup of coffee. I trudged through the living room, appreciating the warmth from the fireplace. Roy was in the kitchen reading the *New York Times* he had purchased the day before in Ennis. Warm scones and soft butter were on the kitchen table. A mug full of hot water was next to the coffee maker.

"Nice touch," I said, emptying the mug and pouring myself a cup of coffee. "I may keep you around."

Roy ignored me. "Titans and Redskins in the Super Bowl."

"Damn, I had completely forgot about the playoffs. I'm glad the Titans made it."

I stirred cream and sugar in my coffee, buttered a scone, and sat down with my map. Roy had his map from his rental car to make notations on. After a few more minutes of reading, he put down the paper and moved his chair beside mine.

"I'm sending you north today, if that's okay," I said.

"Fine with me."

"First, check out Connemara Golf Club. It seems to be on everyone's top ten list. It's located west of Ballyconneely," I said, pointing to the map. "Then come back into Galway and check out Galway Golf Club then Galway Golf & Country Club. Galway Golf Club is west and Galway Golf & Country Club is southeast near Oranmore. If you have time, swing over to Gort and check out the Gort Golf Club."

Outside the kitchen window, night was giving way to early morning. Roy picked up his jacket, poured himself another cup of coffee in a Styrofoam cup, and plucked his car keys off the kitchen table.

"I'm out of here," he said. "See you tonight."

I returned to my coffee and scones while studying the map and planning the day. My main destination was Old Head Golf Links, a new golf course with an old-sounding name. Built in 1997 and thanks to a lot of publicity and expensive green fees, Old Head was on everyone's must play list. I would also check out Cork Golf Club, a highly respected course on the banks of the Lee River at Cork off route N25, past the Shannon airport and beyond Limerick. That should make for a full day. I drained my mug and headed to the shower. Comparing an Irish shower to an American shower is like comparing a misty rain to a torrential downpour. The water trickles out, and if you're lucky, it stays hot. A few minutes later, with my map and a cup of coffee for the road, I was on N85 going south toward Ennis.

I REACHED THE Cork Golf Club around ten-thirty. I spent an hour talking to the starter, a few caddies, pro shop staff, and the two waitresses on duty in the grill. No one recognized Joey Avanti, not even a maybe.

As I was leaving the parking lot at the Cork Golf Club my cell phone rang. "I hope you're not lost," I said.

"I'm just getting ready to leave Connemara and I've got to hand it to you gumshoe, our boy was here."

I felt a rush of adrenaline. "You don't say!"

"I do say. Positive ID, a waitress in the grill. Our boy flirted with her, tried to pick her up, or so she says, then left a big tip. It was the big tip she remembered."

"How about a name?"

"Sorry, no name."

"Damn. Well, you did better than I did. No luck down here so far. I'll see you back in Doolin tonight. Call me if you find anything else."

So the alias Ronnie Fairchild did come to Ireland. It was a good bet that he was no longer here. The question was, Where did he go? And how, and using what name? The name would be the key. I had to get the name.

I WENT BACK into Cork on N25 and took N71 West to Inishannon and followed signs to the village of Kinsale. In Kinsale signs directed me to Old Head. I was beginning to get hungry when I pulled into the parking lot at Old Head Golf Links so I went straight to the grill. I ordered fish and chips, which turned out to be very good. I talked to the waitress on duty but she did not recognize the photo of Joey. She did direct me to other people I could ask. I finished and left a big tip. Maybe *I* would be remembered.

"I remember this guy," the starter said when I showed him the photo. "It was a very nice day in November and we were a little busy. He slips me twenty Euro and I put him with a twosome that had been hanging around trying to get off. They were all happy as clams." He drew nearer to me and said in a quite tone, "The scheduler always keeps a couple of tee times open for walkups and we split the tips. We can make a little extra that way. You understand."

"I sure do." I said, slipping him a twenty. "Do you remember this guy's name?"

"I'm sorry, but he never gave me one. They were off the book, you know."

"Thanks," I said and went back to my car. What a character. I wondered just how happy a clam could be.

ON THE WAY back to Doolin, I called Mary. It was two-thirty Irish time, which meant it was seven-thirty in Mountain Center. She answered on the fourth ring.

"Top of the evening to ya," I said in my best Irish brogue, which was pretty good if I do say so myself. After all, I had been here three days.

"Who's this?" Mary teased.

"Your friendly international private eye," I said trying to do Bogie. Bogie was harder. Rich Little I was not. "How are you?"

"Missing you."

"Good to hear."

"Don't you miss me?"

Oh Christ. "Of course I do."

"No, you don't. You just miss the sex."

You got that right. "That too," I said. "But I do miss you and I'll prove it when I get home."

"Am I getting a present?"

"You bet," I said, dodging a bus that was taking up two-thirds of the road.

"No, not that," Mary said. "Another present."

"Sure. And do not ask what. It's a surprise and you'll see it when I get home."

"Okay, I can't wait. Hurry up and get here. How is the trip? Any luck?"

"Fairchild was here. We have positive IDs from two different golf clubs. I am still looking for a name he might have been using. The name will be the key to tracking him. How is Jake?" I asked changing the subject.

"He's pooped. I ran the nature trail with him after work. He is passed out on his bed as we speak."

We talked another ten minutes about nothing in particular then said good-night. We had an agreement never to say good-bye.

Traffic picked up as I neared Limerick but I managed to beat rush hour. By the time I was back in Doolin, it was dark.

THE LAZY LOBSTER is one of Doolin's upscale restaurants. It sits on a side street almost directly a block behind McGann's. Roy and I had a table by the window. The restaurant was about half full. I sipped on a Harp while Roy nursed a Guinness. We had exchanged stories of how our days had gone over a couple of beers at the cottage. Other than the fact, confirmed at two locations, that the alias Ronnie Fairchild had been in the west of Ireland and had played golf, we had no other leads.

"I talked to Mr. Fleet this afternoon," Roy said. "He wants me to come back if you have no further need for me. I think we have done about all we can do here and I am getting tired of driving on the wrong side of the road."

"Not a problem," I said. "Ronnie is probably no longer in Ireland and I do not need a body guard. I have one or two more things to check out and then I am on my way back. Couple of days at most."

The food arrived. I had a special salmon dish with a dill sauce and Roy had shrimp sautéed with a garlic and white wine sauce sprinkled with basil. The food was excellent as evidenced by our attention to it and the lack of conversation.

"Something about this place is depressing," Roy said.

"The restaurant?"

"No," he said with a sad smile. "The country. Poor really. Bare bones. Raw weather."

"Well, it is a lot nicer in the summertime. When I was here last, it was late May and early June. We stayed a month and had a ball. Of course, I was looking at it through the eyes of a junior in college."

"College boy, huh."

"Yep, University of Connecticut. Chief, too."

"Billy is a college grad?" Roy asked, his surprise showing.

"Degree in art."

Roy nodded. "Yeah, that fits. How did he end up in prison?"

"Long story. He'll tell you one day. Billy likes you, but as you have observed, he doesn't talk much."

"What was your major?"

"Economics."

"That fits too. I guess you are a pretty smart guy."

"And occasionally," I said, "dumb."

Roy finished his last shrimp and smiled. "Aren't we all?"

After we returned to our cottage, Roy used up most of his remaining minutes on his cell phone with Aer Lingus while changing his flight. Changing a reservation on an international flight is like dealing with your local motor vehicle department, nearly impossible.

45

The next morning a chill wind was blowing and it was still dark thanks to a heavy cloud cover that refused to let dawn arrive . . . in other words, a typical Irish morning in late January. I shook hands with Roy at the front door of our rented cottage, and then he was gone. I had a momentary sense of loss. Separation anxiety? I shook it off.

Back at the kitchen table I had a second cup of coffee with a toasted English muffin and looked at my map of Ireland. England and Scotland were on the other side of the map. I flipped it over. I drank coffee and studied the cities, towns, and roads of England and Scotland. I had a fleeting thought of checking out the golf course at St. Andrews until I picked up the cell phone and dialed Aer Lingus. A frustrating half hour later, I had learned there was no direct service from Shannon to Edinburgh, Scotland, the closest airport to the world-famous St. Andrews links.

There was nothing better to do than go back to Lahinch and hope that the vacationing Mary Kathryn had returned. I bumped and bounced my rental car back over the hill and down to Lahinch. The same border collie lying in the same driveway chased my car. Maybe he was practicing.

Few cars were in the parking lot of the Lahinch Golf Club. Only the crazy golfers would play on a a cold, overcast, windy day like today. Three crazies were on the first tee as I climbed the stairs and headed toward the pro shop. James was folding and stacking golf shirts on a table marked *sale*. I looked at the prices. The Irish do have a sense of humor.

"Good morning, Mr. Youngblood."

"Good morning, James," I said. "I just dropped by to see if Mary Kathryn might be here."

"As a matter of fact, she is. Let me take you to her."

I followed him out the pro shop door, across and behind the first tee to the clubhouse on the other side. The three crazies, with their heads down into the wind, were pulling their clubs on carts up the first fairway. *For love of the game.*

Mary Kathryn was an attractive, full-figured, freckled, red-haired woman that I guessed to be in her early forties. She had a quick smile that made her eyes sparkle and she rose to her feet as we approached the desk I had sat at a few days before.

"Mary Kathryn, I would like for you to meet Mr. Youngblood from the United States. Mr. Youngblood is a private investigator working on a case that has brought him all the way to Ireland."

"A private investigator," Mary Kathryn said. "Oh, how exciting. Please sit down, Mr. Youngblood,"

"Well, then," James said, "I'll leave you to it."

I explained to Mary Kathryn that I was looking for a man who might have killed his wife and might have come to Ireland to play some of the famous golf courses. I showed her the picture of the alias Ronnie Fairchild.

"Oh, my," she exclaimed.

"You recognize him?"

"Yes, a real charmer, this one, and good-looking. He was here in November, I think. Let me look." She started thumbing through the ledger. "Here it is. November the eighth. I put him with this twosome here," she pointed.

"Please tell me you have a name," I said.

"Oh, yes. See," she pointed. "Ron Childress."

I saw the name *Ron Childress* written in the margin with a line drawn down to a twosome in the ten o'clock time slot, *Figgins* and *Marshall*. I felt that old adrenaline rush. I stared at the name. Ronnie Fairchild to Ron Childress. It made sense. Similar names. Joey was used to being called Ron or Ronnie. I silently prayed that he had used that name to leave the country.

"Thank you very much, Mary Kathryn. You have been a big help."

"My pleasure," she smiled.

I CALLED STANLEY Johns's unlisted number on my international cell phone. I didn't bother counting the rings.

Stanley finally answered. "Hello."

"Hello from Ireland," I said.

"Is that you, Don?"

"Who else would it be, Stanley? How many people have this number?"

"Two or three, but you could have been a telemarketer. That's why I let it ring so long. Telemarketers won't let it ring more than eight times."

I had long since given up trying to comprehend Stanley's logic. Sometimes he made sense in an oblique sort of way. Other times I could only shake my head and wonder. We got into a discussion one time on why Stanley did not have caller ID. When I ripped away all his arguments, what was left was that he did not want to spend the extra few dollars a month even if his company picked up the tab. It made sense to Stanley.

"Very smart, Stanley. Now listen, I need your help. Sometime after November the eighth try to find out if a passenger traveling under the name of Ron Childress flew out of Ireland. If you come up empty, try England and Scotland. If you still come up empty, try Paris, France."

"That's going to take some time, Don." Stanley sounded a little stressed.

"Don't worry about it, Stanley. Take your time. I'll be home tomorrow night. I'll call you in a couple of days."

THE NEXT MORNING, with my bags packed and in the rental car, I drove down to the main house and knocked on the door. The door opened to Anne Frawley holding a black cat. She smiled and put the cat down and it ran past me into the driveway.

"Mr. Youngblood. What can I do for you?"

I handed her three hundred euros. "I'm leaving today and Roy left yesterday. Here is the full payment for the week."

"This is too much," she said counting the bills. "You only stayed three nights.

"Keep it, Anne. Even for three days it was a bargain. I'll be back some day and I'll be sure to stay with you."

"Well, okay then," she said smiling. "Have a safe trip."

I HAD NOT bothered to change my return flight. Rather than spend time on the cell phone I decided the best plan of action was to show up early at the airport and take my chances. After I dropped the rental car, I went to the Aer Lingus counter and within minutes was booked in first class on a noon flight to Boston.

With two hours to kill and plenty of time left on my international cell phone, I decided to make a few calls. I went through security and found an empty gate area to wait in. I started to call Roy but remembered the time difference, so I read a little first. I was deeply absorbed in the latest Marcus Didius Falco mystery when I heard my flight called. I waited a few more minutes until the final call, then walked casually to the gate and into first class without any wait. Timing is everything.

Once I was settled in, I called Roy and let him know when I'd be arriving. He promised to send the Lear Jet. I realized I could get used to this.

"Did you do any good after I left?" Roy asked just as the cabin doors closed.

"Yes. I have a name. I have to go now. I'll fill you in later."

I ended the call, turned off the cell phone and went back to my mystery novel. First class was only half full and the seat next to me was vacant.

It was a quiet flight and in Boston a chauffeur holding up a card with Youngblood on it greeted me as I exited the secured area of the concourse. A fast limo ride to the Fleet Industries' Lear Jet and a quick trip to Tri-Cities Airport followed. Roy picked me up and I filled him in on what I had found out on my second trip to Lahinch. Then he dropped me at 5300, where I changed clothes, took Jake out for a short walk and headed directly to Moto's. On the way I called Susie at the police station and told her to radio Mary that I was back and headed for Moto's.

BILLY APPEARED OUT of nowhere on the machine to the right of me.

"I see you're back," he rumbled. "How was the trip?"

"Nothing wrong with your eyesight, Chief. How are you doing?"

"I'm well."

I brought Billy up to date as we began working up a sweat. Roy appeared on the machine to the left.

"I could use a good workout," he said. "How are you, Billy?"

"No complaints," Billy said.

We continued in silence and picked up the pace. After half an hour, I left Billy and Roy alone on the elliptical machines and headed for the bench press.

"Hey, big boy." The voice from behind was and is unforgettable.

I turned to face the blond goddess and got a passionate kiss for my efforts.

"I'm sweaty," I said.

"Who cares," Mary said. "You better save some of that energy for later. When I get you home you are going to get another workout."

"Why wait?"

"Why indeed?"

WE SKIPPED DINNER and went straight to dessert for a couple of hours. Aerobic dessert. Low fat.

"Wow," Mary said lying in full splendor beside me on our king size bed. "Maybe you should travel more often."

"Maybe I should."

"But I don't like being away from you," she said and paused in thought. I knew the look. "Maybe we could just pretend you had traveled."

"How often am I going to travel?"

"Every day."

"Lot of traveling."

"Too much?"

"Food for thought," I said. "I'm more into spontaneous travel than planned travel."

"Speaking of food, I'm starved."

"What strikes your fancy?"

"Quiet and intimate."

I pondered that for a minute. "Let's go to the club. They serve until nine and it will be practically empty."

"Give me ten minutes," Mary said as she got up and headed toward her bedroom.

I watched that lovely figure vanish out of sight and wondered why the fates had smiled on me and put this lovely, caring creature in my life. My father had always told me that God has a way of turning bad into good. Mary Sanders was definitely one good thing to come out of the Sarah Ann Fairchild case. For that, I owed Joseph Fleet closure and I was determined to get it.

46

T. Elbert and I sat underneath the heat lamps on his front porch on a cold, late January day drinking coffee and eating bagels with cream cheese while I recounted my Irish adventures. There was a dusting of snow on the ground and the gray cloud cover threatened more. Things had been quiet for a couple of days while I waited to see if Stanley uncovered anything on Ron Fairchild/Childress. Stanley said it was a slow process since he was dealing with foreign airlines and had his own job to do. So far he had finished with Aer Lingus and turned up nothing.

"You should be proud of what you have accomplished on this case," he said. "You have the gift for investigating. If you stay serious about it, you're going to be one hell of a P.I."

"Thanks. I've been lucky so far. If my luck holds, I'll find Fairchild."

"Luck is the residue of hard work. Keep digging and you'll come up with something. If I can help, let me know."

I finished my coffee and bagel and cleaned up after myself. I was racking my brain to come up with something T. Elbert could do for me. He needed to feel useful.

"You might try to find out if there are any known forgers in the area. I sure would like to know if Fairchild had a driver's license and passport in the name of Ron Childress. Be nice to have confirmation."

I suspected that he did. I also suspected that if he did, he probably had them done in the northeast between the time he had disappeared and the time he had resurfaced in Ireland. In any event, it was worth checking out.

T. Elbert was no dummy. "Long shot," he said. "But what the hell, I've nothing better to do."

I SPENT THE AFTERNOON in the office catching up on the market and reviewing client portfolios. I usually reviewed five portfolios a day on a rotating basis unless something drastic was happening on Wall Street. Today I reviewed ten. I had a lot of catching up to do. Jake was asleep on his bed in the corner and Billy was in the outer office working on his latest painting when the phone rang.

"Cherokee Investigations," Billy answered from the outer office. "Good, how are you doing? Hang on."

"T. Elbert," Billy rumbled with a little extra volume.

I picked up the phone.

"I have a name for you," T. Elbert said before I could say hello.

"That was fast."

"Well, like I said, I had nothing better to do. According to my sources, a guy in Knoxville is the best forger in the state but he is supposed to be retired. He is very smart. Went to Harvard or some place like that. Been in prison twice so he would be very careful if he did work for anyone and it would be expensive."

"How would our boy track this guy down?"

"From state to state these guys all know each other. If Ronnie Fairchild knew someone in the northeast that gave him a name down here and vouched for him, then he might have made contact," T. Elbert said. He then gave me a name and an address.

"Thanks," I said. "I'll check it out."

"Be careful. This guy lives in an okay neighborhood but he still might have some friends around and he probably will not want to talk to you."

"I'll take Billy with me."

"Sounds like a good idea."

EARLY THE NEXT morning, I had the cruise control set on a reasonable seventy-five miles an hour with a cup of coffee in the console and an extremely large full-blooded Cherokee Indian in the passenger seat. We were thirty miles outside of Knoxville. The name T. Elbert had given me was Amos "Teaberry" Smith. I had downloaded directions to his street address and Billy and I had been discussing how to approach him since we left Mountain Center. I had decided on the name-dropping approach. *It is not who you are, it is who you know.*

Forty-five minutes later I was knocking on the door of a baby-blue split-level with white shutters in an upper-middle-class neighborhood. Billy waited in the Pathfinder.

A lean black man in his late forties to early fifties, with John Lennon-style wire-rimmed glasses, opened the door.

"Mr. Smith," I said, handing him my business card, "I wonder if I might have a word."

He studied the card. "Private investigator," he said in a very sophisticated accent. "Now, why would I want to have a word with you?"

"Carlo Vincente said you might be able to help me. That is, if you know who Carlo Vincente is." I was gambling that he did.

"I don't live in a closet. Of course I know who Carlo Vincente is. The question is, how do I know that you know him?" He said looking me up and down.

I handed him Carlo's card. "I'll call the office number if you want confirmation and you can talk to the man himself."

"Step inside," he said looking at the card. "What's this number on the back?"

"One you had better forget you saw," I said taking the card back from him.

"Raise your arms," he said.

I did as he asked. He efficiently patted me down.

"No wire and no gun," he said.

"Relax," I said. "I don't need any work done. All I am after is information. Say the secret word and win five hundred dollars."

"Groucho Marx," he smiled. "I watch the reruns on TV Land. So, what is the secret word?"

"Two words," I said, handing him a picture of the alias Ronnie Fairchild.

"This man might have needed your expertise. I need the name on the documents he might have required."

"I do not do documents anymore. I am retired," a bigger smile this time as he handed the picture back to me.

"I had heard that. Too bad. But you might as well take a guess. You know, for the five hundred dollars." I handed the picture back to him and reached in my pocket and took out a wad of bills. I started peeling off hundred-dollar bills.

He studied the picture. "Well, if I had to give this dude a name, and mind you I have never seen him, I would probably name him Ron Childress."

Bingo!

I handed him the five bills. "Guess you got lucky, Teaberry," I said.

He laughed. "That is very good, man. You do your homework. Got that nickname in prison from chewing the gum all the time. Stuff is hard to find now."

"One more thing. If you had seen this guy, how long ago might you have seen him?"

"Probably would have been a couple of years. If I had seen him."

I opened the storm door and stepped out and Amos Smith followed.

"Pleasure doing business with you," he said, pocketing the money. "You really know Carlo Vincente?"

"I do."

"I knew you were not the law," he smiled. "Your clothes are too nice. If you ever need anything, let me know. For the right money, I might come out of retirement."

"I'll keep that in mind. But if I were you, I'd stay retired."

I CALLED T. ELBERT on my way back to Mountain Center to let him know his lead paid off and that I had a confirmation on the name of Ron Childress. He was surprised but pleased he had made a contribution. I let Billy drive back as I made some phone calls. I let Stanley know we were on the right track. I let Mary know, through Susie, that I was on my way back and that this trip constituted travel. Susie laughed like she knew the joke.

I sat back in the passenger seat, leaned against the headrest and gathered my thoughts. Joey had the phony ID made a couple of years ago. Maybe for a good reason or maybe just as a precaution. He had used Eddie Romano's name to skip the country. He had used Ron Childress's name at the Lahinch Golf Club and those two things did not make sense. Why not use the Ron Childress name to leave the country? I would probably have never made that connection. Was I being led by a trail of bread crumbs? If so, why and by whom? Something did not feel right.

Billy and I agreed to meet later at Moto's. I checked e-mail and phone messages then drove to 5300 and took Jake for a walk. Then I changed into my workout clothes and took Jake with me to the gym. So far it had been a good day. I had hopes it might get even better later on.

47

Three days later, pizza in hand, I pulled into Stanley Johns's driveway. Stanley was mysterious when he called me earlier. Bring pizza, he said, and he would tell me all about it. Hadn't Stanley ever heard of pizza delivery? I guess he had—Don Youngblood's pizza delivery service.

Once inside the inner sanctum of Oz, I spread the pizza out on a table. Stanley had prepared drinks and cleared the table. He was eager to chow down. We started to eat. I took a drink of a cold Michelob Amber Bock. I dared not look at the *born on* date.

"So tell me what you have," I said casually.

"I found a Ron Childress who flew out of Paris on November twenty-second on Air France. Guess where he went?"

More guessing games. I played along. Stanley and Scott Glass should meet each other. Something clicked in the back of my mind from a conversation I had with Scott Glass. *Joey was heavily into the drug business.* I had not connected it before but now maybe it made sense.

"South America?"

Stanley looked disappointed. He took another bite of pizza and recovered.

"What country?" he asked, munching away.

"Colombia."

Stanley looked annoyed. "Okay then, what city?"

"Bogota, I guess."

"Why did I do all this work if you already knew?" he asked somewhat petulantly.

"Because I only remembered this second something someone said about Ronnie. And I couldn't be sure he was using the name Ron Childress until you confirmed it. Without your work, I would never have made the connection. What you did was extremely important and much appreciated."

Stanley seemed satisfied with my little speech. He celebrated with another piece of pizza. I was lost in thought. *Now what?*

THE NEXT MORNING I called Raul Rivera. Although his family moved to Miami when Raul was small, he still had strong ties to Colombia through relatives and business. If Joey Avanti was in Colombia, and it made sense that he might be, then Raul would be the one to help me find him. I had not talked to Raul since I called to thank him for the package of goodies used in apprehending Teddy Earl Elroy. Now I was calling for another favor.

"This is Raul," the voice answered.

"How goes life in paradise?"

"Life in paradise is always good, my friend."

"What's happening, Raul?"

"Status quo, Donnie, you know, just another day in paradise. Nothing much is new here. How is the lovely Mary? Did you get her problem taken care of?"

"I did. The problem is dead and buried." *Literally.* "I'll tell you the whole story next time I see you. In the meantime, do you want to hear another fascinating story?"

"Always. Speak to me."

"This story will take some time," I said. "Do you have a few minutes?"

I heard Raul on his intercom ask for his calls to be held. Then, "Okay, Donnie, I am, as you say, all ears."

I told Raul the entire story of Sarah Ann Fairchild and Joey Avanti. He listened without interruption. When I had finished there was silence.

"You are chasing a very bad man, Donnie. And it looks to me as if he just might want you to find him."

"I agree, Raul. I just can't figure out why. How would he know I would be searching for him?"

"Not you specifically, but someone. Maybe he likes the thrill of being hunted, of living on the edge."

"If I ever catch up with him, I'll ask. Any ideas?"

"I have many friends in Colombia. Finding this man may take some time, but if he is in Colombia, I will find out and you and I will avenge the death of Mrs. Fairchild. Send me a picture of him, please. But Donnie, do not go to Colombia by yourself. Colombia can be a dangerous place for Americans traveling alone."

"Thanks, Raul. I'll remember that and I will send you a picture."

"Be patient, my friend. All good things come to he who waits."

Raul, the philosopher.

48

A mid-February warm up had prompted me to run the eight-mile Mountain Center loop. The next morning my legs were reminding me that I was not in particularly good running condition. In fact, my quads hurt with every step. I crept around the office like an old man, enduring major teasing from Billy who ran three times a week regardless of the weather. Not me. In the dead of winter I retreated to the gym, but elliptical machines, stair steppers, treadmills, and exercise bikes were no substitute for the real thing.

I settled into a game of computer solitaire while I drank a second cup of coffee. I played seventeen cards before I had to turn one over in the stack. I was on a roll when the phone rang. *Figures.* Billy answered. He got into a low conversation with somebody and I went back to my game. I had twelve cards up when Billy called out, "It's Raul."

It had been two weeks since we talked. I had heard nothing. "How goes life in paradise? I was just wondering when I was going to hear from you, Raul."

"Life in paradise is always good, my friend. I have located this man you are looking for."

I felt an adrenaline rush.

"Tell me."

"He is involved in a drug cartel and living on a large estate owned by a known drug lord about fifty miles outside of Bogota. He stays close to the estate most of the time, but every now and then he comes to Bogota to visit a high-class prostitute. I have a plan for taking him, if you are interested."

"Of course I am, Raul, but you do not have to get involved in this."

"Oh, but I do have to get involved, Donnie. You cannot do this by yourself but if you try to and get yourself killed, I would die from the guilt."

Raul, the drama king.

"Okay, Raul, I wouldn't want that to happen. But please tell me that there are reasons other than my impending demise."

"There are other reasons, my friend."

"Okay. What's next?"

"Meet me at the Miami airport next Monday. Ship back those items that you ordered from me for your other adventure. We will need them. I'll make arrangements for our stay in Bogota. Bring old clothes, nothing new and nothing fancy. And pack your favorite form of protection."

"Condoms?"

Raul laughed. "It is good to see you have not lost your sense of humor, my friend. You may need it on this trip."

"Are we flying commercial to Bogota?"

"No, we are not. Miami Imports-Exports has a private jet."

Why was I not surprised?

"I would like to bring Billy and one other person, if we can use them," I said.

"That would be desirable. Especially Billy."

"I'll let you know our arrival time," I said.

"Take care, my friend. I look forward to seeing you."

ON THE FOLLOWING MONDAY MORNING, Roy, Billy, and I were jetting south toward Miami on the Fleet Industries private jet. Mary had given me all sorts of grief until I reminded her that her job could be just as dangerous as mine. She calmed down when I told her Billy, Roy, and Raul would be with me. We were all wearing jeans and T-shirts and carrying lightweight jackets. The weather would be relatively warm in Bogota since it was summer in South America. I had packed my Beretta since we did not have to fly commercial. Roy had his Glock. Somewhere on his person I was sure Billy had a knife or two. Roy and Billy carried small gym bags from which they produced their latest reading material. I had brought my laptop in a special leather carrying case designed to double as a briefcase. I reached for the private phone and dialed Raul. He answered on the second ring.

"How goes life in paradise?" I said.

"Life in paradise is always good, my friend. Where are you?"

"About an hour and a half outside Miami."

"What airline?"

"Private."

Raul chuckled. "You are full of surprises, Donnie. Can you identify the aircraft for me?"

"It's a Lear Jet with Fleet Industries on the tail."

"Fleet Industries. Yes, I have heard of them. Is this your client, Donnie? The woman Sarah Ann was a Fleet?"

"Yes, Raul. You catch on fast."

"Indeed I do, Donnie. But I have many more questions. I will have a car waiting for you to bring you to our hangar. See you then."

As promised, a limo was waiting when we landed in the private aviation section of Miami International Airport. We drove a short distance to another hangar and pulled in next to a Canadair Jet. Raul came down the stairs and walked toward us. He was wearing faded tan Dockers and a long-sleeved, light-blue cotton button-down shirt with the sleeves rolled up. He embraced me with a big hug and pat on the back.

"Donnie, my friend, so good to see you. And good to see you, too, Billy," Raul said shaking Billy's hand. "How have you been?"

"No complaints," Billy answered.

I introduced Raul to Roy while the limo driver was loading our luggage into the cargo hold. On the luxury jet's tail was Miami Imports-Exports Limited. A smaller version of the logo was on the side of the aircraft.

"Let's board," Raul said. "There's no time to waste and we have a long flight."

Raul was the last up and he secured the stairway and locked down the hatch. A pilot and co-pilot were in the cockpit. In Spanish, Raul told them we were ready.

The cabin was impressive. We sat in large beige leather chairs that swiveled and rocked. Two chairs faced each other on either side of the aisle, with small wooden tables in between. Behind us was a beautiful couch covered in light fabric with a Mayan design. The couch would easily seat three or four people. Opposite the couch was a dining table with two leather chairs on each side. The aircraft would comfortably seat eleven or twelve people.

"Beautiful aircraft, Raul."

"Thank you, Donnie. It serves us well."

I watched through the window as we taxied toward the runway and shortly the jet had lifted effortlessly into the clear blue sky toward the ocean and banked slowly southward.

"How long is our flight?" Roy asked.

"Usually about three hours and forty-five minutes," Raul said.

"I know nothing about Colombia," Billy said. "Tell us what to expect."

"Colombia is like many third-world countries," Raul explained. "There are many poor and a few rich. A lot of the rich are in the ruthless drug cartels. Some of the rich, like my family, run honest businesses and try to give something back to our country. We contribute to churches, schools and hospitals. Our employees have many benefits and are very loyal. We take care in hiring and usually find very good people.

"Colombia can be a dangerous place for foreigners, especially Americans. Take care when we get there and do not wander off without letting me know. I suggest we stick together. I have reserved four suites on the top floor at one of the best hotels in Bogota. Our warehouse and offices are nearby. We may spend some time with my uncle at his home outside the city, depending on how long it takes to accomplish our mission."

The four of us chatted amiably as we winged our way to a part of the world that was as foreign to me as outer space. In the quiet intervals, I pondered what, besides our friendship, was motivating Raul to help me find Joey Avanti. I knew that Raul hated drugs and the Colombian drug cartels. Raul had often told me in college that when people found out he was from Colombia they automatically thought his family was involved in drugs, and no amount of explaining could change that. I was sure that had something to do with his explaining the family history. I guess we all have our crosses to bear.

IN A FEW HOURS we touched down at a private airstrip adjacent to a huge warehouse complex north of Bogota. Raul had told me that the complex was spread over fifty acres, all of it within a twelve-foot high chain-link fence with barbed wire at the top. The security system was sophisticated, Raul had said, because theft was a problem and many of the items warehoused were very expensive. I could see armed guards patrolling the perimeter. I had the feeling I was not being told the whole story. In fact, I did not want to know the whole story.

We taxied to a private hangar with a Miami Imports-Exports Limited logo over the opening. Every building I could see had a Miami Imports-Exports Limited logo on it somewhere. A white Range Rover with a small Miami Imports-Exports Limited logo on the door was parked in one corner of the hangar. On the other side of the hangar was a Lear Jet with the same logo. I had known Raul came from money, but until now I hadn't realized the magnitude of his family's wealth.

We loaded our luggage in the Range Rover and drove toward Bogota. The weather was overcast and cool and threatened rain. Raul drove at a leisurely pace. About fifteen minutes later we had arrived in an area sprinkled with old houses, small shops, office buildings, and banks. Raul pulled up in front of a nice-looking hotel, the Casa Medina. Two valets immediately descended on our Range Rover.

"Buenos dias, Señor Rivera," one valet said.

"English, please," said Raul. "Our guests are from the United States and are here on business with my company."

"Sorry, Señor," the valet said in perfect English. "Welcome, gentlemen."

"Gracias," I said.

Raul smiled. At UConn, he had taught me Spanish in exchange for my tutoring him in economics. *"How much do you remember?"* he asked in Spanish.

"Most of it," I replied in kind. *"Perhaps I will have a chance to refresh my memory of your language while I am here."*

"Not bad. But let's speak English in front of the others."

"Agreed," I said.

On the elevator going up to our rooms, Raul handed each of us cell phones with a list of each others' numbers taped to the backs.

The elevator doors opened and we stepped out into the elegant hallway and Raul pointed out our suites.

"I apologize but I have some business to take care of and have to leave you now. I've arranged for you to have dinner in about an hour in the restaurant downstairs," he said. "They specialize in French cuisine."

We nodded agreement and went our separate ways. I realized Roy and Billy had been quiet since we landed in Bogota but I knew they were merely being observant. Those two didn't miss much.

49

The next morning we met in Raul's suite to discuss the plan for taking Joey Avanti. Raul had a detailed map of Bogota spread out on the dining room table. There was coffee, juice and pastries on the bar. There was a quiet reverence in the room. We were eating, drinking and listening to Raul who spoke in a subdued voice.

"We are here," he pointed at the map. "The bordello this man Avanti frequents is here," he pointed again. "It is about twenty minutes from here in nighttime traffic. Avanti does not come to Bogota on a regular basis, but the next time he comes in, I will get a call. We will have to be prepared to go within an hour of the call. I suggest we take him as he leaves.

"The bordello is in a residential area off a main street. There are a few streetlights but visibility is limited. We will take the night-vision goggles just in case. Avanti always travels with two bodyguards and we do not want any surprises coming out of the shadows. We will also take the tranquilizer pistols to take care of the guards and to subdue Avanti. We will need to dress in dark colors. I will have a van at the ready and a couple of locals to occupy the guards once we subdue them. Any questions?"

"I don't want anyone getting hurt, Raul," I said.

"Unless, of course, it's Joey Avanti," Roy said.

"Do not worry, my friend. The guards are only doing their jobs and once they lose their man they will not want to return to the estate. They will vanish on their own."

"So what do we do now?" Billy asked.

"We wait," Raul said.

So we waited.

While we waited we explored the immediate area around the hotel. Raul had been specific on where we could and could not go. We visited shops, ate at nearby restaurants, walked the streets and worked out in the hotel's health club. Sometimes I went online and took care of business. Raul was never with us. He was taking care of business at the warehouse complex, but he made it clear he was only a cell call away if we needed anything. A day passed, then two, then three. When I was not with Roy and Billy, I spent time reading, shopping for Mary, and swimming in the hotel pool. I even got a massage.

On the evening of the fourth day, while we were having dinner in the hotel restaurant, my cell phone rang. I made it a point never to take a cell phone into a restaurant but for this trip I had to make an exception.

"Yes," I answered softly.

"Be ready in one hour," Raul said.

I felt that adrenaline rush. "We'll be ready," I said.

I disconnected. I looked at Billy and Roy.

"One hour."

RAUL PARKED THE van two blocks away from the bordello. The side streets were nearly dark. A few street lamps glowed weakly on the corner nearest us. There were intermittent lights in the windows of the houses on the block and a few porch lights were on, but the light cast by these was minimal. There were six of us. Our group of four and two locals who were trusted employees of Raul and who spoke only Spanish. All of us were dressed in black and wearing headphones with mouthpieces to communicate. We slipped out of the van. Another van rounded the corner, parked, and turned off its headlights and motor.

Raul put his hand on my shoulder. "Ours," he said through the headphones, nodding toward the van. "Transportation for the guards once we subdue them. They will be held at another location and then released."

I nodded back.

"Follow me," said Raul. "Stay in the shadows and spread out."

We followed Raul down the street and around the corner and across the next street. He stopped in the shadows of some very tall shrubbery and waited for the group to catch up.

"Put on the night-vision goggles and move slowly behind me," he said. "We must locate the bodyguards."

We did as we were told, moving slowly in the shadows down the street into an alley where again Raul stopped.

"Wait here," Raul said. He pointed to the two locals and motioned for them to follow. The three of them disappeared down the ally into the darkness. A few minute later Raul returned.

"The guards are just inside the gates of the bordello parking area, leaning against a black Range Rover, talking and smoking. They are not paying much attention to what is going on around them. My men are in place. You and I will take them down. Let's go."

I turned to Roy and Billy. "Wait here," I said softly through my mouthpiece.

Raul and I moved slowly down the right-hand side of the alley and beside a wrought iron fence built into the top of a stone wall. As we approached the gate, I heard the low voices of the guards and music coming

from inside the house. The guards were leaning against the front of the
Range Rover with their backs toward us. They wore khaki uniforms and
hats. Raul slipped around the other side of the vehicle.

"Ready?" he said softly through my headphones.

"Ready," I whispered back.

"I've got the one on the left. On three," Raul said.

I took aim at the back of the guard on the right.

"One, two, three."

I heard the spurt sound of the darts leave the pistols. The guards yelped
as they were hit by the darts. A second later, Raul's men had their hands
over the mouths of the guards, dragging them away into the darkness.

"Good thing that music is playing," I said. "They might have heard
us."

"Music is always playing," Raul said. I did not ask how he knew.

A few minutes later Raul's men were back dressed in the uniforms of
the guards. They took positions around the Range Rover, being careful
to keep their faces out of the light. I felt a tap on my shoulder. It was
Billy.

"I'll be nearby," he said. "Roy is watching our backs."

"Now we let the hunted come to the hunter," Raul said.

We watched a few clients come and go but did not see Joey Avanti.
After an hour I began to wonder if Joey was in there. Maybe he had seen
us and left by another entrance. Or maybe he was spending the night.
I was getting antsy.

"Raul," I said quietly. "Do you think he spotted us?"

"Patience, my friend."

We waited another hour. I was ready to storm the place when a
figure appeared at the top of the stairs that led to the second floor. A
man was silhouetted in the light. He lit a cigarette, and in the glow of
the lighter I saw the unmistakable face of the alias Ronnie Fairchild. I
felt my heart pound.

"He's mine," I said through my mouthpiece.

"Affirmative," said Raul. "Let him come to you."

Avanti blew a long stream of smoke out and started down the stairs. He was humming to the music as he reached the bottom of the stairs.

"*It is a beautiful night*," he said in almost perfect Spanish in the direction of the guards. His voice was deep and cultured and slightly sinister, I thought.

"*Si, Señor,*" answered the guard closest to me, and he turned away to open the back passenger-side door. The other guard turned his face away and opened the driver's side door, but I noticed the interior light did not come on. Someone was thinking ahead.

I shot Joey Avanti about the time he reached the front bumper.

"Shit," he exclaimed. No other words escaped his lips because Billy materialized from nowhere and clamped a giant paw around Joey's mouth, and seconds later Joey was out cold.

ON THE THIRD FLOOR of the Miami Imports-Exports Limited warehouse complex, I was looking through a window into the purchasing office. The shades had been drawn and angled so I could barely see in. A single desk lamp was angled toward the far right corner. There, duct-taped to a chair, slumped the unconscious Joey Avanti. The angle of the light, the position of the shades and the darkness of the hall in which we stood made it impossible for Joey to see us. We could see him but he could not see us. Roy stood beside me. Billy and Raul were in the cafeteria. We had been checking on Joey off and on for the last three hours to see if he was awake. He might try to play possum for a while but he could not do that forever, and I was in no hurry. The search was over.

"Why don't you just let me go in there and put a bullet in his head? We'll dump him somewhere over the Atlantic and be done with it," Roy said.

"Too easy," I said. "I want this son of a bitch to know he is caught and who caught him."

Joey's head moved slightly.

"Did you see that?" Roy asked.

"I did. He is starting to wake up. Let's go get some coffee and give him time to stew a little."

We walked down the hall to the cafeteria. Raul had called for a few cafeteria workers to come in early and at five o'clock in the morning things were jumping in the kitchen.

"How is our guest?" Raul asked.

"Starting to come around," I said. "I want him to sweat a bit before I talk to him."

"A little psychological torture," mused Raul. "I like it. You continue to be full of surprises, my friend."

"We all have a dark side, Raul. And you are about to see mine full on."

Raul smiled. "It is not college any more, is it, my friend?"

"No, it's not."

"Whatever happens cannot be more than that man deserves, my friend. I have ordered breakfast for all of us. Let's relax and enjoy."

In silence, we ate traditional Colombian food. Calentado, which is made from leftover beans and rice, was served with scrambled eggs, Colombian chorizo, and arepa, a cornmeal-based substitute for bread. The food was delicious and I could not believe how hungry I was. When I finished, I told everyone what I would like them to do as I interrogated Joey Avanti.

I wanted him to admit that he had killed Sarah Ann.

Raul and I walked back down the dark hall to the window of the office that held my prey. He was fully awake and looking around. I saw no panic in his dead dark eyes.

"Hello," Joey hollered. "What the hell is going on?" He paused as if to listen. "Is anyone there?" he asked loudly.

Joey waited.

We waited.

Joey got more agitated.

"I'm sure there has been has been a mistake," Joey said firmly. "My employer does not want trouble between us. You better let me go now while you still have the chance."

"What's he talking about?" I asked Raul.

"He thinks he has been taken by a rival drug cartel. He's surprised because the rival cartels usually have an understanding between them."

I let Joey squirm a few minutes more and then I went in with Billy.

Joey looked confused when he saw me but he recovered quickly.

"Something tells me you are not in the drug business," he said looking directly at me. "But I have seen you before, Mr. Youngblood, and your Indian friend. A private investigator, I believe. Now what brings you two to Columbia?"

I was hoping to evoke a more fearful response but he seemed much too pleased with himself. I would see what I could do about that.

"Hello, Ronnie," I said. "Or should I call you Joey?"

A look of surprise passed across his face but he recovered quickly.

"Very good," he said smugly. "Score one for your side. But I ask again, why are you here?"

"To take you back to Tennessee to stand trial for the murder of Sarah Ann," I said.

"Sarah Ann is dead? I'm shocked," he said with mock surprise. "Who could have done such a thing? As far as taking me back goes, there would not be enough evidence to convict me, even if you could get me out of the country, which you cannot. I work for important people. They will be looking for me. All the roads and airports will be covered. You are trapped. Sooner or later they will find us and you will die. I suggest you get out while you can and give my condolences to Joseph Fleet."

I could feel my blood pressure rise. At that moment I had a vision of wrapping my hands around the throat of Joey Avanti and choking the life out of him.

"I might just shoot you myself and be done with it," I said. "Or I might let Billy cut your throat." Billy thumbed the blade of his knife.

Joey laughed. "You do not have the stomach for cold-blooded murder. I am sure of that."

I glanced toward the window and back at Joey. The door opened behind me and Roy came in.

I watched Joey's eyes and saw fear for the first time. Roy walked toward Joey. His jaw was hard set and his eyes were piercing. He slapped Joey hard with an open palm. I could hear the echo in the room and I knew it had stung like hell.

"That's enough," I said and Roy backed away.

"Maybe I don't have the stomach for it, but I'll bet Roy does," I said.

Joey recovered and regained his composure. "I am sure he does. I am equally sure you will not allow it."

"I guess we will have to take you back to stand trial or maybe give you back to the FBI," I said. "And I definitely think we can get you out of the country." The FBI crack got a visible response from Joey. The smugness was evaporating.

At that moment Raul walked in. I now saw more than confusion on Joey's face, I saw concern. He fought to cover it up. Joey obviously knew Raul and how powerful his family was. Raul was the wild card that Joey had not counted on.

"*Mr. Rivera*," Joey said in Spanish. "*An honor.*" The smile was back as the patronizing began. "*What on earth are you doing with these foreigners? You know my employer will not be happy when he finds out.*"

Raul smiled and said in English, "We are asking the questions, Señor. And I doubt that anyone will ever find out anything about what happens to you."

The smile on Joey's face had now been replaced by a look of panic. Roy and Raul stood by the door. Billy leaned against the far wall. Joey's smugness was long gone.

"I think we can come to some sort of an agreement," he said.

I could hear the controlled desperation in his voice, a rat trying to negotiate his way out of the trap. "I don't think so," I said.

"I can make you rich. I really can," he pleaded.

"I'm already rich, Joey. Have a nice life."

I picked up the tranquilizer pistol off the desk.

"Don't do this," he screamed.

"Now you know what it feels like to plead for your life, Joey." I hissed at him. "Remember Sarah Ann on your way to hell."

I fired a fully loaded dart into Joey Avanti.

"Don't . . ." Joey screamed and then passed out.

IN THE HALLWAY I turned to Raul. "I think he was surprised to see me," I said.

"I think he was, too, and he didn't want you to know." Raul said. "The man is a psycho, arrogant and unbalanced. Remember, he got away once. In his mind he had gotten away again. I don't think he can come to terms with the fact that you found him. You can never be sure what is in the mind of a crazy man."

Raul the psychiatrist.

"Think they can track him here?" I asked.

"It would not matter," Raul smiled. "He is inconsequential to them. He overestimates his importance. That was his big mistake. His employer would not go up against my family to regain him."

"You are sure about that?"

Raul smiled, "I am positive, my friend."

"I need a place where I can take time to think this out and maybe make a few phone calls," I said.

"Come with me."

Raul led me to the end of the hall to an elegant corner office. I noticed his name on the door.

"Take all the time you need. You will not be disturbed."

Raul left and closed the door behind him. I looked at my watch. It was still on Eastern Standard Time. It read six AM. I called Mary at the condo. The phone rang four times.

"Hello?"

"Did I wake you?"

"Hey," Mary said. "No, I was just getting into the shower. How are you?"

I had a mental image of Mary getting into the shower.

"It's over," I said.

"You have him?" she asked, surprised.

"You doubted me?"

"I'll never doubt you, Don. But it is incredible that you tracked this guy halfway round the world and finally found him. So what are you going to do with him?"

"That's the question I am trying to answer. Any ideas?"

"Give him to Roy and come home." Not an answer I had expected, but a cop's answer, a very tough cop's answer.

"Probably not a bad idea, but for Roy's sake I cannot do that."

We talked for a while longer and Mary caught me up on events in Mountain Center since I had been gone. Jake was fine. There had been an attempted robbery of a convenience store that failed when the getaway car would not start—a nominee for the America's dumbest criminal award—and a couple of traffic accidents. I promised to be home by tomorrow night.

HALF AN HOUR LATER, after much debating, I called Scott Glass at his FBI office.

"Glass."

"Good morning, Professor."

"Blood, where are you? You sound close."

"The miracle of modern technology," I said. "I am nowhere close. I have a hypothetical question for you, Professor."

"I do not like this already," Scott said. "Go ahead."

"What would the FBI do with Joey Avanti if they caught him?"

"Don, what the hell is going on? Do you have Avanti?"

"Answer the question, Scott."

I waited through the silence.

"Well, the FBI would probably cut him another deal for all the information he could give us if it was worth anything and then put him in the witness protection program. If not, we would put him behind bars."

"How much time would he get?"

"I don't know, Don. Ten years, maybe."

Ten years.

Witness protection or ten years. Ten years for killing Sarah Ann and all the other nasty things he had done in his pathetic life. Ten years and he would be out, if he got ten years. He would probably charm his way into the witness protection program again and get nothing. I could not allow that to happen.

"Good-bye, Scott."

"Don . . ."

I disconnected and made another phone call.

LATE IN THE day I waited in the hangar with Raul while our luggage was being placed on Raul's private jet. Roy and Billy were already on board. A comatose Joey Avanti was duct-taped to a wheelchair locked in position near the far right side of the hangar opening. Joey had a plane to catch. The Lear Jet touched gently down on the tarmac and taxied near the hangar. The World Wide Imports logo showed clearly on the tail.

WHEN THE ENGINES had shut down, Raul gave the high sign to the refueling crew and they went to work. Everything had been prearranged. The stairway unfolded from the side of the jet and two familiar figures emerged and descended the stairs. The larger of the two walked over to me and extended his hand.

"Carlo sends his regards and says to tell you we owe you," Frankie said as we shook hands. "Any time, any place. And I personally echo those sentiments."

"My pleasure," I said. "Give Carlo my regards. Take good care of the package. If he gives you any trouble give him a shot of this." I handed Frankie one of the tranquilizer pistols.

"Cute," he laughed. "I always wanted to fire one of these."

Gino wheeled Joey to the stairs and he and Frankie carried him up, wheelchair and all. The refueling was finished. Frankie turned and gave me a quick thumbs up and I waved back. The stairs folded up and a couple of minutes later Carlo Vincente's Lear Jet was airborne. Raul and I watched it disappear in the distance.

"Joey Avanti is in for quite a surprise when he wakes up," Raul said.

"Indeed," I said. "It would not have been possible without your help, Raul. I thank you."

He smiled. "A happy ending is thanks enough. Now go home to that lovely lady who is waiting for you."

There was an idea I could get excited about.

50

On a cold, gray Monday morning, Roy, Billy and I were in my office drinking coffee and enjoying bagels. The wind blew snow flurries past my window. Almost a week had passed since we returned from Bogota, private jets all the way. I would be forever spoiled when it came to air travel. I had been thoroughly greeted by Jake and Mary. Especially Mary. We spent that weekend at the lake house doing nothing but eating, drinking, some running and getting reacquainted.

I finally had to come back to the office to get some rest.

"How is Fleet?" I asked Roy.

"Making a comeback."

"Catching Joey Avanti probably helped," Billy said.

"That and the package he received," Roy said.

"What package?" I asked.

"A package from New York. Whatever was in it pleased him. It must be of some value. He locked it in the safe."

"Something he ordered?"

"I don't know. Does World Wide Imports have mail order?"

LATER THAT DAY I had a visitor. Since Jake did not growl when the office door opened, I knew it was someone familiar. The big man walked in uninvited and sat down.

"Heard you were back," he said.

"News travels fast in this town," I said. "But then again, you are the Chief of Police."

"True," Big Bob said. "But sometimes I am the last to know."

"Unusual for you to just drop in. What's up?"

"Two things. First, the Sarah Ann Fleet case is an open murder investigation for the Mountain Center police force. I'd like to know whether to keep this case open or go ahead and close it. I'm not looking for any of the details, just thought I'd ask." He stared at me and waited for an answer.

"I'd close it," I said.

"It's closed . . . sometime I *would* like to hear the details."

"Sometime you will," I promised. "You said two things."

He handed me a slip of folded paper and I opened it. It read: Science Hill Riding Academy, Telford, Tennessee.

"What's this?"

"The ghost of high school past," Big Bob said cryptically.

My stomach did a somersault. "Explain."

"That riding academy is owned by Marlene Long."

I felt my jaw drop. "*The* Marlene Long?"

"One and the same."

"You're sure?"

"Hell, yes, I'm sure. I'm the Chief of Police."

"And you are telling me this because?"

"Because I am your friend. You have had your head up your ass over this girl for over twenty years. And now you have someone in your life that can finally rival that memory. You need to go see Marlene and get this out of your system one way or the other."

I had not heard Big Bob put that many words together at one time since he took the oath of office. I stared at the slip of paper and refolded it neatly and stuck it on my bulletin board with a pushpin.

"I'll think about it."

"You do that," the big man said getting to his feet. "You owe me a beer and a long story about that trip to South America."

"How did you know I went to South America?"

Big Bob gave me the famous stare.

"Right," I said. "You're the Chief of Police."

51

Telford is like many small towns in Tennessee. If you drive though it too fast and blink, you'll miss it. I knew where Telford was because one summer when I was home from college, I dated a girl who lived there. *Jane, or was it Joan?*

Somewhere below Jonesborough I took a left turn that looked familiar and worked my way over toward Telford. I found a small gas station and asked the attendant if he knew where the Science Hill Riding Academy was. He did and was kind enough to share his knowledge with me. A few miles beyond the gas station, I saw the sign and took another left. A hard-packed gravel road stretched for about a mile to a large barn. I got out of the Pathfinder and realized what a nice day it was. East Tennessee. If you didn't like the weather, wait five minutes. Winter had briefly retreated and allowed an early February thaw. Yesterday, snow flurries. Today the temperature had to be in the upper fifties, but I was comfortable in jeans, dark brown boots, a beige turtleneck and a brown leather bomber jacket. I caught my reflection in the window of the Pathfinder and smiled. Never hurts to have confidence.

A dozen cars were scattered in the gravel parking lot. I took a deep breath and walked toward and through the open double barn doors. I was standing in a wide corridor at least a hundred yards long with at least twenty stalls on each side. Four horses were in the corridor being groomed and two more were being saddled by young riders. A door to my right read Office.

I started to reach for it when out of one of the stalls came an image that sent my mind reeling. It was Marlene. I quickly realized that it couldn't be Marlene. This young lady was no more than nineteen or twenty years old but she was the image of Marlene at that age. She had to be Marlene's daughter. She walked toward me and smiled.

"Can I help you?"

"I'm looking for Marlene Long," I said. "Is she around?"

"I'm Jessica," she said, "her daughter. Mom is in the Gunsmoke corral giving a riding lesson. She should be finished in a few minutes. Go back out the way you came in and walk to the right. You can't miss it."

I followed her directions. I walked past the Bonanza corral and the Ponderosa corral and then found the Gunsmoke corral with Marlene Long in the center of it giving instructions to a young red-headed girl that I would guess to be about ten years old. The years had treated Marlene well. She had put on some weight but in all the right places. The voice, the smile, the dark curly hair, all were still the same. I tried to assess my emotions. All I could come up with was excitement and anticipation. She glanced and saw me watching but showed no reaction. A few minutes later the lesson was over. She looked at me again and walked my way.

"Hi," she said.

"Hello."

"Are you waiting to see me?"

"Yes."

"Can I help you?"

No recognition. My ego took a serious blow; so much for confidence. All these years and she probably hadn't given me a second thought. Of course, I rationalized, I had the advantage, I *knew* who she was. Could I have picked her out of a crowd after twenty plus years? Maybe, maybe not.

"You don't recognize me, do you?"

"No, should I?"

"Well, we did go to high school together."

She stared hard at me. The wheels were turning. Memory was being accessed.

"Don? Don Youngblood? Is that you?"

"It is," I smiled.

"God, how long has it been?" Then more memories kicked in. "Oh, Lord. The last time I saw you was the night after . . ."

Her voice tailed off and a hand went to her mouth.

"Yeah, that's the last time, Marlene. I always wanted to know what happened to you."

She put her hand over mine.

"I do owe you an explanation," she said gently. "Come on, let's have a cup of coffee."

I walked with her in silence back the way I had come, and through the door marked Office. Inside the office door was a reception area with a couch, a few chairs, and a coffee stand. There was an inner office with

Marlene's name on the door. We poured coffee. I didn't bother with cream and sugar. I hadn't come for the coffee. I could sip black coffee and listen.

Marlene closed the door behind us and went around her desk and sat down. I sat in a chair facing her.

"I am a little embarrassed, Don. I do not know really where to start," Marlene said in that soft Southern belle accent.

"Well, I'd like to know two things," I said. "One, what happened in my car the night before, and two, what happened to you the next day."

"The night before," she said almost to herself. "Yes, well I think I seduced you and got more than I bargained for. It took me years to get that night out of my mind. I thought it was pretty special. As to why I did it? You were right the next day. I thought I was pregnant and I thought you were the best candidate to be the father. I was eighteen years old and stupid. I liked you a lot as a friend, and after that night I was even more convinced it would work, that I could love you. I wasn't very subtle, was I?"

"Not very," I smiled.

"You were always real smart, Don. You saw through my scheme in short order and I had the typical female reaction. I got mad and stormed off. I went to my mother and told her the truth and the next morning I was on a plane to California to stay with my aunt. Two days later I got my period. My mother was so mad at me for being sexually active that she did not want me back, and my liberal Aunt Marie was so understanding I decided to stay. I went to Sacramento State and graduated with a degree in equine studies. I married an Air Force captain soon after I graduated and we had Jessica soon after that. I worked for an exclusive riding academy near Sacramento until my husband died of cancer two years ago. I wanted my own academy but California was too expensive to start one, so Jessica and I packed up and came back here. Jessica loves horses as much as I do, and she was very excited about having our own stables. She is going to East Tennessee State in the fall and will enroll in their new equine program. That's my story. I'm glad I finally got to tell you how sorry I was about what happened." She took a deep breath.

I started to say that I wasn't that hard to find, but what would be the point? She hadn't cared enough to track me down, and now that I had finally found her all I felt was a slowly growing anger. I was angrier with myself than with Marlene. I had built that night into more than it had been, two kids having sex in parked car. Happened all the time.

"No big deal," I said casually. "I heard you were back and I was in the neighborhood with some time to kill and thought I would look you up and say hello."

"Well, I'm glad you did," she smiled and then turned serious. "I heard about your parents, Don. I'm sorry. That must have been hard."

A little more fuel on my fire. *Not sorry enough to get in touch with me.* "That was a long time ago. I got over it."

We were running out of things to say and Marlene did not seem to want to prolong the conversation. I stood and she followed my lead.

"Well, look me up if you are ever in Mountain Center, Marlene. It was nice seeing you again."

"I will do that. It was nice seeing you again, too."

The phone rang and saved what could have been an awkward moment. Marlene picked up the phone and answered it as I waved and backed out of the door. She waved back and turned away.

I took the back roads home. I was in no particular hurry and I wanted time to digest my encounter with Marlene Long. I alternated between anger and relief—anger at myself for being so stupid and not realizing that you cannot live your life in the past and relief that another search was over. Maybe Big Bob knew what I had not, that present-day reality could rarely match twenty-year-old memories. The big man was pretty smart. He knew that when I saw Marlene I would finally resolve that night that had haunted most of my adult life. I felt light. A burden had been lifted. I almost laughed out loud. I drove on, back to the woman I knew was my destiny.

THAT NIGHT MARY and I sat on the floor leaning back against the couch in front of the fireplace, enjoying a bottle of Merlot. The shadow dance of the flames cast a soft glow around the room. No other lights were on. I told her the entire Marlene Long saga. She listened without interruption until I finished. "And what did you learn today?" she asked.

"I learned what everyone else already seems to know."

"And that is?"

"That you're the one."

Mary laughed. "I could have told you that, but you had to learn the hard way. A typical man."

"Would you have me any other way?"

She put her wine glass down and moved as close to me as she could get and kissed me gently. "Of course not," she whispered and kissed me again. "Of course not."

52

Two days later temperatures dropped into the teens and snow flurries returned. Though renovated, the Hamilton Building had an antiquated heat system that was never a match for bitter cold snaps. I supplemented with a space heater that struggled against the chill. Jake was curled into a tight ball on his bed. Billy was in Cherokee, North Carolina, visiting "a friend." Billy had spent a lot of time in Cherokee lately. I knew that in his own time he would tell me. I wrapped my hands around a warm mug of coffee and read the market report on the

Internet. I had just hung up from talking to Trent Fairchild IV and, as promised, letting him know the outcome of my investigation. I left out the details he did not need to know, but he got the gist of it.

The phone rang. "Cherokee Investigations."

"This is your friendly FBI agent," Scott Glass said.

"Hey, Professor, what's happening?"

"I have some news I thought you should know. Guess who was found floating in the East River in the Big Apple?"

"The mayor?"

"Funny. Try Joey Avanti."

"Really?" I tried to act surprised.

"Really," Scott said snidely. "You, of course, wouldn't know anything about that, would you, Blood?"

"Absolutely not."

"Well, I thought you would like to know. I guess this closes your case."

"And then some."

"Say, Blood, why don't we get together at Singer Island soon? Run on the beach, drink a few beers, eat some good food, get laid."

"Sounds good, Professor, but about the getting laid part, I need to give you an update." I told him the whole Mary story.

"Being an FBI agent and all, and trained to interpret clues," Scott said, "I would say you have bitten the dust."

"Could be. Think we can make it a foursome at Singer?"

"Not a problem. There is a cute little trainee I have my eye on. How is April?"

"I'm flexible. April is good," I said. "We'll firm it up later."

"Okay, Blood, got to run. Hey, I almost forgot, Joey Avanti was missing his right hand. Chopped off clean."

A package from New York, whatever was in it pleased him. It must be of some value. He locked it in the safe. "Ouch," I said. I felt a little queasy.

"Ouch, indeed," Scott said.

Epilogue

In early April, Mary was granted two weeks of vacation so we could meet Scott Glass and his new trainee flame, Melinda, at Singer Island. I tried to talk Mary into quitting police work altogether but she would have none of it. *It's what I do,* she had told me, *and what I like to do.* It's hard to argue with female logic.

My life had returned to normal. I went to the office, played the market for various clients, ate breakfast at the Mountain Center Diner, worked out at Moto's Gym, and continued to develop a deeper relationship with Mary. No other big cases came my way nor was I looking for them.

Two days before we were to leave for Florida I was in the office early playing solitaire on the computer. I had all four aces up and six spades and was desperately was trying to find the remaining deuces when I ran out of cards. I stared at the screen. *Three deuces down.* I had a sudden chill. Three deuces down would forever remind me of Sarah Ann Fleet. I needed a new game to play.

My melancholy faded as I heard the front door of the office open. Jake growled his less-threatening growl.

Seconds later a rather unkempt young girl stood in my doorway. She was wearing jeans, beat-up tennis shoes, a navy pea coat that was too big for her, and a wool cap pulled down over blond hair. She pulled off the cap and stared at me with piercing blue eyes that looked old beyond her years.

"Can I help you?" I asked.

"I need you to find someone . . ."

Author's Note

LIKE MOST WRITERS of fiction I have drawn from past experiences, my many travels and the people that have crossed my path as I have journeyed to this point in time. I have borrowed a few names from that past and even a few personalities and I thank those that have loaned them out even though they did not give permission. However, this is a work of fiction. None of it is true.

Well, very little.

Like Donald Youngblood, you will have to determine what is true and what is not.

— KEITH DONNELLY

You may contact the author at ThreeDeucesDown@aol.com.